ON A QUIET STREET

SERAPHINA NOVA GLASS

GRAYDON
HOUSE

GRAYDON HOUSE®

Recycling programs for this product may not exist in your area.

ISBN-13: 978-1-525-89975-1

On a Quiet Street

Graydon House
22 Adelaide St. West, 41st Floor
Toronto, Ontario M5H 4E3, Canada
www.GraydonHouseBooks.com
www.BookClubbish.com

Printed in U.S.A.

Praise for the novels of Seraphina Nova Glass

"Bold, racy and masterfully plotted, *Such a Good Wife* kept me guessing from the very first page to the scorching, jaw-dropping conclusion."

—Rose Carlyle, #1 internationally bestselling author of *The Girl in the Mirror*

"*Such a Good Wife* hooked me from page one and didn't let go... Clear your calendar because once you open this book you won't want to close it until after you've read the last page!"

—Amber Garza, author of *When I Was You*

"In *Such a Good Wife*, Seraphina Nova Glass weaves a deliciously dark tale... If you think you've figured out the culprit, think again. A sly and pulse-pounding murder mystery set in steamy Louisiana."

—Kimberly Belle, internationally bestselling author of *Stranger in the Lake*

"A juicy tight-rope of a thriller that sees a woman teetering on the perilous line between lust and love as deception, betrayal and murder threaten to destroy her seemingly perfect life."

—Katie Tallo, author of *Dark August*, on *Such a Good Wife*

"*Such a Good Wife* is a terrifically engaging thriller. I couldn't turn the pages fast enough!"

—Emily Gray Tedrowe, author of *The Talented Miss Farwell*

"Glass remains a writer to watch."

—Publishers Weekly on *Such a Good Wife*

"Glass weaves a taut web of suspicion, murder and revenge in this chilling tale... Add *Someone's Listening* to your must read list!"

—Liv Constantine, internationally bestselling author of *The Last Mrs. Parrish*

"Unputdownable. I found myself suspecting everyone at some point. Twisty, original and a must-read—highly suspenseful and cleverly written."

—Karen Hamilton, bestselling author of *The Perfect Girlfriend*, on *Someone's Listening*

"A taut and intriguing suspense that held my attention from the very first page... A stunning and impressive debut."

—Alessandra Torre, *New York Times* bestselling author, on *Someone's Listening*

Also by Seraphina Nova Glass

Someone's Listening

Such a Good Wife

For Dianna Nova and Julie Loehrer

ON A
QUIET
STREET

PROLOGUE

Nothing ever happens in Brighton Hills. Well, nothing you can see, anyway. It all happens in whispers and behind closed doors: it swirls around in rumors and sideways glances, even though the surface is glossy and calm. Underneath, though, it's filled with desperate women who turn their heads from their husbands' affairs so they can keep their Gucci and Birkin, and dads are buying recreational coke from a high-school kid to get them through soul-stealing jobs they hate. It's Abby Rosen, whose nanny stole her three-karat diamond to sell and replaced it with a cubic zirconia, and Abby never found out. It's Martin Landry, who eloped with his seventeen-year-old stepdaughter. It's a million stories like that that make up this lonely, unknowable place. Who knows what's true? The people seem too beige and plastic to be that interesting, but something is indeed happening beneath the manicured facade. When you walk down the sidewalks of Brighton Hills, it's green and tidy and…a lie. People are polite, and it's always so quiet, but on this night, something very loud happened.

He just wanted to talk, but instead he found himself yelling, his voice choked with tears—he needed help. The rain fell in torrents, and the thunder forced him to scream over the noise, but he wasn't trying to be threatening. It just sounded that way. As he stood in front of the car, dripping in the rain, he pleaded for understanding to the figure sitting inside it. He apologized for everything, but it wasn't enough.

There was a gunshot, he thinks. Who shot it? He felt far away from himself and couldn't piece together what was really happening.

All he could see were headlights in the darkness, suddenly coming toward him. The figure hit the accelerator, wheels howling against the wet pavement, barreling toward him. There was no time to run: it happened too fast. He felt the impossible weight of the bumper crash into his hip, and then he was flying, floating.

He hit the ground so hard his head didn't even bounce. He felt his skull crack and soften, and then warm blood pooled around the base of his skull. He closed his eyes against the black rain on his face and told himself it would be okay, he wasn't going to die. As the car pulled away, another must have passed as it pulled into the community, and he thought maybe he would be helped: he could be saved still, he was certain. The car stopped. It stopped to help him! Doors opened and closed, and he heard the voices of two people, a man and a woman.

"Oh, my God!" the female voice said. "Call— Oh, my— Jesus, call for help." And just then the wail of sirens could be heard, blaring in their direction; he was sure they must be coming for him.

"Let's get outta here!" the male voice said.

"What?" The woman kneeled next to Caleb, and he tried to reach out his hand but couldn't make it move. The man pulled her away.

"Help is coming. We can't be here," he said. He could feel her hesitate but then sensed that she wasn't there anymore. He heard the car pull away, and tears escaped the corners of his eyes, washed away by the rain. Had the gunshot made the neighbors call the police? They were probably coming. He waited, alone, the cold permeating his clothes and making him tremble.

"I'm sorry," he whispered, but before help could arrive, he was gone.

1

PAIGE

Paige stands, watering her marigolds in the front yard and marveling at how ugly they are. The sweet-potato-orange flowers remind her of a couch from the 1970s, and she suddenly hates them. She crouches down, ready to rip them from their roots, wondering why she ever planted such an ugly thing next to her pristine Russian sage, and then the memory steals her breath. The church Mother's Day picnic when Caleb was in the sixth grade. Some moron had let the potato salad sit too long in the sun, and Caleb got food poisoning. All the kids got to pick a flower plant to give to their moms, and even though Caleb was puking mayonnaise, he insisted on going over to pick his flower to give her. He was so proud to hand it to her in its little plastic pot, and she said they'd plant it in the yard and they'd always have his special marigolds to look at. How could she have forgotten?

She feels tears rise in her throat but swallows them down. Her dachshund, Christopher, waddles over and noses her arm: he always senses when she's going to cry, which is almost all the time since Caleb died. She kisses his head and looks at her now-beautiful marigolds. She's interrupted by the kid who delivers the newspaper as he rides his bike into the cul-de-sac and tosses a rolled-up paper, hitting little Christopher on his back.

"Are you a fucking psychopath?" Paige screams, jumping to her feet and hurling the paper back at the kid, which hits *him* in the head and knocks him off his bike.

"What the hell is wrong with you, lady?" he yells back, scrambling to gather himself and pick up his bike.

"What's wrong with me? You tried to kill my dog. Why don't you watch what the fuck you're doing?"

His face contorts, and he tries to pedal away, but Paige grabs the garden hose and sprays him down until he's out of reach. "Little monster!" she yells after him.

Thirty minutes later, the police ring her doorbell, but Paige doesn't answer. She sits in the back garden, drinking coffee out of a lopsided clay mug with the word *Mom* carved into it by little fingers. She strokes Christopher's head and examines the ivy climbing up the brick of the garage and wonders if it's bad for the foundation. When she hears the ring again, she hollers at them.

"I'm not getting up for you people. If you need to talk to me, I'm back here." She enjoys making them squeeze around the side of the house and hopes they rub up against the poison oak on their way.

"Morning, Mrs. Moretti," one of the officers says. It's the girl cop, Hernandez. Then the white guy chimes in. She hates him. Miller. Of course they sent Miller with his creepy mustache. He looks more like a child molester than a cop, she thinks. How does anyone take him seriously?

"We received a complaint," he says.

"Oh, ya did, did ya? You guys actually looking into cases these days? Actually following up on shit?" Paige says, still petting the dog and not looking at them.

"You assaulted a fifteen-year-old? Come on."

"Oh, I did no such thing," she snaps.

Hernandez sits across from Paige. "You wanna tell us what did happen, then?"

"Are you planning on arresting me if I don't?" she asks, and the two officers give each other a silent look she can't read.

"His parents don't want to press charges, so…"

Paige doesn't say anything. They don't have to tell her it's because they pity her.

"But, Paige," Miller says, "we can't keep coming out here for this sort of thing."

"Good," Paige says firmly. "Maybe it will free you up to do your real job and find out who killed my son." Hernandez stands.

"Again, you know we aren't the detectives on the—" But before Hernandez can finish, Paige interrupts, not wanting to hear the excuses.

"And maybe go charge the idiot kid for trying to kill my dog. How about that?"

Paige stands and goes inside, not waiting for a response. She hears them mumble something to one another and make their way out. She can't restrain herself or force herself to be kind. She used to be kind, but now, it's as though her brain has been rewired. Defensiveness inhabits the place where empathy used to live. The uniforms of the cops trigger her, too; it reminds her of that night, the red, flashing lights a nightmarish strobe from a movie scene. A horror movie, not real life. It *can't* be her real life. She still can't accept that.

The uniforms spoke, saying condescending things, pull-

14

ing her away, calling her *ma'am*, and asking stupid questions. Now, when she sees them, it brings up regrets. She doesn't know why this happens, but the uniforms bring her back to that night, and it makes her long for the chance to do all the things she never did with Caleb and mourn over the times they did have. It forces fragments of memories to materialize, like when he was six, he wanted a My Little Pony named Star Prancer. It was pink with purple flowers in its mane, and she didn't let him have it because she thought she was protecting him from being made fun of at school. Now, the memory fills her with self-reproach.

She tries not to think about the time she fell asleep on the couch watching *Rugrats* with him when he was just a toddler and woke up to his screaming because he'd fallen off the couch and hit his head on the coffee table. He was okay, but it could have been worse. He could have put his finger in an outlet, pushed on the window screen and fallen to his death from the second floor, drunk the bleach under the sink! When this memory comes, she has to quickly stand up and busy herself, push out a heavy breath, and shake off the shame it brings. He could have died from her negligence that afternoon. She never told Grant. She told Cora once, who said every parent has a moment like that, it's life. People fall asleep. But Paige has never forgiven herself. She loved Caleb more than life, and now the doubt and little moments of regret push into her thoughts and render her miserable and anxious all the time.

She didn't stay home like Cora, she practically lived at the restaurant. She ran it for years. Caleb grew up doing his homework in the kitchen break room and helping wipe down tables and hand out menus. He seemed to love it. He didn't watch TV all afternoon after school, he talked to new people, learned skills. But did she only tell herself that to alleviate the guilt? Would he have thrived more if he had had a more normal day-to-day? When he clung to her leg that first day of preschool, should she have forced him to go? Should she have let him change his college major so many times? Had he been happy? Had she done right by him?

And why was there a gun at the scene? Was he in trouble, and she didn't know? Did he have friends she didn't know about? He'd told her everything, she thought. They were close. Weren't they?

As she approaches the kitchen window to put her mug down, she sees Grant pulling up outside. She can see him shaking his head at the sight of the cops before he even gets out of the car.

He doesn't mention the police when he comes in. He silently pours himself a cup of coffee and finds Paige back out in the garden, where she has scurried to upon seeing him. He hands her a copy of the *Times* after removing the crossword puzzle for himself and then peers at it over his glasses.

He doesn't speak until Christopher comes to greet him, and then he says, "Who wants a pocket cookie?" and takes a small dog biscuit from his shirt pocket and smiles down at little Christopher, who devours it.

This is how it's been for the many months since Grant and Paige suffered insurmountable loss. *It might be possible to get through it to the other side, but maybe not together,* Paige said to Grant one night after one of many arguments about how they should cope. Grant wanted to sit in his old, leather recliner in the downstairs family room and stare into the wood-burning fireplace, Christopher at his feet, drinking a scotch and absorbing the quiet and stillness.

Paige, on the other hand, wanted to scream at everyone she met. She wanted to abuse the police for not finding who was responsible for the hit-and-run. She wanted to spend her days posting flyers offering a reward to anyone with information, even though she knew only eight percent of hit-and-runs are ever solved. When the world didn't respond the way she needed, she stopped helping run the small restaurant they owned so she could just hole up at home and shout at *Jeopardy!* and paper boys. She needed to take up space and be loud. They each couldn't stand how the other was mourning, so finally, Grant moved into the small apartment above their little Italian place, Moretti's, and gave Paige the space she needed to take up.

Now—almost a year since the tragic day—Grant still comes over every Sunday to make sure the take-out boxes are picked up and the trash is taken out, that she's taking care of herself and the house isn't falling apart. And to kiss her on the cheek before he leaves and tell her he loves her. He doesn't make observations or suggestions, just benign comments about the recent news headlines or the new baked mostaccioli special at the restaurant.

She sees him spot the pair of binoculars on the small table next to her Adirondack chair. She doesn't need to lie and say she's bird-watching or some nonsense. He knows she thinks one of the neighbors killed her son. She's sure of it. It's a gated community, and very few people come in and out who don't live here. Especially that late at night. The entrance camera was conveniently disabled that night, so that makes her think it wasn't an accident but planned. There was a gun next to Caleb's body, but it wasn't fired, and there was no gunshot wound. Something was very wrong with this scenario, and if the police won't prove homicide, she's going to uncover which of her bastard neighbors had a motive.

She has repeated all of this to Grant a thousand times, and he used to implore her to try to focus on work or take a vacation—anything but obsess—and to warn her that she was destroying her health and their relationship, but he stopped responding to this sort of conspiracy-theory talk months ago.

"What's the latest?" is all he asks, looking away from the binoculars and back to his crossword. She gives a dismissive wave of her hand, a sort of *I know you don't really want to hear about it* gesture. Then, after a few moments, she says, "Danny Howell at 6758. He hasn't driven his Mercedes in months." She gives Grant a triumphant look, but he doesn't appear to be following.

"Okay," he says, filling in the word *ostrich*.

"So I broke into his garage to see what the deal was, and there's a dent in his bumper."

"You broke in?" he asks, concerned. She knows the Howells have five vehicles, and the dent could be from a myriad of causes over the last year, but she won't let it go.

"Yes, and it's a good thing I did. I'm gonna go back and take photos. See if the police can tell if it looks like he might have hit a person." She knows there is a sad desperation in her voice as she works herself up. "You think they can tell that? Like if the dent were a pole from a drive-through, they could see paint or the scratches or something, right? I bet they can tell."

"It's worth a shot," he says, and she knows what he wants to say, also knows he won't waste words telling her not to break into the garage a second time for photos. He changes the subject.

"I'm looking for someone to help out at the restaurant a few days a week—mostly just a piano player for the dinner crowd—but I could use a little bookkeeping and scheduling, too," he says, and Paige knows it's a soft attempt to distract her, but she doesn't bite.

"Oh, well, good luck. I hope you find someone," she says, and they stare off into the backyard trees.

"The ivy is looking robust," he comments after a few minutes of silence.

"You think it's hurting the foundation?" she asks.

"Nah," he says, and he reaches over and places his hand over hers on the arm of her chair for a few moments before getting up to go. On his way out, he kisses her on the cheek, tells her he loves her. Then he loads the dishwasher and takes out the trash before heading to his car. She watches him reluctantly leaving, knowing that he wishes he could stay, that things were different.

When Paige hears the sound of Grant's motor fade as he turns out of the front gate, she imagines herself calling him on his cell and telling him to come back and pick her up, that she'll come to Moretti's with him and do all the scheduling and books, that she'll learn to play the piano just so she can make him happy. And, after all the patrons leave for the night, they'll share bottles of Chianti on checkered tablecloths in a dimly lit back booth. They'll eat linguini and clams and have a *Lady and the Tramp* moment, and they will be happy again.

Paige does not do this. She goes into the living room and closes the drapes Grant opened, blocking out the sunlight, then she crawls under a bunched-up duvet on the couch that smells like sour milk, and she begs for sleep.

2

CORA

Nobody will eat the chocolate chip pancakes, but they complete the breakfast table. If I take the yolks out of the egg bake, then it will make up for pancake calories. Nobody will drink the orange juice either, but it looks nice in tiny glass cups next to the coffee, and it's Sunday, damn it, so everything should look nice, even if it's just the three of us and I'm the only one who cares. It's the same thing as making your bed in the morning. You don't leave it messy like a slob just because it will only get used again that night. You make it so when you pass by the room, everything looks tidy and put together and right.

When Mia trudges into the kitchen wearing flannel pajama pants, she grabs a piece of toast and keeps walking toward the door.

"Where are you going?" I ask. I didn't expect fanfare over the breakfast spread, but maybe at least a *Good morning.*

"Sasha's."

"In that?" I ask, and she looks down at her pajamas but clearly doesn't see a problem. "Yeah. Can I take the car?"

"It's Sunday," I say, trying to keep the annoyance out of my voice. She knows that's the unspoken rule that even if we miss meals during the week, with Finn's late nights and her volleyball practices, on Sundays we make time. Mia looks past me to the table.

"Oh, but you're doing Weight Watchers again, I thought," she says, matter-of-factly. She's not trying to be hurtful. I am doing the program again, but explaining that you still actually eat meals on it seems pointless. She eyes the stack of chocolate chip pancakes and goes to take one off the top.

I hand her the car keys. It's good to see her getting out of the house and seeing friends, if I'm honest. She's been moping for months since her breakup with Josh or John or whatever his name was. How she can date the guy for too little a time span for me to recall his name but can cry over him for an eternity is beyond me.

"You can have the car, but help me with something."

"What?" she says, hand on one hip, ready to be inconvenienced by whatever it is I have to ask.

"There's that charity dinner next week. It's at Paige and Grant's restaurant in town. Come down and help me with the silent auction or serve tables or something."

"Ugh" is all I get from her.

"I'll take that as a yes. Be home by dinner. We're eating at the table."

When she's gone, I catch a quick look at my reflection in the sliding glass door that leads to the deck. Before I can scrutinize whether Weight Watchers is working, I see past my image and into the backyard of the elusive Georgia Kinney, who is as rare a sight as a snow leopard in the wild. I run out to the edge of the deck and open the camera on my phone, zooming in, to get as close a view as I can. She's lifting her baby into a swing, the plastic kind with the foot holes and safety bar. She pushes her, mindlessly. She doesn't coo at her, and she doesn't scroll on her phone, ignoring her, either. She just stares off, absently.

If I were that freaking gorgeous, I'd be thrilled all the time. I'd live in strappy tops without worrying my back fat would squish through them like a tube of biscuits you whack against the counter to split open. I'd wear my sunshine-colored hair loose down my back and never expose my porcelain skin to the sun, not once. Granted, she is a good fifteen years younger than me, and her husband for that matter—the youngest mom in the neighborhood, I think. She's in her mid-twenties, it looks like.

It might be pathetic, but I don't get why she doesn't want to make friends with any of us. I mean, it's a little snotty. Finn hung out with her husband, Lucas, a couple times, so I know she's from England. Maybe she thinks she's better than us if she's English, and she probably is, calling gasoline *petrol*, and a cell phone a *mobile*: they always sound so fancy. But they have been living across the street over a year now, and she hasn't even said more than a quick hello. She didn't even write a thank-you note for the mascarpone pound cake I dropped off when they moved in. It won a prize at the state fair, for God's sake. She could have at least returned the plate. Still, she looks so glamorous, and her husband's a judge, and I will win her over.

"Are you spying on them?" Finn asks, and I jump and clutch my chest. I whip around to see him standing in the open doorframe, smirking at me.

"No! Of course not." I push past him and shut the door, a little annoyed at the interruption.

"Then, what were you doing?" he asks, amused.

"Finn," I say firmly as if that's an answer to his question. I click the lid down on the Keurig and listen to it sputter and drip.

"Look at all this," he says, sitting at the table and filling his plate with egg casserole. I place his coffee in front of him and sit, serving myself a pancake.

"I thought you were doing the Weight Watchers thing again."

I clench my jaw and look at the ceiling, then exhale loudly in annoyance.

"Sorry," he says, flashing his palms in defense. I decide to change the subject so we don't start the day with tension.

"It's just that I find it off-putting that they're so antisocial. The O'Briens lived there eleven years before the Kinneys moved in, and they were over all the time. It feels—I don't know—uncomfortable that they can't be normal. I like to know my neighbors. We should all be friends, look out for each other."

"He seems normal," Finn says. "Well, we only had a beer a couple times, but he seems okay. I think she's a—whatchamacallit—a wallflower."

"What?" I laugh.

"She has that phobia where she's afraid to leave the house, I think," he says.

"Agoraphobia?" I suggest.

"That sounds right," he says, buttering a piece of toast.

"Um. Wait, wait, wait. Are you kidding? He actually told you that?"

"Yeah. Well, I don't think he used that word, no, but something like that," he says, and I smack his arm a few times.

"Why would you not tell me that! Are you serious? Tell me exactly what he said."

"Jeez, Cora. I don't know. She had some trauma happen, and now she has to be within, like, spitting distance of her house or she freaks out and panics." He eats his triangle of toast in two bites, opens his phone, and starts scrolling.

"Finn, oh, my God. That's— He told you this, and you didn't tell me?"

"We were having beers. I forgot. I'm not the one obsessed with her, so it didn't seem like headline news I had to rush and tell you," he says.

"And he just opened up and told you this out of the blue?"

"Uh…no, I don't know. I think I suggested they come over or you two get together, and that was the reason she couldn't."

"Oh. My. God," I say, picking up my phone.

"Cor, don't." He stops me.

"What?"

"Don't tell Paige. Just—"

"I'm not," I lie and put my phone back down. "At least it's a good reason. I just thought she was a bitch."

"Maybe she is. She could be an agoraphobic bitch. Why do you care so much?" he asks.

"Are you gonna hang out with Lucas again? Our house is within 'spitting distance' of hers, right? Maybe she'd be comfortable coming here. Maybe it's in the comfort zone, y'know?"

"I don't know how it works, but he didn't make it sound like that was an option."

"Just—do you have plans with him again?"

"We mentioned golf in a couple weeks. The club is having an amateur tournament. I said he should come."

"Oooh. When is it? I could invite her over. It would be a way to start the conversation. 'Since the guys are abandoning us for golf, you should come over for a glass of wine' sort of thing. Perfect. When, when, when?" I push, and he shrugs, mumbling through a mouthful of food that he's not sure.

"Can you check?" I ask.

"Now?" He looks at me with a mix of amusement and annoyance.

"Yes, please."

"You're obsessed," he says but places his napkin on his now-empty plate and goes to grab his day planner. He's the sort who needs to write everything down in neat, blocky ink letters into a physical datebook, says his phone can be unreliable and a successful man always has a backup. He comes back and sits down again, sipping his coffee and paging through it.

"The thing at the club is on the nineteenth. But, Cor, maybe take a hint if she doesn't wanna be buddies."

"Um, for your information," I say, "she would be very lucky to know me. I still know every teacher at the elementary school, my book club has a waiting list, and I can tell her who all the good parents are in the neighborhood and which ones to avoid—"

"I think she wants to avoid all of them, right?" he interrupts. I look at him a moment, then stand and start to clear the table.

"You know what your problem is?" I ask.

"I do not. Please, do tell." He smirks, but I'm getting genuinely annoyed with him.

"You give up too easy when things get…challenging," I say.

"Since when do you think that?" he says, but he's only half listening. He's back looking at work emails on his phone. He's not someone easily rattled.

"Since, I don't know, always."

"Example?" he asks, looking at me now.

"You want an example?"

"I would like an example, yes." He crosses one leg over the other and folds his arms, amused, but also challenging me to come up with something. I stop scraping plates into the disposal and give him my full attention.

"The dog we got that you returned after he peed in the house a few times," I say.

"It was a foster dog for a reason. You see if it's a good fit. And there was more than peeing, he was—"

"Fine. The basketball team you joined at the Y and quit after your first practice."

"I don't need a concussion, Cor."

"Okay," I say. "Spanish lessons, tennis lessons, building the shed in the backyard, the downstairs bathroom reno—"

"Okay." He stops me, and I stop rattling off my list, although I could have gone on. I wanted to end my list with *and* us. *You gave up on us when you did what you did*, but he still denies it, and I pretend to believe him.

"Fine, you wanna stalk Georgia Kinney from across the street, enjoy yourself. I'll stay out of it."

"Thank you." I smile. "It's not stalking, it's called making an effort." But my smile quickly fades when I put down my tea towel and walk over to kiss the back of his head. I see what's written in his planner for tonight: *Drinks with C.*

He said he'd be out tonight because Benny Waller was retiring and everyone from the office was getting together for a send-off. I asked him why on a Sunday, and he said that's just how it worked out for everyone's schedule. And then he went on to say it's weird that going out on a Sunday seems odd but not a Thursday. You still have to get up for work the next day. I let it go.

Who is *C*? It's not *Cora* because I wasn't invited, of course. *Carrie, Cheryl, Claire, Chloe.* Do I know anyone with a *C*

26

name? One of his assistants is *Celine*, I think. Or *Chelsea*? I feel my face flush and heat prick up my spine.

"You okay?" Finn asks, picking up his coffee, about to head up to his office.

"Fine," I say, and he smiles and heads upstairs. I can't do this to myself. *C* is probably for *coworkers*. Yes. It's probably *colleagues*. Yes, yes. It's a weird way to write it, though; it seems like a name. Short for *Drinks with Connie* or something, right? It's weird. Wouldn't he write *Work party* or *Benny's retirement*? It doesn't sound right.

If I knew where the event was, I would go and find out myself, but he's careful not to tell me these details anymore after I showed up that time and humiliated him, causing irrevocable damage to his reputation. I can't ask either. I won't ask because we cannot go back down the road we were on a couple years ago. I almost ruined everything once, accusing him, and I was wrong. I was obsessed with catching him. Maybe that was a dig just now, when he said I was obsessed with Georgia.

It almost ended us the last time I started thinking like this. I take a deep breath. It's nothing. I stare at his planner on the table. I won't open it. I take a step closer, though. I think maybe I could open it quickly. I sit at his place at the table and stare down at it. I lift my hand tentatively...and just then Finn appears out of nowhere.

"Jesus!" I clutch my heart.

"Whoa," he laughs and picks the planner up off the table. "Sure you're okay, Cor?"

"Fine. Great. You just scared the shit out of me," I say, and he heads back to the stairs. Did he just come to get that so I wouldn't see it?

"Hey," I call to his back. He turns.

"I was thinking dinner out tonight. What do you think?"

"Oh, I'm out tonight. I thought I told you," he says.

"Oh, maybe I forgot. What do you have, again?"

"A thing with the office. Birthday drinks."

"Ah, right. You probably told me," I say, and he disappears up the stairs. I sit at the kitchen table. My ears are hot, and my hands shake. He's lying to me. He forgot to be consistent. It's a retirement party, Finn, you bastard, not a birthday party. It's happening again. *Who the fuck is C?*

3

GEORGIA

The days stretch long when you don't have distractions outside the house. Even as October brings shorter days and a welcome change in the air, I find myself wiping down already-clean surfaces, anxiety baking, and pacing. An acting teacher in college said never to pace onstage as an acting choice, because people don't pace in real life. You must have a reason to go one way or another. It's a cliché, she said. But I pace.

I watch Avery napping. She's finally sleeping through the night, and her naps are shorter in the afternoon. I like it better when she's awake, but I'm careful not to jostle her too much as I carry her to the front porch and lay her in her playpen set up there. I sit on the porch swing and watch Paige Moretti rake up piles of wet leaves a few doors down. She instructs her wiener dog to poop on the Carlsons' lawn, and she gives him a cookie from her pocket when he obeys. I smile, but only to myself. I ache for her loss, and I wish there were something I could do or say to her. I never even formally met her, really. Probably because everyone on the block knows there's something wrong with me. The only one who goes out of their way is the blonde who is always looking over here and brought me baked goods once, but I think my aloofness has put her off by this point.

It wasn't always this way. It was only three years ago, when I was working in the south of France at a luxury resort during the summers. I served drinks at a swim-up bar in the infinity pool overlooking the Mediterranean. I was tanned and lean and made a fortune pouring Rosé Royale to sun-kissed, tipsy guests by day. And at night, I swam in the saltwater pool and ate boeuf bourguignon and gougères beachside under strings of twinkling lights and met fascinating people from all over the world who were there on holiday.

Lucas was one of those fascinating people. An American with a big, fancy job. Well, *I* was fascinated by it, anyway. He was visiting his parents, who had retired there, and treating them to a week of couples' massages and day drinking at the hotel. I was normal then. Better than normal. I was vibrant. I was shiny hair and sundresses, lip gloss, and joy. I was twenty-six and planning on graduate school back in London after another year of working and saving money at the resort. Lucas saw that person—the person I was then.

One night, after it had gotten dark and all the guests had long abandoned the beach, I sat in an oversize sweater on one of the beach recliners. There were rows and rows of empty recliners, and I pulled one right down to the black waves and looked out at the water, surprised when Lucas appeared. I'd seen him chatting with a few couples in the pool earlier. I saw him see me as well, but he didn't approach me then or order a drink, so although I found him dangerously attractive, I didn't give it much thought after that.

"Evening," he said, and I instinctively looked around to make sure I wasn't too far away from safety if he was some lunatic. It's an instinct every woman on earth has, I'm sure. It was nothing to do with him, just a knee-jerk reaction, but he picked up on it.

"Sorry. I didn't mean to scare you. I was…" he gestured down the shoreline, and then I saw his earbuds and running shorts "…and I saw you here. You're the bartender from the pool, yeah?" he asked, and that was it. We talked for an hour before I fetched a bottle of red and two plastic cups, and he grabbed some towels from the beach stand, which we covered up in like blankets, and I was head over heels. He was thirteen years older than me, and I can imagine if my parents were still with me that might have given them pause. My friends thought it was weird at first, the age difference, but they also thought it was so sexy that he was American and rich and hot. That's not what drew me to him, though. Well, of course, I'm sure that played a part, initially, but he made me feel very safe in an unexplainable way.

It wasn't even a question when he asked me to marry him six months later. He'd visited Marseille again, and we fell asleep talking over video chat many nights when he was away. He was so settled and grounded—everything I wasn't. I had spent my years since college traveling and taking jobs like infinity-pool bartending all over the world. I wanted to travel and be free, but I was getting to a point where fitting everything you owned into one suitcase and a carry-on, never staying anywhere long enough to create real connections with people, was getting tiresome. He was the opposite of all that: he was all hedge funds and real-estate investment and dinner parties, and I was ready.

So he took a few weeks off work, partly to spend time with his parents and buy up their condo building for a real-estate opportunity—to fix it up. He did that, and while he did, I finished out my contract at the resort. We had an intimate beach wedding with just his family and a few of my friends from the resort. It was too good to be true. I should have known it was all a little too fairy-tale to be real and something would ruin it.

But shortly after I moved to this country that I have no business being in, the terrible night happened, and everything changed. I changed.

I stare down the street, and my eyes rest on the block where all the street's mailboxes are stacked on top of each other next to the security gate, wondering how I got like this. It seems impossible that not long ago, I would just walk out my door and into cars and restaurants and shops, that I could get on a plane and go to another country alone, that I was free and wild, and now I can't imagine being in a world outside this block.

"Jesus!" I'm thrust back into the present moment by a figure appearing out of nowhere.

"Oh, I'm so sorry. I didn't mean to startle you!" It's the woman from across the street. I don't remember her name, but she always seems to be carrying plates of baked goods.

"Uh…no, I just… It's fine," I stammer, instinctually backing away from her and looking over my shoulder as if we're engaging in an illegal activity. That's who I am now. Jumpy. Paranoid.

"Sorry, I didn't see you walk up," I say, and I didn't, which is hard to imagine. She's very shiny with her sparkly tops and sleek blond bob, and whenever I see her interacting with other neighbors or walking to or from her car, she's always humming or giggling. She might be the happiest person I've ever met. I try to recall her name. *Carolyn*, maybe.

"Brown Betty," she says and smiles, shoving a plate at me.

"Oh, Brown Be… I thought your name was C…" I trail

off, confused. She laughs so loud I glance over into Avery's playpen and make sure she didn't wake up.

"Cora, yes. No, I was referring to my apple brown Betty."

"Oh." I blush, taking the plate she still has extended toward me.

"It's all brown sugar and butter, but you're just a pretty little wisp of a thing. It can't do any harm," she says giggling.

"That's very sweet. Thank you." She's not leaving, and her presence is starting to make me uneasy. I have to try to appear normal. What would the previously normal me do? I'm supposed to invite her in, I think. But I can't.

"I'd invite you in, but..." I gesture to Avery. She stifles a squeal of delight upon seeing her and goes up to take a closer look.

"Of course, of course. What a little angel."

"Thank you." I smile and wonder if I said it in a way that indicated a close to the conversation. She doesn't look at me, just continues to coo over Avery.

"Oh, I just have baby fever. Mine is seventeen, so I've pretty much had baby fever since she was a toddler. How old is this little sweetheart?"

"Almost seven months," I say, not used to having someone gush over her, since I never take her anywhere. It's nice for a moment.

"Well—" she turns around "—she's perfect. You know who to call anytime you need a sitter. No charge, I just wanna kiss her little face off," she says to a sleeping Avery in a quiet baby voice, then turns to me again. "Hey, why don't I cut us a slice, and we can sit out here." She starts to take the dish back from me as if she's going to march right in the screen door and make herself at home, looking for forks and plates in my kitchen. I pull it away, on autopilot.

"Oh, please sit. I'll get it," I say, having little other choice.

My hands are shaky as I go through the screen door and walk barefoot down the hall to the kitchen. I start to have irrational thoughts as I clumsily dig in the drawer for forks. *What if she's one of those women you read about who snatch babies because of their—what did she call it?—*baby fever. I force myself not to run back down the hall and check. That's crazy. She practically emits sunshine. But wait, isn't that what the sociopaths do—appear so normal, maybe even a little overboard on the nice? *Stop. Pull it together. Shit. Okay.*

I bring silverware and plates and sit perched on the edge of a wicker lounge chair across from Cora, as she has taken my chair. She takes over quickly. It's as if she can't help but take the role of the one entertaining, even though she's at my house. She scoops generous servings of the whatever-she-called-it and plates them, licking the excess off her thumb as she hands me one. I will Avery to wake up and start wailing so I have an excuse to run her inside and shut down this visit, but she lies peacefully, her perfect, damp little curls clinging to her head, her rosebud mouth pursing and releasing, lost somewhere in a dream, maybe. What could a baby possibly dream about? I wonder.

We sit across from each other. I smile. I know I'm supposed to say something nice about the brown dish, but American desserts are too sweet for my taste, and I don't want a second bite.

"Lovely," I lie.

"Oh, thanks. Old family recipe."

"Oh, nice," I reply, and we eat in silence.

"It's white sugar," she giggles, her round cheeks flush.

"I'm sorry?"

"The secret in the recipe. White sugar instead of brown, so I guess I should call it a white Betty. Oh, and a little squeeze of orange."

"Oh." I smile.

"It's not really a secret, I guess. I can give you the recipe if you want."

"Oh, gosh, I don't really bake, but that's very sweet of you to offer," I say, and she makes a wave gesture, indicating it's no problem. It's silent again. Then…

"Do you know, our husbands have gotten together a few times, and I can't believe this is our first time hanging out," she says. I didn't realize we were *hanging out*. It feels more like a trap I'm trying to free myself from. But I nod, having no other response.

"I just— I see you driving in and out all day, figured you must be a very busy lady," I manage to say, like a normal person making conversation.

"Oh, my goodness. Mia is involved in everything. Volleyball, violin lessons, dance. Then there's the PTA, the food bank, the toy drive—year-round, mind you. The list would bore you, but yes, you have that right. I'm sure I make you dizzy with the back-and-forth all day." She laughs, and her cheeks redden again. She seems to be nervous for some reason. "Oh, but never too busy for my neighbors, of course," she adds.

"Sounds really exciting, actually," I say, and then her face changes.

"Oh, no. No, it's not, it's just…dull actually." She looks down at her plate and pushes the crumbs around with her fork. Shit. She knows. Lucas must have told her husband or whoever about me—that I can't leave the house—and the news has reached her. This is a pity visit, and she thinks I'm a freak.

"Well, a little bird told me that your Lucas might be playing a golf thing with my Finn in a couple of weekends. I thought I'd invite you and sweet little Avery over for some cake and wine. Of course, I guess you guys would call it *afternoon tea*."

She does a bad English accent when she says this and laughs at her own joke. "Oh, wait" she continues. "You call lunch *dinner*, and you call dinner *tea*," she says, laughing.

I don't know what to say. If Lucas told her about me, then why would she think I could possibly go to her place? He probably explained that I can go to the small community park behind our house when it's empty and can sometimes walk as far as the mailbox without a panic attack, and she thinks that means that anything between here and there is home base, therefore okay—not a trigger. I've thought about this a lot. How he has to explain it to friends. What they must think.

She's been very kind, if not a little pushy, and I still don't know how to handle this conversation. She sets her plate on the ground by her chair and wipes the crumbs off her maxi skirt. She looks at me expectantly. I can't say that I have to check my schedule or that I'm busy. Lucas has taken those excuses away by telling her.

She notices that I'm taking too long to answer. I can feel a rash of heat blotch my chest, and just then, Avery starts to cry glorious, screeching howls. I rush over to her and pick her up, rocking her on my hip and cooing at her.

"Well." Cora stands, taking it as her cue to leave. "You just let me know, sweetheart," she says kindly, touching my arm, but she looks visibly disappointed at the same time, and I can't help but wonder why in the world she cares. I'm the odd stranger across the street. Why all the effort? She takes Avery's little bunched-up fist between her thumb and forefinger and kisses it. "Aren't you the sweetest?" she says, and then, "You keep the rest of that Betty, and I'll get the dish another time," and then she's off.

I try not to think about the fact that she's left herself a reason to return. I watch her walk across to her house. She waves to Paige and pets one of the neighbor's outdoor cats that's sunning himself on her front step, before a teenage girl runs out, handing Cora her purse, saying they'll be late. Mia, I assume. They get in her Lexus and drive off.

I watch the taillights turn past the mailboxes and security gate and onto the main road. I kiss Avery's head and close my eyes. I make a silent promise that that will be me—us: mother and daughter, carefree on a drive to soccer practice. That I will find a way out of the personal hell I've gotten myself into somehow, and maybe she'll never even have to know I was ever like this.

4

CORA

The next day, I think about Georgia while I dump baskets full of clean clothes onto the couch and sit to fold them. I limit my soap-opera viewing time to the space it takes me to fold the laundry, so I take my time. Today, Marco Devine has woken up from his coma only to find out that his evil twin, Blaize, has impersonated him while he was sleeping and stolen his lover. So today, I match the socks with extra care so I can see if Bianca Lovewright will reveal who her heart belongs to. Even as she weeps at Marco's bedside once she finds out he's alive, I still find it's hard to focus. Georgia seemed so glossy and exotic, but now, I don't know what to make of her. She looks…I want to say *ill*.

I can't imagine life inside my house all day. We live on the Oregon coast for the exact opposite reason, in fact. The Douglas fir and hemlock dwarf the neighbors' and make the minimansions along the coast look like hobbit houses beneath their majestic canopy. The houses on our side of the road have woodsy backyards that slope slightly to meet the lakefront. Each long dock stretches out into the clear water, and most have recreational boats attached for lazy weekend rides up to Dockside's country club on the other side of the lake a few miles down. Georgia's side of the street backs onto a forest of Douglas firs with a clearing, which holds a picnic table and a swing set passing for a small park. The air perpetually smells like moss-covered tree bark, sandalwood, and pine, and it's paradise, if you ask me, so how she could be afraid of all of this and not leave the house is baffling.

I wonder what the thing was—the trauma that happened to her. What an odd way to handle a trauma. I watched *My 600-Lb Life*, and they'd all had a trauma and then comforted themselves with cheese fries and beef brisket until they had to be forklifted out of their house and sent to Houston for gastric bypass surgery. I could see that. And the hoarders, who have a dumpster full of stuffed animals and nineteen cats but no litter boxes. I could even see that, sorta—the need to pad yourself with things you find comforting—but poor Georgia. No beef brisket or Care Bears to comfort her. She's all alone all day. Well, she has the baby, but that little, unknowable person cannot be a comfort at that age. The opposite, I would think. I mean, I love babies. No one loves babies more than me, but it's not healthy to be locked away like that with no help.

I could help her. I mean, she's a little weird, but I think I could get through to her and get her out of the house. I took social psychology my sophomore year, and people really respond to me, I think. I'm not tooting my own horn, but I am a people person. I have practiced listening to the woes of my girlfriends for years. I was the one they came to: even back in college, I held their hair back in the bathroom of a dirty bar countless times when they got too drunk and threw up after a rejection from some co-ed. I picked them up from the apartments of one-night stands so they could avoid the walk of shame, and now that we're older, who does Connie Wilkinson call when her son escapes from rehab and we need to drive through the neighborhood in search of him? Who does Vivian Fletcher call when Steve goes on a bender? And the school, whenever they need costumes sewn for the fall play or scones made for the volleyball bake sale? People rely on me. So I just need to figure out how I can show Georgia that she can, too.

As I try to decide whether I'll make rhubarb squares or lemon meringue to bring over to her for a follow-up conversation, I feel a small, crinkly object fall from the still-warm bath towel I'm shaking out. I stare down at it—the half of a rolled joint lying on the couch cushion—and my chest tightens. I sit down and pick it up, examining it. There's a faint pink circle of lipstick around the edge. I don't know whether it's worse if Mia is smoking it or if Finn has a special friend.

When I found a bag of pot in the garage back in January, Mia said it was her friend's and promised she'd never tried it. She might have been lying, but it didn't feel like it at the time. Mia, however, never wears lipstick. She has pink and champagne-colored glosses, but this is Pepto Bismol pink.

Could it belong to whoever *Drinks with C* is? My hands tremble a little as I place the joint on the coffee table and take a deep breath. Stop it. I have to be reasonable. If the pot really belonged to one of Mia's friends last time, maybe the same pot-smoking friend wears pink lipstick. Rational. Be rational. That doesn't explain how it got into our laundry, but it's just as possible as it belonging to Finn's lover, right?

I misread things, and I get carried away. And it gets me into trouble. I can't overreact here. I know what that does. A couple years ago when I saw a text on Finn's phone, I went down the rabbit hole. It said, Hey, babe, can't wait to see you tomorrow. His wife of twenty-two years should have every right to react any way she likes to seeing a message like that, but he explained that it was from Janet Palmer, and that she's the cool lesbian from Accounting and calls everyone *babe*, and that she was looking forward to seeing him at a company mixer because they were planning a funny prank on the managers.

I'll give it to him that if he were lying, it was detailed and very quick thinking. At the time I was sobbing and screaming at him, demanding to know the truth. When he asked me if I wanted to see the texts before that one—the ones where he asked her whether Andy Keat was stopping for the supplies or if he needed to get anything, I pushed his phone away and threw it at him, then ran upstairs and locked myself in the bathroom.

He was going to prove the conversation was innocent, but I ruined my chance to know for sure. Now, I wonder if he really was going to show me the text thread. He knew I was hysterical and how I respond when I'm like that. I don't think he ever planned on showing me the exchange. He would have found a way out of it even in the heat of the moment, waving his phone in my face, denying everything. I don't know how, but I know he would have.

I wouldn't let it go. I showed up at his job, to *surprise him* by taking him to lunch, trying to get a glimpse of lesbian Janet, but I never did. He saw through my attempts, of course, and every time I found him at a work dinner and peered through the front window to make sure the attendees were who he said, or each time I followed him to the gym only to wait in the parking lot to see if he left with some muscly bimbo, he pushed me further away, and the screaming matches became a nightly event.

It was the little things that added up—all the *Drinks with C* sort of notes when it should really say *Retirement party*. There was always an explanation, though, so I was always just the crazy and paranoid wife. I felt that way, anyway. Between accusations, I sobbed and asked for forgiveness every time he proved himself innocent. I told myself that I was wrong and, if I wanted to stay married, I had to let it go, but I always had this shadowy feeling, and it was almost becoming an addiction, trying to catch him.

Then one night Paige texted. She was purchasing wine for the restaurant at a little bottle shop/tasting-room place downtown, and she snapped a photo of Finn sitting at a candlelit table with a waifish redhead. I remember feeling paralyzed, sitting there at my bedroom vanity, plucking my eyebrows and sipping ginger tea. I stared at the photo. I could see that glossy, shy look in his eyes—the kind accompanied by an audible swallow and a nervous laugh. I know that glint. It's a touch of insecurity masked as self-assuredness. I looked at their wineglasses, their hands too close together, then I looked at the silver watch on his wrist that I'd given him on our second wedding anniversary, brushing the side of her impossibly thin arm, and lost my mind.

I have little memory of driving to the bar. I just remember knowing it was my one chance to catch him in the act. I was right. I had been goddamned right all along, and this was it. Thinking back to what a cow I must have looked like, storming in there in a terry-cloth robe and slipper socks, I could just about die with the shame of it. Not to mention I was not wearing makeup and had dots of eye cream beneath my eyes.

"You wanna call me crazy now? Am I still fucking delusional?" I screamed when I reached their small table by the front windows. The place was a small, moody wine bar with only a few other tables, and of course everyone stopped and looked. I didn't care. Tears blurred my eyes, and my life of single motherhood and perpetual bitterness, and the pity of everyone, was all that flashed before me, blinding me.

"Cora, let's go outside. Come on," Finn said, leaping to his feet instinctively, like I was some unhinged wife and he had to do this kind of thing all the time. He shot the redhead an apologetic look, and that's when I really lost it.

"Don't fucking touch me," I yelled, yanking my wrist away from his grip. "You liar. He's a fucking liar," I said to the small woman, who just sat there, still holding her wine, with her mouth agape. "Did you know he was married? Yeah, the son of a bitch is married with a kid to boot. Did he mention that?"

"Cora!" Finn snapped and tried to grab my arm again. The man from behind the bar came over and started to ask something stupid like "Is everything okay?" but I don't recall exactly what.

The small redhead picked up her handbag and started to say "Maybe I should…" but I broke away from Finn's grip and flipped the table. Both glasses of red wine smashed, smattering onto the woman's pale silk blouse. Some of the glass cut through the material and into the tops of her forearms. She sat in silent shock, looking like a murder victim who had been stabbed through the heart but hadn't fallen over dead yet. The bartender screamed at Finn to get me out of there while someone else called a medic. He said they were calling the police, but the redhead insisted they shouldn't. Then, suddenly, I was outside.

Finn pulled me into the car and told me if I didn't stay there and settle down, he'd call the police himself and press charges and I'd be headed for a psych eval. I stayed there, sobbing, beating the dashboard as he went back in to take care of his little slut girlfriend. Half an hour later, he returned. He said he'd drive me home in his car because I was in no state to drive. He didn't look at me or speak for a long time.

Then, when we were almost home, he said, "What the fuck is wrong with you?"

I didn't answer.

"You're lucky. She *should* press assault charges. But at least the glass didn't… It could have been a lot worse. You could have…" He stopped and took a deep breath, then just shook his head.

"I don't care," I said defiantly, looking out the passenger window. "You should go stay somewhere else tonight."

"Oh, I plan to."

"Good," I said, and then silence again.

"You just cost me, *us*, a lot of money, you know that? 'Cause you had to act like a paranoid psychopath. She was a top client who was discussing her company expansion, which would have been a huge chunk of business for me. I can't even believe what you just did. Is this just how you are now? Look at you!" He slammed his hand on the steering wheel, and I became painfully aware of how much I must have resembled a fat, demented Xena, Warrior Princess, flipping a table like that with one hand in my giant pink robe and eye cream. My suspicions gave way to immeasurable shame when I realized what I had done.

And if I'm honest, we've never been the same since. I went to therapy, and he finally said he forgave me after months of silent dinners and avoidance. It was probably because she only had minor cuts on her arms and ended up giving him her business anyway, no doubt out of pity, and because they had laughed and bonded over his pathetic wife who must be such a burden to bear. Nonetheless, things slowly went back to near normal.

Now, two years later, I cannot afford to ask him if this joint belongs to the redhead who may or may not really have been a client or if it belongs to *Drinks with C.*

I decide to ask Mia about it instead. Shortly after I found that bag of weed in the garage months ago, she had an incident with the car. She hit a pole while pulling into a Trader Joe's parking lot. She seemed removed and distracted around that time, too. Maybe she *was* lying to me about it? Something was going on.

I abandon my pile of laundry and go upstairs to have a look in her room. Her laptop sits open on her desk, but I tell myself that looking would be an invasion of privacy, and at this juncture I'm not willing to cross that line yet—not unless I think she's in real trouble. Also, I don't have the password. Otherwise, if I'm honest, I probably would. Just to check on her well-being, of course. But before I can even open a drawer, I hear a key in the door and footsteps lumbering up the stairs. I barely exit her doorway before Mia is in front of me, tossing her backpack on the floor and stopping to look at me.

"Hi!" I say, too loudly, accompanied by a forced, too-big smile.

"Why are you being weird?" she says, looking me up and down. When I don't quickly come up with an answer, she gives a sort of shrug.

"'K. I'm gonna go in here now," she says in that condescending teenage way and then flops on her bed, already with phone in hand. I remember then that there's a teachers' conference, so it's a half day, and no, she didn't sense my spying somehow and materialize just in time to hide her drugs.

I stand in her doorway, holding the joint that she hasn't noticed yet and wait for her to look up from her phone. She finally senses me looking at her and raises her eyebrows at me.

"What?" she asks.

I wave the joint back and forth.

"Oh, my God. Are you smoking pot?" She sits up, cross-

45

legged on her bed with wide eyes, staring at me, confused but almost sort of excited.

"Am I— What? No. Mia. I found this in the laundry."

"You think it's a good idea to smoke something you don't know where it came from?" she asks matter-of-factly. "It could be laced."

"What do you know about drugs being laced?" I say, much louder than intended.

"Uhhh, I'm seventeen, and I have a pulse. I think those are the only requirements for knowing what *laced* means. What, now I'm getting yelled at for knowledge I have no control over having?"

"I'm not yelling at you. I'm asking if this is yours," I say.

"I thought you just said it was yours," she says.

"Oh, my God, Mia…" I stop and take an exaggerated breath, then speak slowly, an annoying motherly habit I picked up somewhere along the line. "It is clearly not mine. I found this in the laundry. I am asking if this belongs to you."

"You found it in my laundry? No way."

"I found it in *the* laundry. Can you just answer me, please."

"So you assume it's mine. I'm not the only one who lives here."

"That's not an answer," I say, keeping my tone controlled. "Last time I checked, your father and I don't smoke."

"Are you sure?" she says, propping herself against her headboard and picking up her phone again.

"What's that supposed to mean?" I ask, taking the phone out of her hand.

"It's not mine. I don't smoke pot. You wanna know why? Because pot makes you eat everything, and when you eat everything, you get fat. Are you calling me fat?" she asks.

I mutter *Oh, my God* under my breath and give her her phone back.

"Libby Patterson became, like, a total pothead, and now she shops at Hot Topic and gained, like, a million pounds. Annie Brewer called her Libby-McSaturated Fatterson, instead of Patterson, during study hall, and the nickname stuck. And then someone left a stick of butter in her locker. You think I want that to be me? No way. You should be way more concerned about whether I'm drinking and let the pot thing go." She gives me a look that somehow punctuates her monologue and goes back to her phone.

I don't even say anything. I just stand there, trying to process it all. I turn and leave, knowing she's telling the truth. And knowing what it means that she's telling the truth. I throw the joint in the big garbage behind the garage and go back to finish folding the laundry. I missed finding out which twin Bianca Lovewright will choose, and I don't even care.

Later that evening, I take a bottle of Pinot Grigio over to Paige's, and we sit in Adirondack chairs in her garden like we do a couple times a week. Since her son's tragic death, it's become less often, but I make a point to still pop by, though I try to sense her mood before making myself comfortable. Paige never talks to me about Caleb. I mean, I know that she is certain it was murder and that she suspects all the neighbors and spies on everyone for clues, but she never talks about *him*. He's in all the photos that line every bookshelf and mantel in the house: the tiny Caleb standing in tall weeds at dusk, holding a lightning bug in a jar; the Caleb who was gifted at art but didn't want to pursue it, who drank Mountain Dew for breakfast and broke his left wrist jumping off a dock at Eagle Cliff Campgrounds; the Caleb who was a football star in high school but also watched reruns of *The Golden Girls* with his mother; the Caleb who hated bullies and loved collecting Pez dispensers. This is the son she never talks about, at least not to me.

47

We silently watch a yellow cat named Arnie balance on the wood fence around the backyard. The neighborhood is quiet at dusk, as it always is. A wind chime made of seashells makes a hollow tinkling sound in the breeze, and a dog barks in the distance. I pour us two large glasses of cold wine and place the bottle on the cement pad next to my chair. I want to cry.

"I think he's cheating," I say to the trees, then take a deep breath and blow it out, hard.

"Oh, honey," Paige says, looking at me.

"For real this time. I found a joint with lipstick on it in the laundry. And no, it's not Mia's. It was like a ballet slipper color. She hates pink. And I asked her, so, I mean, it's someone's. I'm not imagining it."

"Cor, you don't have to convince me. I believe you."

"You do?" I look at her, feeling a flood of something. Relief, I think.

"Of course. Just because you haven't caught him all those times you suspected doesn't mean you're wrong. You trust your gut. That doesn't make you paranoid, it makes you smart." She places her hand on mine and squeezes it a moment.

"Thank you," I say and take a large gulp of wine.

"So tell me again why you don't just leave the bastard?"

"Oh, no. He's not a— I could be wrong. I mean, I really could. Maybe it's me. And I don't know, it's just not…"

"Not what?" she prompts.

"Well, not that easy," I say, and she shakes her head and scoffs.

"'Course it is."

"There's a prenup," I say tentatively.

Paige purses her lips and says, "Ah!" as if she gets it now, without me needing to say anything further, but I do anyway.

"It's not what you think. I wanted it. I wanted a clause

added that there would be—" I make quotation marks with my fingers "—*a substantial penalty paid out if infidelity is involved.*"

Paige looks half-impressed and half-confused.

"What would make a madly in love twentysomething girl think to ask for that?"

"I caught him sneaking out of one of my girlfriends' dorm room at three in the morning the spring before the wedding. I just had a sense about him, about his…nature, I guess," I say.

"His *nature*. Is that what we're calling it?" she asks humorlessly, but she doesn't question why I still married him. "So when you say *substantial*, what exactly does that mean?"

"Well, the way it shook out, it's about a half-million-dollar payoff."

"If he cheats?" she clarifies.

"Yeah, but if I just leave for seemingly no reason, I mean, they say you get half, but I have never worked, you know like a job outside the house, and Mia will be off to college so it will just be me and my financially noncontributing self. Everything is in his name…and he can pay for the best lawyers. I talked to a lawyer once. I could be left with next to nothing. Which, you know what, is bullshit."

"If I remember right, you gave up a career in journalism to move here and take care of pretty much everything else," Paige says, sipping her wine and staring out into the inky air.

"I don't want it to sound like… I'm making it sound… Those were my choices, and maybe I'm wrong about him," I say, and then we just listen to the cicadas a moment. It *was* my choice. It wasn't a time when I was expected to be a stay-at-home mom. But I did tell myself that if life allowed me the stability to make my child my full-time job, nothing could make me happier. And when I met Finn, somehow the stars aligned.

My own single mother worked squirting perfume at people at a Dillard's by day and took overnight shifts at Shady Brook Nursing Home at night, spending the weekends on the couch recovering from her stressful week with tumblers of peach Boone's Farm. I was able to do the exact opposite. And I get to help people every day. I get to run charity drives and volunteer. It seems more useful an existence than shoving a mic in someone's face just to be the first vulture to get a statement so I can boost my career. It really does. I'm needed rather than being a success-hungry nuisance to everyone I meet like I might have been in the journalism world. Paige thinks I just say this to be at peace with the simple life of a so-called housewife, but that's not true. I mean it. I have never regretted giving up my career for the life I have.

Now, though, if Finn breaks his side of our promise, his life goes on as it is and I lose it all. He still has his career, money, the house. All of it. My contributions are what we agreed was best for our family, but on paper I'm worthless, aren't I? It's incredibly cruel and unjust. The cheating is one kind of betrayal, but being stripped of everything else is quite another. I sigh and sip my drink, then say, "But I don't think I am."

"What?" she asks.

"Wrong about him. I don't think I am."

"Well, you're not very good at catching him, are you?" Paige says.

"Because I'm probably wrong—just being a paranoid psycho."

"So wait. Back up a sec. Why would Finn, twentysomething in love, agree to this clause?"

"Mostly because he wanted clauses that said he keeps such and such investment. He was already doing well out of college and wanted to protect his money, so I got to have a clause, too. Also, he knew he was sort of caught with the dorm-room girlfriend, so I almost didn't marry him at all. It was a strange negotiation for that age, you're right, but that's how it all rolled out over those months when I was ready to walk away from him. Funny, I thought that him agreeing somehow proved that he didn't mess around with my friend like he was insisting he didn't, but...now I wonder if he just knew he was really good at sneaking around. Or maybe that he could easily talk me into staying if he got caught. I don't know anymore."

"Sorry, Cor," she says. What else can she say?

"I actually put away some money to hire a private investigator. God, that's so crazy, right?"

"But you didn't do it yet?" she asks.

"No, 'cause I feel like it—I don't know—crosses, like, a big line. I just— I don't know."

"Well, maybe I can help," she says, looking at me. I turn to look at her, taken aback.

"Uh, really?"

"Grant thinks I need a hobby," she says, and we both laugh at this. "Maybe some time focusing on something else wouldn't be a terrible idea."

"Okay," I say skeptically. "Not sure how you could help. I've tried, like, everything."

"I'm gonna need you to be open-minded here," Paige says, with a look like she's about to deliver bad news. I raise my eyebrows at her.

"Okay..." I say, waiting to hear more.

"I could follow him. I mean, instead of you hiring some stranger you don't know if you can trust, I could...sort of set a trap."

"Like, what do you mean? How would you do that?"

"Well, first I'll follow him—see if I can catch him. If I can't find anything, then...I try to, you know, make a pass—seduce him. See if he bites," she says, as if she didn't just say something shocking. My hand flutters to my mouth, and I feel a surge of nervous energy rush through me.

"Are you kidding?" I ask.

"You want proof? I'll have a camera and a firsthand account. Bam!" she says, a little too into this idea. I think about it for a moment. Paige, with her Pilates body and sweep of long chestnut hair, could probably seduce anyone. I haven't consciously felt jealous of her beauty until this very minute, while I'm forced to think of her in bed with Finn. My Finn.

"I won't actually let it go too far," she adds, as if reading my mind. "Just enough to get you what you need." I don't ask where those lines lie, exactly. I just sit in stunned silence for a few minutes. I want this. I need to know. Would he go as far as to cheat with one of my closest friends? Would it only take a few drinks and one sexual advance to just throw away everything we have? If so, yeah, I guess I want to know.

"I don't know," I say. "It's…crazy."

"Yep," she says. Spoken like a woman with nothing left to lose in life, which is exactly what she is. "Think about it," she says, pouring another glass.

We drop the subject and talk about the squirrels stealing from the birdfeeder and how she hopes the sod she laid isn't too shaded by the oak tree.

I think about how she was so crippled with grief she had to stop working. She and Grant had a chain of restaurants once upon a time. They paid for this house in cash and had a cabin in Puget Sound. They vacationed in Thailand and Fiji. And now? The one restaurant they kept is keeping them afloat, probably only because the house is long paid off, but the property taxes alone have to be a struggle. Maybe there's money I don't know about, but still, I'd rather pay her than a stranger. It feels less dangerous somehow—more of an act of solidarity. And then out of nowhere I blurt, "Okay! Yes!"

and she chuckles and takes another sip. "I'll pay you the same if you can get proof."

"You only pay me *if* I get it, though," she says.

"Okay," I agree. I'd have it to spare if this all goes down the way I pray it won't. My hands are trembling, and I should tell her no, that this is absolutely insane, but I think it might be my only shot. So I shakily raise my glass and clink it against hers.

"Okay," I say. "I'm in."

5

GEORGIA

Sometimes, I completely forget I'm in this prison I've made for myself. Right now, as I peel the brittle paper on a bag of English breakfast tea and put the kettle on the stovetop, I forget and feel, just for a moment, like a normal, very lucky woman with a handsome, caring husband and the gift of a new baby. I live in an enormous house and should be nothing but happy and completely untroubled. But that only lasts for seconds, usually. Or sometimes, when I wake up in the morning, I get to hang on to the wisps of a dream and stay suspended in that place between sleep and wakefulness, and I get to forget a little bit longer than I would if I were fully conscious.

I try to remember who I was before I deteriorated into whatever this version of myself is. Flashes of long-ago happiness comes in disjointed bursts. I remember a much-anticipated birthday party at Skateville when I was twelve: lace-up tan skates when I wanted the white ones, personal pepperoni pizzas and Dr. Peppers at the concession stand, the dizzying dots of light moving across the skate floor. I remember the sneaking out of the house for nights on the beach in Cornwall with friends, sitting around firepits, drinking peach wine coolers, and laughing. My parents' house in the city and the last Christmas there before they passed. We drank ginger wine and watched *It's a Wonderful Life*. The day I sold my beloved 1997 VW Jetta because I was off to take on the world. My BA in hospitality and tourism would first take me to a six-month contract in Cordillera and then who knew where.

I push the memories away and sit on a kitchen chair to take a deep, mindful breath and keep it together. This is interrupted by my growl of frustration when I see the dirty-laundry basket sitting outside the door to the basement. I planned to have it done now so Avery would have her favorite blanket clean, the one that she puked up on earlier. She won't go down easily without it.

She smiles at me from her playpen set up in front of the TV, where a *Teletubbies* rerun plays a song that sounds like the moment in a horror movie before an evil doll comes to life and slaughters everyone. I want to turn it off, but she squeals at it in delight and pumps her little chubby fists in the air, trying to dance along. I tell her I'll be right back and go to the laundry basket, hesitantly. I fling open the door to the basement and peer down the steep staircase into the darkness. I feel for the chain that turns on the overhead light and pull it. These old houses are all renovated and pristine, from the open floor plans to the white quartz kitchen islands, but the basements are still dungeonesque. I'm sure the only reason Lucas never bothered to move the laundry to the main floor the way every HGTV home-makeover show does is because he doesn't actually do the laundry, so why would it be on his radar?

I tread carefully, the laundry basket bouncing on each step behind me as I inch my way down. It's just laundry. It's just fucking laundry. I'll dump it in the washer, push Start, and go. I pause at the bottom of the stairs. There are rickety wooden shelves on the wall to the right, probably original to the house, filled with rusted paint gallons and ancient oil cans, among other neglected clutter. The washer and dryer are at the end of the cement room under an egress window that doesn't contribute much light to the basement, as it's masked by a huckleberry bush outside of it. I eye the open washer, then look back up the staircase. It's not an irrational fear of ghosts or even rapists hiding in the shadows. I'm not an unreasonable person. But when that sour-basement, dirty-mop-water smell hits me, I'm in that room again. I am in that room, screaming. I'm pleading to get out. I…

There is something backed up in the utility sink near the dryer. I can see the brown water, sitting stagnant. Some has spilled over the sides, and the cement floor is damp where it streamed down the sloped floor to the metal drain in the middle of the room. I gag. Then it comes, completely out of my control. I can't catch my breath. I'm gasping for air. I open my mouth to scream, but nothing comes out. Then, when the tears start without my permission, the sobs follow in uncontrollable hiccups at the top of each panicked hitch. I run, almost crawling up the steep staircase. I hear the tea-kettle squealing on the stovetop, which has made Avery cry, and I can only focus on catching my breath before I'm able to even stand up and go to her. On my hands and knees at the top of the stairs, I try to stop the panic attack. I try to inhale.

Just then, Lucas opens the door from the attached garage and is met with the screeching sounds of the baby, the kettle, and me on the floor, gasping for air.

"Jesus!" He drops his things and rushes to me and puts his

arm around me, helping me to sit. "Hey, it's okay," he says. "Are you okay? Breathe. It's okay, you're okay." He stays with me a few moments until he sees I'm calming down. Then he runs to turn off the screeching kettle and picks Avery up out of her playpen and comes back to sit on the floor next to me.

"See? It's okay," he says to her in a baby voice she likes. "Everything is just fine, right?" He bounces her on his knee, and she stops crying and grabs for his nose, smiling. "Yes, it is." He gives her cheek a raspberry, and she giggles.

"What happened?" he asks. I can't tell him what happened because nothing exactly did happen.

"I don't know," I say, getting to my feet and shakily going to sit on a dining-room chair. He is accustomed to this answer, and he knows there is nothing else he'll get out of me. I open my arms for him to give Avery to me.

"It's okay," he says. "Maybe you should take a few minutes." He puts her back in her playpen, and she is immediately engrossed in her show again.

"I'm fine now," I add. He gives me a look. I know there is some football game tonight that he's talked about a few times, so I try to distract him with that.

"Really. Grab your beer and watch your pregame whatever-it's-called. I'm fine. I'll start dinner in a little bit."

"Why don't you take a bath and relax for a little while first. That always helps," he says. Except that it doesn't, but I don't say that. He's already halfway upstairs to run the bath on his way to change out of his work clothes.

When I've bathed and changed into clean yoga pants and an oversize jumper, I make an Indian curry for dinner with jasmine rice and store-bought naan on the side. We sit on the front porch because the evening is breezy and cool. Lucas pulls Avery's high chair outside and feeds her spoonfuls of carrot puree while I arrange the dishes on the small porch table. We eat quietly. Even though he's recording the game, he often walks over to the screen door and peers through to the TV a moment when he hears cheering or excited sportscaster voices.

I want to talk to him about Cora's visit—her invitation to come over one afternoon with Avery—but I don't, because it's not possible. Even though I fantasize about a life where, if I'm not able to go out into the world like a normal person, maybe I could at least create a small world for myself in the safety of the cul-de-sac and have some social interaction. It's close. It's still safe, I think. But I am too tired for this conversation. My face feels swollen from crying earlier, and it's not a topic I can handle, not tonight.

After dinner I take Avery to the small park behind our house and push her on the baby swing. After my state earlier, I know, without having to look over at the back of our house, that Lucas will peer out the window now and then to check on me. But I wouldn't put Avery in harm's way for anything, so there is really no need.

I see some teenagers over by the small pond. They're doing tricks with their skateboards and drinking cans of something out of a paper bag. Lucas has always said this has turned into a druggy park and to watch out, but I tell him I've never seen anything like that here. I'm squinting my eyes against the low sun and straining to see what they're up to when one of them heads over to me. I instinctively glance toward the house to see if Lucas is there. I stop Avery's swing and take a step in front of her when the kid approaches. He's older than I thought: seventeen or eighteen, maybe. His head is shaved on one side, with floppy bangs that hang down over his eye on the other.

"Hey, can I ask you something?" he says.

"No," I say sternly, picking up Avery and putting her in her stroller.

"Whaa!" He does some kind of bro laugh. "Whoa, I can't ask you something?"

"Are you selling something?" I ask.

"Do you want me to be?" he says, smirking.

"Because only people selling something ask a stranger *Can I ask you something?* Like the guy at a mall kiosk trying to sell sunglasses or the guy outside the grocery store asking who your phone carrier is. I'm not interested in buying the burned CD your band made, but thanks anyway."

"Daaamn. Rich lady got some attitude, for real. Nah, I ain't selling anything," he says and pulls out a tiny bag of weed from his shorts, just enough for me to see what it is.

"What makes you think you can come over here—where there is a baby, mind you—and try to sell me pot? Are you insane?"

"Chicks like you are my best customers. Plus, it's free for you. This one time." He looks around and then reaches out to hand it to me. I stand there with a hand on one hip and the expression on his face grows impatient. He's careful, eyeing the surrounding area to make sure there are no cops or onlookers.

I want it. I *need* it. But what if Lucas is watching right now? How would I explain it? Especially with Avery right here. I couldn't. I can't take it.

"Shove it in my pocket," I say quickly.

"What?" he says.

"Shove it in my goddamn pocket," I snap. He laughs and mumbles some joke about knowing how I like it, but he does as I ask. When he does, I lift my hands up in protest and back away from him. Just in case Lucas sees, I look like I've been forced, assaulted even. I know it's a little much, but I need it.

The kid gives another smirk and then a wink as he leaves, telling me he'll see me again. I put the pot in my bra and walk quickly home, my heart beating hard in my chest.

This could change things. This could change everything.

6

PAIGE

Paige sits in the darkness of her upstairs study and fast-forwards her surveillance video of the Holmons' house on her desktop computer. She stops now and then and zooms the picture in to make sure she doesn't miss anything, even though there is absolutely nothing of note to see. He seems like the kind of slimeball who would sneak his lover out the back door while poor Cora simultaneously, and innocently, comes in the front door from a book-club meeting, tipsy and chatty about her evening, not even noticing him zipping up his pants and smoothing his hair.

The guy is good, Paige has to admit. She'd waited in the parking lot of his office every day this week and followed him after work. Three nights he went right home. One night he went to a fancy-schmancy steak house but was escorted to a reserved private room, so she couldn't see anything after that.

Now, what sort of person gets a private room at a restaurant? Of course, he would say he was courting some important clients and they needed to be able to hear one another talk—that was how she assumed he'd rationalize it. Maybe it was perfectly legitimate, but perhaps it was something else. She'll never know.

The other night he didn't go home after work; he met some people for drinks. Coworkers or clients, maybe. Paige watched, parked on the far side of the bar parking lot and peering in with binoculars. There was a handsy brunette in a tight pencil skirt that she made note of—and took a few photos of with her new Nikon D850 she bought specifically for her new task. All fairly disappointing so far, overall.

Then, Paige sees something odd in the frame and backs it up, leaning in to see what the movement next to the garbage cans is. A damn raccoon. Nothing more. She is so engrossed in her work, though, she doesn't hear the footsteps come up the stairs or the figure stopping at the study doorway until she notes an inhale of breath. She flings her chair around in terror and stands clutching her chest.

"Goddamn it, Grant! You scared the absolute fuck out of me!" But Grant doesn't immediately answer. He stands with a bag full of take-out boxes and stares over her shoulder at the screen.

"Oh, don't get all self-righteous on me," she says, before he can open his mouth to speak. "If I'd had cameras on the neighbors a year ago, we might not be in this situation. What the hell are you doing here, anyway?"

"Pasta puttanesca," he says, innocently holding up the bag.

Downstairs, they eat together in the dark kitchen. The only sound is a cable news show, faintly heard from the living room, where she usually keeps it on in the background for company.

"How is it?" he asks expectantly.

"Good," she says. "It's always good."

"It's for the charity thing tomorrow night. I got the good anchovies. Can you tell?" he asks.

"Martel's?" she asks.

"Martel's? You think these are Martel's? It's Delfino's. Four times the price per tin, and you can't tell the difference?" She knew it was Delfino's, but she likes to rile him up a bit. She still finds it endearing the way he's so passionate about his cooking. She smiles, and she can see him realize she's kidding. She offers him wine, but he declines, so she puts the kettle on for tea instead.

"It's really good," she says again, squeezing his shoulder as she passes behind him, and plucks two mugs from the cabinet. After their meal, they sit out on the front porch in the rocking recliners. Christopher jumps up on Grant's lap, and he strokes the old dog on the top of the head and sips his tea. It's a breezeless night, and the neighborhood is silent. Paige pours a nip of gin into her tea and covers her legs with a blanket.

"Be careful," Grant says out of nowhere.

"With what?" Paige snaps.

"Whatever sneaky snake stuff you're getting yourself into now, that's what," he says.

"Sneaky snake?" she repeats with a look of condescension. He doesn't react, so she waves his comment away with her hand and a scoff.

"I had this memory of Caleb last night," Paige says. "Do you remember when he came home late from some party last year, and he was laughing because he saw Finn Holmon parked on the street and he said it looked like he was getting a blow job?" Paige asks.

"I can't say that I remember that," Grant says with a short laugh.

"Maybe you were at the restaurant, but he said he was pretty sure old married couples didn't do stuff like that."

"I told him it was a cliché for a young person to say old people don't have sex, and also Cora is, like, thirty-nine."

"He said his point was that it wasn't Cora. When I asked how he knew that, he just said, 'Trust me,' and went up to bed. He thought it was hilarious."

"Okay," Grant says, not knowing where this is going.

"I assumed it was Cora, but now that I think about it, he's right. Pretty sure it wasn't her," Paige says.

"And this is our business how?" Grant asks.

"'Cause she's my friend. And the son of a bitch is a cheater."

"Is this how you're spending your time at home all day?" he asks and then sighs, and she can tell he wishes he hadn't said anything about how she spends her time. "I just worry," he continues. He doesn't have to say all the reasons why—that he worries she is unstable, or too isolated, or has been mourning too long, or sleeping an unhealthy amount; the list could go on—so before he says anything else, they just drop it the way they have both learned to do, so it doesn't explode into raging arguments the way it used to right after Caleb's death. Maybe if they'd learned to control the conversations this way earlier, they would still be together and not have said things they can never unsay to one another.

"Why don't you hang out with Finn anymore, anyway? You two used to watch the game together and play golf all the time," Paige says. Grant just shrugs.

"Things change," he says, and they don't say much of anything else, just that Christopher is getting a little fat, the ice maker in the fridge keeps jamming, and Grant could use a haircut, which Paige offers to do for him when he comes over on Sunday.

The next morning, Paige wakes up late the way she often

does these days. She trudges downstairs in her sweatpants and oversize Blondie tank top and starts a pot of coffee, when she sees Finn out her kitchen window, stuffing his golf clubs into the back of the Holmons' Land Rover. She decides, without thinking, that this is an opportunity to follow him. She shoves her feet into slippers, grabs her handbag, and runs to her garage. She times opening the garage and pulling out to just after she hears his car pull away.

On the drive, she very much regrets not pouring a coffee into a to-go mug or putting on real clothes, and she begins seriously doubting that she will obtain any valuable information at a golf course. The last thing in the world she wants to do is sit in a country-club parking lot all day on a Saturday, but she's on a mission, so she'll at least give it an hour or so.

When she sees him take the Greenbriar exit, her pulse starts to speed up, and her hands feel suddenly clammy. The golf course is six miles farther down Lakeview. Maybe he's stopping for gas. Good, she thinks. She can grab a coffee maybe, even though she looks slightly homeless. The fleeting judgment will be worth the caffeine. When he drives right past the Conoco station, and the Mattress Firm, Coffee Central, and a vacant Taco Bell building, she cannot believe her luck. He's driving to the Royal Inn.

She slows down a bit because he must be looking over his shoulder. He must be going to a place like this rather than the Hilton Express or whatever because nobody besides hookers or cheap road trippers would ever stay here, so he's likely to never run into someone he knows. Holy shit, she's got him. She parks in the Antiques Mall parking lot across the street so he doesn't spot her and peers through her binoculars at the motel. He's still sitting in his car.

The Royal Motel is anything but royal, of course. It's a single-story, ten-room building with a low roofline and a broken Pepsi machine out front that looks like it's been there since the 1980s. Each room can be accessed directly from the parking lot, and there are no numbers on the rooms, only a different, boldly colored door for each to differentiate. A few young women are loitering around the yellow door, smoking cigarettes and looking at their phones.

She wonders why he's still in his car. Is the woman he's here to meet inside, or perhaps not here yet? Then, after ten or so minutes of watching him, she sees one of the smoking women flick the butt of her cigarette into the air, fluff her hair, and walk over to his car.

"Shut the fuck up," Paige whispers under her breath as she watches in horror. The woman is wearing a tight leopard-print minidress, exactly like you'd imagine a college girl would wear on Halloween and whose costume is *Stripper*. Except this woman doesn't have sexy, high-heeled boots or anything, but rather, dirty pink flip-flops. She leans into his car, and they talk for a minute. Then—

She cannot believe it. What in the fresh hell is she seeing? The woman takes Finn's hand out the window and puts it into her panties. Paige almost screams, but instead, she takes a photo with her Nikon. And then a few more as Finn and the woman laugh. Then he goes to the front check-in area, which is housed in a tiny, separate building near the entrance, presumably to pay for a room. The girl wanders back to her friends, smokes another cigarette, gathers her purse, and then, a few minutes after Finn enters the green-door room, the woman follows. Paige captures it all.

She smiles to herself as she pulls away from the seedy motel and back onto the main road. She got what she came for. She should bring it directly to Cora and let that be that. She won't do that, though, because there's a bigger picture here, and she has plans for Finn Holmon. A hooker photo is not enough.

When she gets home, she feels breathless and anxious. She makes her coffee and sits in front of her computer, clicking around for YouTube videos to learn how to transfer the data from her complicated camera to her desktop file labeled *Finn Holmon*.

She can't quite believe it. It's not that she didn't trust Cora's instincts, but she expected a mousy receptionist he could easily impress and manipulate, not animal-print-clad prostitutes at the Royal Inn. What the hell was he doing? *If this is what you want, why be married?* is all she can think.

He's always been the type of guy who will comment on the waitress's backside or the nice rack on the blonde news anchor. It's the kind of passive comment designed to make any other woman in his company feel lesser-than. Otherwise, why say anything? Why does anybody care what gives you a boner? Not his wife, she can promise him that. Nobody is interested in who you'd like to stick your dick in, she thinks. But that's really what a comment like that implies, and it takes a certain kind of person—maybe a narcissistic one—to freely make these sorts of proclamations to make those around them feel uncomfortable.

She remembers how he'd once said, while at Paige and Grant's restaurant—and Cora was in the restroom—that the legs on the teenage waitress went "all the way to heaven." Grant never gave the courtesy laugh or grunt of agreement Finn was fishing for, though. He always changed the subject and pretended not to hear him.

She knows the person Finn is. So why does she need more? She thinks she might have finally lost her mind.

That afternoon, Paige calls Cora, even though she knows the kind of frenzied state Cora gets in every time she's helping to host one of her many charity events. She lives for them, and they have to be absolutely flawless. She doubts Finn will be there tonight because it's Cora's thing, or so he always says, and he rarely accompanies her. But where *will* he be? is the question.

"Hey, just calling to see if you need any last-minute help," Paige says to Cora, praying she doesn't.

"Oh, that's sweet, but actually I think it's under control so far."

"Will Finn be joining you tonight?" Paige cuts to the chase and hears the hesitation in Cora's answer: she knows Cora is not completely sure about this whole scheme of theirs.

"Uh, no. He's got plans with some buddies— I think beers at O'Sullivan's." Paige scribbles this down. "Mia bailed, so…"

"Huh. What time?" she asks.

"Sorry?" Cora says.

"The beers at O'Sullivan's," Paige says. Cora is silent a moment.

"Paige, I—" Cora starts to say but then is interrupted by Mia, it sounds like. She hears a moment of muffled conversation, then, "Hey, I gotta go, but you'll be at Moretti's tonight, though, right?" she asks.

"I'm actually a bit under the weather," Paige lies. "I'll see how I'm feeling later." When they hang up, Paige feels terrible. She should be there for Grant tonight, and she and Cora should probably call off this whole crazy plan, she knows that. It was a ridiculous idea that Cora agreed to out of desperation, and now Paige is exploiting that. Something inside her is stirring, though, changing like a vagary of wind shifting directions. Grief is supposed to come in fits and starts, but hers has been unceasing, breath-stealing. It felt like the world was tilting and she had to claw and grip the earth so she didn't slide off—a constant, all-consuming effort every waking moment. So even though she knows it's fucked up that she's finding this flicker of hope—is that what this is?—in Finn Holman, in Cora's husband, she just knows she needs to do this.

She's going to the salon for a blowout and manicure and then to the boutique on Sixth Street to see if that cute silk cami is still in the window.

O'Sullivan's is busy when Paige arrives. She's in skinny jeans and heels with the black silk camisole top from the shop window. She's been told she has Sandra Bullock hair, and when she does herself up, she's quite the knockout. She hasn't changed out of sweatpants in weeks, nor has she applied makeup or taken her hair out of a scruffy ponytail for as long as she can remember—maybe Caleb's funeral was the last time she'd made any effort for any reason. She feels like a different person tonight. Part of it is that she feels human again—more than human, desirable even. She doesn't care about being desirable outside of the necessity of the job at hand, but it does make one feel lighter, a bit confident, even. This new focus—to trap Finn—has breathed new life into her somehow. She walks through the dark pub and sits at the bar. The place smells like years of beer spills dried into the carpet along with a stale, smoky tinge from the decades of smoke yellowing the walls, back before smoking indoors was banned.

She doesn't waste any time. She orders a beer and gulps half of it, less for liquid courage and more to appear as though she's been there awhile and therefore not stalking him. She spots him near the pool tables with a couple guys she doesn't recognize. She half expected him to be with a woman but supposes not even he would do that so openly in a local hot spot. She carries her beer and looks down at her phone, pretending to text as she meanders over that way. *He* has to see *her*, and not the other way around, for this to feel organic. And he does. Well, she's made it impossible for him not to. She lingers close to their table, looking engaged in her phone.

"Paige!" he hollers, cupping his hand around one side of his mouth to be heard over the noise. He holds up a beer and gives a sort of *What are you doing here?* shrug of disbelief.

"Oh. Finn. Hi!" she says, pushing her hair from her face and putting her phone in her purse.

"Hi. What are you doing at Sully's? I've never seen you here before."

"Oh, just meeting a girlfriend for a drink, but her sitter called—a fever or something—and she had to go." She likes how easy and slippery these lies feel: she's playing a character, and it's invigorating. He doesn't ask why she's not at Grant's thing, and she doesn't ask him either. They should both be there, supporting their other halves. Well, at least he should. Paige is separated. There is less obligation. This omission on both their parts seems appropriate for the situation.

"Well, join us," he says with a wide smile.

"Oh, no. That's okay. Looks like a guys' night. I couldn't intrude."

"Look, I've known these sad sacks since college. We have nothing new to say to each other, and if I hear Jesse bitch about his wife not letting him join a rugby team one more time, I was gonna leave anyway. Come on. You'll be a breath of fresh air. I'll buy you a drink," he says.

"Uh, yeah. Okay. I guess…for one," she says, and he waves down a tiny blonde waitress holding an impossibly full tray of teetering bottles and pint glasses.

"When you get a chance," he says and gestures a sort of circle with his finger. "A round of…" He looks to Paige.

"Oh, uh, Heineken," she says, and the girl nods and disappears into the sea of patrons that seem like giants next to her.

They end up sitting on stools at the high pub table next to the billiards area. His friends shoot games, and he is mostly invested in a football game playing on the many flat screens around the bar. He looks like a teenager in his backward UMass ball cap, fixated on the TV and stuffing loaded fries into his mouth. She stares at him, momentarily transfixed. Something about the hat makes her heart flutter. He looks back at her.

"What?" he asks, chewing a mouthful of food.

"N-nothing." She smiles and nervously looks down at a cardboard coaster that she picks at until the drinks come.

She feigns interest and tries to make the right noises when something exciting or disappointing happens on-screen, but she was hoping for a little more conversation in a quieter place that would allow it. She can tell he's getting a little drunk by the increasing amount of high fives he gives her. Also, he doesn't notice her finding ways to dump her beer into other people's empties every time a new round arrives. She needs to keep her wits about her.

Once the crowd thins and his friends leave, she realizes how late it's getting. She has sort of just existed in the background of Alabama Slammer shots and bad referee calls all evening, and that was not the plan, but he doesn't seem to be much of a conversationalist. She isn't sure about the best way to do this. Too blatant an approach could be dangerous, but now that he's nice and loose, she tries to flirt, even though she feels she may have forgotten how.

"I bet you played football in school," she says and immediately wants to gag at how lame it sounds.

"Oh, no. I was a big theater nerd," he says, and she almost spits out the sip of her drink she's just taken. She feels it burn in her nasal passage as she snorts it back.

"Sorry," she laughs. "That's just not what I was expecting you to say. At all. Cora never mentioned that." Damn, she shouldn't have brought up Cora. The last thing she meant to do is remind him she's friends with his wife.

"Oh, yeah. I was gonna be a movie star. Everyone always thinks it's such a geeky thing, but most big actors started in theater classes," he says matter-of-factly, and Paige just cannot picture it. She finds she's staring with her mouth slightly open.

"What?" he counters with a smile.

"No, that's…that's great. I…" She finds herself at a loss. She has only ever seen him playing golf and pickup basketball and cheersing with cans of beer like a big buffoon the times he's been over watching a game with Grant.

"I was in *Annie* in high school," she says, for lack of anything else coming to mind.

"Were you, now?" he says. "What role?"

"Not exactly a role. I got to sit backstage for two hours every night and then walk across stage with a mop bucket during the 'Hard-Knock Life' number," she says. "Kinda deterred me from the craft after that." He laughs at this.

"So what happened to your acting career?" she asks, moving a little closer.

"Y'know, you try to major in the arts in college and then realize you'll never actually have a career and you've shamed your parents, so you change your major to something responsible like business and computer science." He raises his drink and his eyebrows at this, and she thinks she hears a note of bitterness behind his words.

"Right. Well, you've done well for yourself, so…"

He quickly raises his beer to clink bottles at this sentiment, the hundredth clink of the night, she thinks.

"And you. You own a restaurant," he says.

"Past tense. I gave that up," she adds, and his face makes that shape people's faces always make when they remember her son and the way her life crumbled in the wake of his death. "Same, though," she adds before the mood takes a turn. "I was on the business side, the entrepreneur. Grant was the creative, the chef," she says, kicking herself yet again for bringing up a spouse. Finn doesn't seem to notice, and they move on to talk about meaningless things: who would play them in the movie of their lives, why there are no good contractors for bathroom renos, and what's with Janie Nowak a block over who hoards cats, but they laugh far more than she expected, and there are many moments that she forgets why she's there and simply enjoys the company of this increasingly and surprisingly charming man. Then she remembers herself and feels a flush of shame redden her face.

An actor, she thinks, after he excuses himself to the bathroom. Makes sense. She watches him sway slightly as he returns to the table.

"Let me give you a ride home," she suggests, knowing that Zach drove him to the pub and he planned on Ubering home.

"Oh, that's okay. I don't want to put you out," he says.

"We live on the same block." She smiles. "And yes, I'm okay to drive," she adds. He makes a messy *Well, okay, then* gesture with the flick of his elbows and then steadies himself against the table to get his bearings.

A small woman with a missing front tooth and an ironic *Say No to Drugs* T-shirt makes her rounds from table to table, holding a five-gallon bucket of single roses wrapped in plastic.

"A rose for your rose?" she repeats to every guy she walks up to. Most wave her off. One guy in a tank top and a hipster beard buys one for his tiny girlfriend with an impossibly small waist and purple hair. When he goes in for a hug, his exposed armpit hair envelops the woman, and Paige suppresses a gag when she sees a dangling knot of white deodorant hanging from it, right beside the girl's face. Her staring is interrupted when a crinkly plastic object appears in front of her face. Startled, she whacks at it.

"Jeez," Finn says, pulling back the rose he was presenting her.

"Sorry, Sorry! I— You startled me. What's this?"

"It has always been my belief," he says, hand to heart, "that you never turn down a two-dollar rose from a vendor when there is a beautiful lady present." He hands it to her, and she takes it but can't hold back her laugh at the obnoxiousness of it all. She's suddenly a junior in college again at a stinky bar dealing with drunk men who think they're charming. She wonders how many of these roses wilted on her dashboard after nights out at the bar in those days.

"What?" he asks.

"No, nothing. Thank you. That's super nice of you." Shit, she is letting the real Paige slip into the character Paige, and she's gonna blow it. "Really," she adds.

As they drive and he flips through channels and sings along to a Goo Goo Dolls song from the '90s, his arm brushes her thigh. He lets it linger there a moment. Then, as if noticing her for the first time he says, "You look really nice tonight." She gives an involuntary little laugh, and then...

"Um, thanks." Usually she'd say *Shut up* and punch him in the arm, as she is uncomfortable with compliments. Also, he could just be offering this kindness because he just realized it's been a long time since anyone has seen her out of a housecoat and yelling at UPS guys and newsboys. It probably wasn't a flirt. She hasn't been as good at this as she thought.

"So do you," she adds, painfully. She feels him staring at her as she pulls into her dark driveway in the back of the house.

"What?" she asks, shifting into Park and looking back at him, smiling.

"Eh, nothing. You're a hot chick is all. Happy looks good on you, Paige Moretti," he says and then clicks to release his seat belt and moves to open his door. She suddenly panics because she's about to lose this opportunity, so she moves her hand to his inner thigh.

"You don't have to go yet, if you don't want," she says, shocking herself. He seems completely shocked, too. His eyes widen, and then he starts laughing. Laughing! Fucking laughing, which really pisses her off.

"What?" she says, defensively.

"No, nothing, it's just… You're…"

"A hot chick," she says, trying to joke, pulling him to her and kissing him. He kisses her back, passionately, and they grope one another across the console until he abruptly stops it and, to her horror, laughs again.

"Whoa. Okay, maybe you had a few more than you thought and we should have taken a cab," he says. She is perfectly sober and exceedingly annoyed.

"I'm not drunk." She starts to kiss him again, and he allows it for just a moment before pulling away and adjusting his shirt. He flips down the mirror on the back of the visor in front of him and checks his face for lipstick marks. Something he is practiced at, no doubt.

"You're my wife's best friend. This— I don't know what we were thinking. This can't happen."

"Who's gonna tell her?" Paige asks.

"Daymmn," he responds and the frat-boy language coming from a fortysomething, accomplished man sounds ridiculous. She tries not to let her annoyance show.

"Well, it's not safe. She'd find out," he says.

A slip, Paige thinks. It seemed so easy for him to almost admit he'd do it if Paige were someone else—someone not too close to home.

"I mean, not that I would, anyway," he adds quickly. "I know you and Grant are, you know, separated, and I guess that makes you single, but…"

Before she lets him say any other stupid thing, she cuts him off by slipping down the spaghetti straps of her cami and letting them drop, pulling down the front of the shirt and exposing her breasts.

"Oh, my God," he says, exaggeratedly, squeezing his eyes closed and then open. "What are you trying to do to me?"

"Offer's open is all," she says, pulling her top back up quickly and gesturing him permission to go, keeping a modicum of integrity at least by being the one to dismiss him, but he decides to talk.

"Paige," he says, softly, "I think you're…" Then he stops. Holy shit. Is he about to reject her and give her a shitty *I think you're really…whatever* speech?

"You're amazing, but I think you're just lonely right now and you'd really regret this," he says self-righteously. She doesn't know if her mouth is gaping open at the shock of this, as he opens the passenger door and gives a little wave before walking across the street to his house.

"Are you fucking kidding me?" she says out loud after he's gone—the sudden silence of the radio and car creating a ringing in her ears. He slept with a prostitute wearing giant hoop earrings and animal print, and he rejected her?

She put herself on the line, she bought new makeup and suffered through a pub full of complete Neanderthals—she gave up all dignity, and she made sure she looked smoking hot doing it, and this is what he does?

Oh, no, Finn Holmon. This is not how this will go. She will not take no for an answer.

7

CORA

Moretti's is nestled under a canopy of red alder and big-leaf maple trees. A cottony fog threads through the treetops, and it seems out of place against the seaside cliffs, but from inside it has always reminded me of an Italian restaurant out of a movie. The brick walls and featured pizza oven give it a rustic feel, but the oversize wineglasses on each table and the strings of white lights crisscrossing the ceiling give it a sophisticated air. Tonight, each table is filled with people who paid two hundred dollars a head with most of the proceeds going to the local Hunger Project.

Tony Bennett sings "The Very Thought of You" through the dining-room speakers, and couples dressed in evening gowns and dinner jackets clink glasses and speak to each other in low voices across candles and plates of pasta.

A few of the charity's spokespeople make their way up to

the microphone on the tiny stage next to the old Steinway & Sons piano to thank the guests and talk about the mission of the organization. I am stationed at the silent-auction table and supervise the handful of other volunteers who clear plates and refill drinks. The whole event is seamless and lovely. Except I can't stop thinking about Paige. And Finn. And maybe them together.

Imagining a scenario where his hands are on someone else, especially my close friend, makes me physically sick, but what's worse is the emotional betrayal. Attraction to someone else or even sex with them would feel like a punch to the throat, but his heart being elsewhere—his ability to go through the motions of a life with me and not actually want that life—that's so much worse. That's...unbearable.

I realize that I have been staring at the floor, lost in my own thoughts, when a volunteer taps me on the shoulder and I'm jolted back into the present.

"The music's out. There's something wrong with the audio, a short in the wiring, they think. They wanna know what they should do," a soft-spoken young woman says.

I hadn't even noticed Tony Bennett go quiet. I see Grant across the room. His job is to schmooze the crowd. He stands with his hand resting on the shoulder of one of the biggest donors, pointing out selections on a wine list. He pauses to raise an eyebrow at me, asking if I can help, no doubt. I see that the busser is tangled in cables and cords, trying to get to the bottom of the problem. He's barely out of his teens, and looks like someone who knows his way around audiovisual equipment with his Dungeons and Dragons T-shirt and lip piercing, so I leave him to it and quickly make my way to the piano.

The place is always packed on Mondays and Wednesdays when it hosts sing-alongs after dinner, so there is a massive binder of sheet music inside the piano bench. I flip it open and land on "Wonderful Tonight" by Eric Clapton and start to play, filling the quiet in the room. A few people clap, as if I've saved the day. I see Grant shoot me a surprised smile and a thumbs-up from the bar. After about an hour of Righteous Brothers and Elton John, the busser fixes the audio just in time for most people to be gathering their coats and slowly saying goodbyes as they make their way out.

As I'm thanking my young volunteers and giving them all little gift bags for their help, Grant comes over with a plate of the night's special, a tomato risotto, and gestures to the booth next to him.

"You, madam, have pulled off a spectacular evening and have not sat down all night. Please." He motions for me to sit.

"Oh, Grant. That's okay. It's what I signed up for. I'm happy to do it," I say, meaning it.

"You must be starving," he says. "Join me. It's the least I can do," he adds.

So after the last couple people leave and the restaurant is otherwise empty, we sit down and eat warm crusty bread with olive oil and shaved Parmesan with outrageously delicious risotto and lots of red wine. Grant has always been an extension of Paige to me, mostly. With so many restaurants to manage, he was scarcely around, even when he did still live with her, so our coffee-in-the-garden mornings or movie nights usually didn't include him. He seems different than I thought. Maybe I assume all men are like Finn—sort of emotionally unavailable and often distant with a wandering eye and a penchant for one-upping people at every opportunity. The one-upping thing I used to find sort of adorable. He's a successful and confident guy, but his need to be right and always have an answer or a better story showed the crack in his armor, and his insecurity was exposed—at least to me. I liked the vulnerability he was unaware of. The other qualities were not so charming, but those developed slowly over time and snuck up on me, or at least I think so. If they were always there, I was blinded by love, I suppose.

Grant, however, seems to—I don't know—listen without the need to scroll through his phone or trump something I say with a more interesting thing that happened to him, for example. It's very...unexpected. I haven't sat alone with a man besides my husband in years—probably since dating Finn. It feels a bit scandalous, if I'm honest. But why should it? He's separated, and I've basically hired a friend to catch my husband cheating. I'm allowed to enjoy it, aren't I? I'm not doing anything wrong.

"How did I not know you played piano?" he asked.

"I took lessons as a kid and then minored in music in college, actually. I don't play too often these days, but—"

"New Year's, four years ago?" he says, interrupting.

"Uh..." I start to ask what he means.

"You guys threw a New Year's party at your place, and you played 'Auld Lang Syne' on Mia's little keyboard when the ball dropped on TV."

"Yes," I say laughing. "I guess I did."

"So I did know you played. How could I forget such a performance?"

"Right. Then, I guess I'm insulted. It was some of my best work." I smile, remembering how I'd plunked out the clumsy tune with two fingers and sung along to the tinny, electronic hum it made. It's strange how familiar yet distant Grant is to me. It strikes me that if I know things about him from Paige, like the fact that he sleeps on a mattress on the floor in the apartment above this restaurant because he refuses to buy furniture and make it a home, she's probably told him secrets about me, and we likely know each other, in our shared loneliness, better than we think.

I know that, sobbing, he tried to reach into Caleb's casket and pull his lifeless body up to hold him. I wasn't there because they wanted a small funeral with only family, a couple hours north near his grandparents, but I can't get the image out of my mind. I also know the funeral service was delayed because Grant collapsed in grief, and he could barely physically walk into the chapel. I know Paige pushed him away until the couch became the guest room, and now this room above the restaurant, and he became smaller and smaller and sits up there alone every night. She told me she wishes she could stop—stop taking away the only thing he had left: her. But she couldn't. Still, somehow, unlike her, he walks out into the world each morning, and a stranger would never know the debilitating despair he suffers. I feel like *I* shouldn't know.

No matter what she might have told him about me over time, my problems seem pretty pathetic considering what he's been through. It embarrasses me that he might know I haven't had sex in months or that I eat sleeves of Oreos on the back patio at night after everyone is asleep, Oreos I retrieve from their hiding spot in my glove compartment. Or that I went psycho on a woman I thought Finn was having an affair with and couldn't imagine loneliness more acute than feeling simultaneously abandoned and betrayed but also at fault for it because of my crazy paranoia.

I'm sure he knows, and this mutual knowledge of the other's secrets seems oddly intimate suddenly, and I feel like I should go. But Grant tops off our wine and leans back in his seat, studying me a moment.

"Do you miss playing?" he asks. No one has ever asked me that before.

"Uh, yeah, I guess so. I mean, I don't give it much thought. I played a lot of recitals, but never on a bar stage, so it was actually pretty cool," I say.

"Well, I'm looking for someone a couple nights a week. I mean, I know you're the busiest gal in town, but if it's something you—"

"Oh, for piano-bar sing-along," I blurt excitedly.

"Yeah, I thought about getting rid of it," he says, "but folks love it, so…"

"*You* love it," I add. "I've seen you dancing away to a terrible rendition of a 'Don't Stop Believin'' medley more than once, don't think I haven't."

He laughs. "Is it singed into your brain?"

"Causing persistent nightmares, yes," I say, laughing, and he picks up a shaker of Parmesan cheese and sings into it, along with a Frank Sinatra song that's playing.

"'That's life…'" I hear him sing too loudly. I join in, matching his dramatic gesturing. We roar the next line, and then we lose the lyrics and laugh.

I think about the restaurants he and Paige sold and how small his world has become. I know it's just a silly piano night, but it feels like something he shouldn't have to lose.

"What happened to Wanda?" I ask. "She didn't even need the sheet music."

"She got a gig in town, five nights a week," he says, lifting his drink in mock congrats to Wanda.

"Fancy. Well, you can't compete with that." I smile, and we cheers for no reason. I guess because our glasses are already raised.

"I mean, no pressure, Cor. Only if it would be fun for you. Just an idea," he says, with a sort of dismissive gesture, as if waving away the idea.

"No, I mean, yeah. I mean, I don't think I can compete with Wanda, though. They'll all be like, 'Where's the hot, gothy brunette, and why have you replaced her with a ham stuffed into a dress?' and you'll be like, 'No, it's not deli meat, it's just a fat chick who can kinda play the piano…but definitely needs sheet music.'" I laugh, but Grant does not.

I instantly regret the joke. Finn is used to it, so he doesn't feel the need to counter it with a comment. Sometimes he asks if I'm *fishing*. Truth be told, it's just habit. I'm not, at least on a conscious level, seeking a compliment; it's just what I know to say in the moment.

"I hope you don't really think that," he says.

"Sorry, just a joke." I blush, feeling self-conscious now.

"I've always thought you were breathtaking," he says, and I almost want to laugh. I mean, Paige is, by any standard, breathtaking. I know he's just trying to be kind.

"Sorry. I don't— I mean, yeah…" I quickly change the subject. "I could maybe play a couple nights. I'll have to check in with Finn, see if…" but I don't know how to finish that. I don't check with him about much anymore. I take on more than I can keep up with all the time, and I never get his input. Mia is starting to drive herself to practices and friends' houses. Nobody needs to okay this. Still, I don't want to agree quickly to do it. I'd rather be like the aloof Paige and give him a solid maybe, but it sounds thrilling.

"Well, let me know." He smiles. "For real, no pressure."

"I'll do it!" I say, like a total lunatic, but he doesn't seem to notice my overzealousness and gives a *Woot* into his cupped hand. We both laugh.

Some old jazz song comes on that I don't recognize, and he sings, off-key, to the lyrics. It's the wine, probably. Me being flushed and giddy, him singing Sinatra and Dean Martin, but it's really nice. He holds the Parmesan mock microphone across the booth to me when the female part of the duet comes on, and I hold my hands up in protest, giggling.

"I don't know it," I say. Then he gets up and holds out his hand for me to take. I think he's a little tipsy. I know him to be someone who very rarely drinks. In fact, Paige mentioned it more than once—that he can be a bit of a judgy-judger when it comes to people imbibing too much, so I'm surprised. I stand and take his hand, and he pulls me in to dance, still singing bits of lyrics here and there.

I can feel my pulse in my throat and the wine buzzing in my head. Then the playful twirling and humming along to the music stops, and we just sway slowly, holding one another. I don't know why, but I rest my head on his shoulder. It feels like we're barely moving. I can feel the warmth of his breath on my neck and the tapping of his heartbeat against my chest. I can feel my eyes sting with tears that are trying to surface, but I blink them back, not understanding where they're coming from. I swallow, and it sounds loud between my ears. I should go.

When I look up at him, ready to pull away and comment on how late it's getting, our foreheads meet, and we let them. We stand together like that a moment, and then he moves his hand to the side of my face and cups my cheek gently. When our eyes meet, I wonder what the hell I'm letting happen, but then suddenly, synchronously, we don't let it happen.

We don't kiss. He drops his head, and he squeezes my hand almost apologetically. Then he pulls me to him in a hug that feels desperate. We both silently hold on to one another tightly. For a long time. Then, still without speaking, we let go, and I walk to the booth to pick up my coat and bag and go to the door. When I look back, we exchange a joyless smile. I take in the room, the empty glasses and dim light, all the life and noise and laughter that filled the place only an hour ago, and now Grant standing in the wake of it all. I imagine he'll turn off the lights, climb the back wooden staircase with what's left in the wine bottle, and lie down on his mattress, so very alone. My heart races in my chest.

I want to go with him. What would he do if I dropped my

things and took his hand and led him toward the staircase? What would he do if, right here, I kissed him and started to unbutton the front of his shirt? The desire feels overwhelming. I almost move to him, but I feel paralyzed. I open my mouth to say something, and he looks at me expectantly, but I find that I don't know what to say, so I just flash my flat palm as a sort of awkward wave goodbye, and I leave.

By the time the cab drops me off at my house, a slushy rain has started and falls in icy pellets that sound like bullets on the metal of the car. I'm distracted by thoughts of Grant, so I almost don't notice a figure standing across the street, backlit by the garage light. It's Georgia's husband, Lucas. He's standing, glass in hand, his shoulders hunched, staring out into the sleet, which is falling sideways. Even though he's mostly shadowed in silhouette, I see his face when the headlights flit across him briefly, and he looks drenched and upset. When I exit the car, I pop my umbrella, and the cab drives away. I pause a moment before I run inside, not knowing if I should say something. I lift my hand in a tentative wave, but he doesn't wave back. He doesn't move at all. Then I see his garage door slowly close in front of him until I can only see his legs, then darkness as the interior light is extinguished.

8

GEORGIA

On Saturday evening I stand in front of the sink, peeling rus-
set potatoes and flicking the skins into the garbage disposal.
It's getting dark early as November approaches, and it's already dusk before dinnertime. The shorter days make life in
this house seem even more suffocating.

Avery sits in her high chair playing with fists full of ap-
plesauce when Lucas comes through the side door, stopping
to wipe the mud from the bottom of his shoes onto the welcome mat.

"There's my girls," he says, pulling off his coat and going
over to Avery immediately. "Hey there, french fry. What did
you do today?" he asks in a playful voice, and she squeals,
opening and closing her messy hands at him. After a series of
tummy pokes and a raspberry on the head, he comes over and
kisses me on the cheek.

"Sorry, I gotta do two quick calls before dinner. Twenty minutes max," he says, loosening his tie and heading toward his office.

"Yeah, of course," I say, distracted, because out the window I see Cora. She looks quite pretty in her blue velvet dress and peacoat. She's going to a fundraiser. I heard her talking about it—a fancy-dinner event. I feel as if tiny fingers are tapping up my spine at the thought of it. I wipe my hands with a tea towel, lean my head back, and take a deep breath, blowing it out hard. The longing to sit at a dinner table among friends, with posh martinis and live music—such a simple thing, yet there are days I feel the absence of it could kill me.

Lucas is much longer than twenty minutes. When he finally comes down, I have two plates of salmon and scalloped potatoes on the table, and Avery is on a blanket on the floor next to my chair, playing with her shapes toy, cramming triangles and circles into the wrong holes.

I ask him about his day, even though he seems distracted. His cases are always interesting to me. Murder and armed-robbery stories are always an escape for anyone, I suppose. He doesn't tell me about his case, though, and I know something is wrong. When he finishes his food, he pushes his plate away and leans back, smiling at me. My heart drops into the hollow of my stomach. He pulls a tiny bag of weed out of his pocket and tosses it on the table.

"Where'd that come from?" he asks. I feel all the blood drain from my face. I reach down and stroke Avery's hair and play dumb.

"No idea," I say.

"It was in the shed. Poorly hidden, I might add."

"What were you doing in the shed?" I ask, confused. I thought it would be the perfect place because he never goes in there.

"Don't ask me why I went in my own fucking shed!" he yells, slamming his fist on the table, spit spraying from the sides of his mouth.

"Why would you think it's mine? Where would I get that?"

"That's a great question. Druggy park you're always bringing Avery to, maybe," he growls.

"That's— Why would I buy pot? Where would I have even gotten the money? That's— No. That's…"

"Good question. *Great* question!" he yells. I can see Avery is getting ready to cry, but I know I can't ask him to lower his voice.

"Lucas, I swear. Look, all the teenagers around here—they, maybe they… Donna Nichols said she caught two kids having sex in her guesthouse once. Maybe some kids were out—"

He stops me. "Why would you be talking to Donna Nichols? She lives two streets over," he says.

"She jogs by, says hello." I can hear the desperation in my own voice, and I hate it.

"Here's what I think," he says, more quietly now. "I don't know what you did to get it, but I bet you planned to sell it and pull the shit you pulled last time." He waits for a response. "You think I'm stupid?" he screams, and now Avery is crying. He stands and grabs the back of my hair, forcing me up, pushing me toward the stairs to the basement.

"Maybe you need some time alone to think about it," he says, and I howl, pushing my hands against the doorjamb, resisting, screaming for him not to put me in that room. Those basement smells come back—the mop water, my hours locked down there—and I can't control my shaking or the panic.

"Please!" I beg. "Please, I promise it's not mine. I wasn't gonna… Please!" I sob, trying to look back at Avery, who is wailing. I need to comfort her. I can't spend the night in that room.

"I'm sorry! Please. Okay, a kid gave it to me. I didn't know what to do with it. I should have thrown it out. I…"

He lets go of the back of my head, and I drop to the ground. I crawl over to my baby and pick her up. I stroke her hair and rock her while Lucas goes to the sink and dumps the contents of the small bag down the drain, turning on the faucet to wash it away.

"You're not going to that park anymore. You don't think I saw your little act yesterday talking to that kid? I see everything. This is what happens when I trust you. I thought you could handle leaving the house. I gave you a little freedom because I thought you could behave yourself. I did that for *you*." He lowers his voice and looks down at us, a shift from rage to disappointment. "Goddamn it, Georgia. Things could be so good if you'd just stop. Stop fucking everything up all the time," he says, shaking his head, and then he takes a beer from the fridge, pops the cap, and goes into the living room to watch TV.

My knees shake uncontrollably as I try to get to my feet with Avery in my arms. I sit with her on a kitchen chair and just shush her gently and rock her for what seems like close to an hour before she is calm and finally falls asleep. I heard Lucas behind me getting himself another beer a while ago. When his footsteps paused, I thought he'd hit me maybe, but not with Avery in my arms, thank God. Now, the laugh track from an old sitcom is the only sound in the house, so I quietly take Avery upstairs to her room, lay her in her crib, and sit in the darkness on her SpongeBob beanbag chair and try to think. *To think.*

This plan, like many before, has been stopped in its tracks. I thought maybe if I could sell that stupid dime bag to some kid at the park for ten bucks, it would be enough for bus fare to town. Three months ago, I found an old ring that looked vintage—maybe his grandmother's—in the bottom of a box in the garage, which was a lucky find, because everything valuable is stored somewhere else. He knows I look. He's thought of everything. Absolutely everything. I thought I could get to a pawn shop to sell the ring. Even though the house is outfitted with cameras in every room and motion sensors so he can keep tabs on me all day and alarm the police if I try to leave, telling them I plan to harm myself or the baby, I have figured out how to trick one of the cameras. I've been waiting for this opportunity.

There is only one security camera in the community, and that's at the front gate. It works about half the time, from what I'm told. He, of course, doesn't have access to that footage. Some neighbors have Ring cameras on their front doors, but all those will show is a limited area in front of their house and, again, he wouldn't have access to those. There is little surveillance in this neighborhood. These rich people probably want to feel like they live in a safe area and aren't being watched all the time. The only house outfitted with intense surveillance is ours.

So I was elated when I realized that I can freeze the image on the porch camera. It only points inward, toward the porch, not out to the street. I would think the neighbors would find that odd, but I guess nobody looks at stuff like that. But it's there to make sure I don't get farther than the front step without him knowing.

One day I noticed a tiny remote, taped with clear packing tape, to the side of the camera. I stared at it for weeks before I got up the nerve to just grab it, to just trust that he is not watching all the time and the odds were good he wouldn't see me do it. He didn't. As far as I know, he forgot it was even there and has no idea I have it. So now, if I take a nap on the front porch daybed with Avery in her playpen, I can freeze the image on both of us asleep. It would only give me an hour or so—a believable length of time for a nap—but we could slip out while he thinks we're there, asleep. If he studies that camera closely and notices the images of us were suspicious, I'd be totally fucked, but it's a risk that I'd have to take. The weather is only going to get colder, and porch naps can't last much longer, so I need to plan my move.

I don't know how an hour would be enough time, with bus transfers and a baby in tow, but it's the first glimmer of hope I've had in months. And it might not be much, but if I could get a few hundred dollars, it would be a start...of something, maybe. But there's no chance of that now. I know he sees Cora visit, and he hears everything. I keep it as light as possible when she's here, but I can only pray he doesn't have it out for her. He hasn't mentioned her visits, which I've learned is worse than a confrontation in the long run.

Moonlight shines through the window of her bedroom and casts farm animal–shaped shadows across her floor from the *Charlotte's Web* mobile hanging above her crib. I blink back tears. It's not a time to cry. It's a time to rethink my escape.

I think about how he was too good to be true when we met. Even the night everything changed and his eyes went dark and empty, I'd never have believed that he planned all those months in France to sweep me off my feet so when he got me here, he could destroy my passport with no way for me to get a new one. It's so outrageous, absurd. Runaway teenagers get trafficked, I'd always thought. Not a world traveler, an educated adult.

I tried once. To order a replacement passport. In the early days, before I knew how trapped I really was. Before I knew that he had put a bug in the ear of his colleagues and friends that I was depressed and unstable, so if I ever went to anyone for help, I'd be the crazy, antidepressant-popping wife and he'd be the judge with decades of established relationships and good standing in the community. I can't imagine what it must have taken for him to put it all together.

I had money at first, money I'd saved from my jobs—a lot. When I began to realize what was happening, I ordered a replacement passport online. This was my very first mistake. Of course he checked the search history on his computer that I'd used after he'd fallen asleep. Of course he intercepted the mail and then subsequently had all mail go to a PO box after that so he could control it. These were things I can't believe I was naive enough to do back then. *Back then*. It feels like years, but it's been barely a year now.

Back then, though, was before I knew that he had full control over all of Avery's birth documents, and unless I found a lot of money and some shady people to provide me with fake ones, this was now our life.

I have dreams sometimes of telling Cora, or Donna who jogs by and coos at Avery on the front porch sometimes, but it's not that easy. Of course, I thought I could just go to the police. I could call 9-1-1 or run to a neighbor and tell them everything. What rational person wouldn't think to do that? Lucas thought that was a great idea. The first time—the night everything changed, and he pushed his thumb into my throat so hard I saw stars and blacked out—I said I'd call the police. I was pregnant; we'd just arrived in the US. It was only a matter of months before the man I married choked me up against the bathroom wall for telling him he'd used up the hot water.

He laughed at me when I said I'd leave, go for help. He handed me his phone to call the police. When they came, he welcomed them in. He laughed with them, explaining my depression and fragile state of mind. It didn't matter that it wasn't true. They called him *sir* and shook his hand.

If I am to escape him, there can be no chance that I'll be stopped by police or reported as missing before I can get very far. I have to get far enough away in one go, and that will take money. I think about Cora on our porch. It's the closest I've been to another person besides Lucas and Avery in so long. There was a moment I thought, *What if I opened my mouth and the words came out and I asked her to help me?* But I already know how that fantasy ends because all the cameras have audio and he gets alerts on his phone anytime they pick up any voice in the house. I learned that the hard way. And I cannot spend nights in that room in the basement again for some attempt that will never work.

I pull a pink knitted blanket from the back of the rocking chair in the nursery and lie on the floor beside Avery's crib. I still don't cry. I don't feel anything at all. I just stare at the unicorn night-light plugged into the wall across the room and pray for merciful sleep.

9

PAIGE

Paige stands in her dark kitchen opening a can of tuna fish for Christopher, who dances around on his hind legs impatiently. She's teetering on spiky high heels in a too-tight skirt she can barely walk in, and he almost knocks her over with his excited jumps.

"Take a pill, Christopher," she says, nudging him off her leg and leaning down to feed him the tuna, which he eats in two bites. She has to hold the side of the sink to stand back up, in the stupid getup she's forced to wear. She hates dressing up. Adults should not dress up for Halloween. Period. She hates theme parties where she's required to come as a flapper girl or in some grass skirt for a backyard luau. *Guess what, Brian? Adding pineapple to your burger on your shitty backyard grill and throwing some plastic leis around for decoration does not a luau make.* This might not be a costume, but it feels like one.

The annual Museum of Art Ball should also not be called a *ball*. There's a karaoke room and a bunch of twentysome-things throwing up into garbage cans by nine o'clock after too many free margaritas. Most people make an effort, though, in their tuxes and puffy dresses, even though it looks a bit like a 1980s prom exploded, and then there's a handful of people who come in jeans, for Christ's sake, but fine. It's a *ball*. She and Grant have always gone, and of course Cora and most of the community have, too. Like most events they attend, it's for charity. She would not be going at all this year if Finn were not going to be there, but Grant is excited to pick her up and go together, so she'll pretend to be trying to have a normal evening. In fact, Grant is stunned that she agreed to go at all. She knows he's hopeful that she's finding a way to move on with her life, if even just a little bit.

The Sapphire Hotel is decorated with sparkly paper snow-flakes hanging from the ceiling and balloons floating in between them. There are little bar carts set up around the enormous room. Well, more like folding tables with black tablecloths over them, and some bottles of booze and plastic cups scattered about, but it will do. Giant double doors stand open and lead into a few other rooms, one where a live jazz band is playing and a decent crowd of people are out on the makeshift dance floor already. The other banquet room has round tables set up around the plush, carpeted space, hold-ing hors d'oeuvres, like deviled eggs and crab puffs. There's an ice sculpture of what she thinks was probably a swan but now has melted a bit and looks more like a demented pigeon.

Grant points out Cora and Finn standing in a circle of con-versation with a few couples near one of the bar tables. They make their way over and exchange pleasantries with everyone. She avoids eye contact with Finn. She's not sure what her face might give away in front of the others. She's not accustomed to making out with married men, so she isn't certain she'd mask her guilt well on the spot. She needs a minute.

"What the hell is that?" Paige says, pointing to Cora's drink, which looks like a snow cone.

"A Blue Lagoon," she says.

"Is that a gummy bear?" she asks. Not waiting for an answer, she takes it from Cora and sips, then makes an exaggerated face of disgust and hands it back. She feels Finn's eyes on her.

"Well, don't you two look like a Disney couple," she says, reluctantly meeting his gaze and then quickly giving her attention to Cora, who gives a giggle and little mock curtsy, although, really, her outfit makes Paige wonder if Cora has realized this is not her quinceañera.

"I need a martini with a blue-cheese-stuffed olive immediately." Paige pulls Cora over to the bar with her, having asked the group to excuse them. Paige pokes at the olive in her drink with a toothpick as they glance around the party together.

"God, Harry Kilgore's breath just comes right at ya, doesn't it?" Paige asks, looking back over at the growing circle their husbands are still standing in.

"I had to sit in a car with him once for a PTA thing. I had to throw my coat out after. The dry cleaner couldn't get the smell out. Poor guy has no idea," Cora says.

"I feel like someone should tell him," Paige says, and Cora looks to her as if she's clearly the only person capable of such bluntness.

"Someone close to him. Not me. Hey, who's that?" Paige asks, pointing to a couple newcomers to the husbands' conversation.

"Oh, Charlotte and Tony," Cora says. "Very cool couple. She's like an art teacher, you know the kind where you paint real naked people, and he works with Finn. He's in a band. Well, you know, like a garage sort of thing on the weekends, but I think he's the drummer. I should tell you next time we have them over. You'd like them." Paige doesn't have to give Cora a look that says meeting new people and attending dinner parties are the furthest thing from her mind. Cora just tacks on, "I mean, at some point. We don't see them too often, anyway."

"Right." Paige smiles, wondering if Charlotte is the *Drinks with C* woman Cora told her about.

"I guess nothing yet or you would have told me," Cora says, fidgeting nervously with her straw and dunking her vodka-soaked gummy bears into the blue depths of her drink.

"Not yet, sorry," Paige says, avoiding her eye, feeling a muscle in her cheek twitch. Cora nods and gives her a tight smile.

"I figured last weekend when you didn't come to the restaurant for the event that night, maybe you… I don't know."

"Yeah, I followed him a bit here and there and haven't seen anything, you know, red-flaggy yet. I'm trying to be careful so he doesn't catch on, of course. But I'll keep trying," Paige says. She notices Cora looking longingly over at Finn. "If you want me to," she adds.

"Yeah. No, I mean, I think so. But that's good, right? He is where he says he is, so that's a good sign. Maybe I am being psycho doing this. That's what he would call it if he ever found out. I mean, we'd be over. Shit. What if you come on to him and he…says no. I hadn't even thought about how forever awkward that would be between all of us. Then, what if he suspects I put you up to it? God, I don't know. I don't know anymore." She blows out a heavy breath and stares into her drink.

"He won't say no," Paige says, curtly.

"What?"

"I just mean, I'll make sure I'm getting the right signals. I'm not just gonna lunge at him. I'll, you know, make sure I know he's gonna take the bait," she says. Cora looks at the floor and swallows hard.

"Yeah," she says.

"He might not, Cor," she says more softly. Cora blinks back tears and gestures to a few moms she knows from Mia's school across the way.

"I should go say hello," Cora says, painting a smile across her face and moving through the crowd of people, bumping folks in the backs of the knees with her giant feathered skirt. Paige watches as Vanessa Hammon's knees buckle and she reaches her hand out so her drink spills on the floor and not on her dress. Cora is clueless of the domino effect of spills she's caused and the glares she leaves in her wake. Paige would usually be delighted by this, but instead she feels tiny pricks of heat spread across her chest, creating blotchy red marks. Is it guilt or excitement? She can't tell.

People start to get messy after a couple hours. Grant sits with Paige at a table in the banquet room with the band. They passively listen to the music and watch Cora and Finn and a few of their friends dance. Charlotte is out there, seemingly drunk and a little handsy. Paige has learned she goes by *Char* like *Cher* but with an *a*, so Paige has made sure to pronounce it *Char* as in *charbroiled* and pretends not to hear when someone corrects her. Char is doing that thing where she drops it low or twerks or whatever the hell and then tries to share a laugh, insecurely, like she was just kidding, just pretending to do a silly move, but is secretly trying to push sexual boundaries to see what kind of attention she can get.

Grant pops a white Laffy Taffy into his mouth and chuckles.

"What?" Paige asks.

"I think Sequin Dress over there forgot to wear underwear,"

he says. She doesn't have to look to know the only one in a skintight sequined dress is Char.

"Dinner and a show," she says jokingly.

They're sitting at a table with a three-tiered glass dessert-stand centerpiece that is filled with all-white candy for some strange reason. Paige has collected meringue drops, rock-candy sticks, and gumdrops and piled them on a plate in front of her.

"Did you even know they made white M&Ms?" she asks, pushing one into his mouth.

"Whoa, I got a taffy goin' on here. That doesn't go," he says, spitting it into a napkin.

"What the hell flavor is *white* taffy?"

"Eggnog?" he says with a shrug. She looks at the wrapper.

"*Macadamia.* You can't tell the difference between eggnog and macadamia. Both of which go with chocolate, FYI." She pushes another M&M at him, and he smiles, keeping hold of her hand a moment. She smiles back. After a beat, she pulls away and continues her meaningless observations.

"And why would they choose the rarest color of candy for this thing? Is that how they spend their money? It's a charity event. Maybe their candy budget could have gone to, I don't know, the sponsored charity."

He looks at her plateful and gives her a look that says *If you say so.*

"What's the charity, again?"

"A Child's Wish Foundation," he says.

"Jesus," she scoffs. *"Sorry we can't help your child's dying wish come true. We had to buy a storage unit full of..."* she examines the candy in front of her *"...piña colada jelly beans. Our bad!"*

Cora comes over and plops down, exhausted, at their table. She takes off her heels and dabs at a bit of sweat on her brow with a napkin.

"Almond bark?" Paige offers up her plate.

"Oh, I shouldn't," she says but continues to look at it. Paige hates Cora's fat complex. She's a perfectly curvy, average-size person, and she needs to get over herself. She looks great.

"How's the piano stuff going? Grant told me, and I forgot to say anything," Paige says and watches Cora's cheeks go red and a shy smile spread across her face.

"Haven't started quite yet, but it will be good. Really fun."

"Can I get you a refill?" Grant asks, standing.

"Oh, no, I've had too much. Thanks, though," Cora says with a giggle as Paige simultaneously holds out her glass and says, "Martini. Extra olives."

Cora gets shy and apologetic. "Oh, God, sorry, I thought you were talking to me. Us. Never mi— Of course you were asking her. Ha ha! Sorry."

Paige finds this behavior odd and looks at her a moment.

"I was asking whoever was thirsty," Grant says, graciously, taking the outstretched glass and heading to the bar.

"You okay?" Paige asks.

"Yeah. 'Course. Sorry. I think I'm just... It's a lot with all the Finn stuff. Just trying to keep it together, y'know."

Paige pulls her mouth into a tight line and gives an empathetic nod. They sit, watching the party awhile.

A woman with a selfie stick takes glossy-eyed photos of herself in front of a giant margarita glass and poses like she's drinking it. A group of women create a circle on the dance floor and have discarded all their shoes in the middle of it as they dance overdramatically, in a style that doesn't match the music. Lucas Kinney, Paige just notices, is standing in a tux near the stage, a drink in hand, chatting with a couple lawyers she vaguely knows from years of these events. Cora strains to see him. She cups her hand above her eyes to deflect the glare of the dance-floor lights.

"What?" Paige asks.

"Lucas Kinney is here," she says.

"How exciting," Paige says dryly. Cora stands for a better look. "Uh…you can see him any given day, rubbing his BMW with a diaper in his driveway or jogging around the neighborhood with short-shorts on. Why the staring?"

"You think he's, a bit, I don't know…"

"What?"

"Off?" Cora asks.

"You're asking the wrong person. I think everyone in the neighborhood is off. Except you guys, of course," Paige says, and Grant returns, handing her a full martini.

"Who's off?" he asks, sitting between them and slurping the foam off a fresh beer.

"Lucas Kinney," Paige says. "I thought he was gay."

"He's married," Cora says.

"Yeah, before that. He lived there a couple years, and I never saw anyone come and go from his house, so I figured *gay*."

"So," Grant says, "if you never saw anyone go in or out, then you also didn't see men go in and out. How does that equal gay?"

"Dunno. 'Cause he was hiding it, big judge and all that," Paige says, all of them peering over at Lucas now.

"So now he's a closeted gay man just because you don't see people come in and out. He could have dated a thousand women and stayed at their places," Grant says.

"A thouuusand? Yes, well, if he dated a thousand women, I probably would have seen one or two walk-of-shame themselves to their cars at least once," Paige says.

Grant turns his attention to Cora.

"I thought he was great, the once or twice I joined Finn and him for a drink. Why, what'd he do?"

"Nothing, really. A little unfriendly, maybe. Just wondering if it was just me."

"I think he's off. He wears chinos that are too short and shoes with no socks," Paige says.

"You think everyone is off," Grant says.

"Yes, we covered that while you were gone, thanks."

"I think that's stylish now," Cora says. "On *The Bachelorette* all the guys have ankle pants with no socks. It's a thing," she adds with authority.

"It's idiotic, and he's not a twenty-two-year-old reality star."

"I fear what you two say about me when I'm not around," Grant says jokingly. Cora laughs too loud and gives him a playful, dismissive gesture with her hand, but Paige is distracted. She's spotted Charbroil following Finn to the bathrooms. Paige noted earlier that the bathrooms that line the main corridor near the kitchen are the unisex, single-stall kind. Probably for kitchen staff, not patrons, but since food service stopped a while ago and the kitchen is in a frenzy of dishwashing and packing up catering gear, she thinks it might be a private place for lovers to meet.

"Oh, there's Claire. Haven't seen her in ages. I'll be back," Paige says. She knows it's completely out of character for her to pursue social interaction, and this might be interpreted as fishy, but both Grant and Cora want her back to being herself, so they probably won't bat an eye at her departure.

Paige does her whole pretending-she's-lost-in-a-text walk, looking down at her phone so she's never caught spying. When she reaches the dark hallway leading back to the bathrooms, she sees them talking in the yellow rectangle of light from the open bathroom door. Char has slid down the wall with her head in her hands and is crying. God, Paige hates women. Why are they always crying around men? She ducks back around the corner, against the wall, and stands listening.

She can only hear muffled voices from this far away. Damn. She dares to peek around the corner to see what's going on. Finn tries to guide Char up by her shoulders. She lets him for a minute. He tries to hug her, but she pushes him.

"Always gonna be like this!" is the only thing Paige hears as Char turns toward her and comes barreling down the hall, away from him. She quickly turns and walks a few steps away. She holds her phone up to her ear and pretends to be on a call as Char huffs past.

"Oh, yeah. We're getting ready to leave. No, no. Yeah, yeah." Paige has no idea what she's doing—no real backup plan, but Char pays no attention to her. She just breaks into an emotional sprint back to the banquet room.

There's an unexpected opportunity; she has to decide what to do in a matter of seconds. She has a very drunk Finn on her hands. Maybe a just-broken-up-with Finn. Vulnerable? Check. Would it be morally wrong to take her shot? Yes. It would.

She waits a minute, expecting him to appear, but he doesn't, so she turns down the hall and sees him leaning against the wall, smoking a cigarette. When he sees her, he drops it and crushes it out with his foot in an instant.

"God, you scared me. I thought you were..."

"Who?" Paige asks.

"No, I—don't— What are you doing over here?"

"You smoke?" She changes the subject.

"Not usually. Someone gave it to me, and I don't know. It seemed like a good idea."

"Nobody smokes anymore," she says. Acting coy last time didn't work, so why not be herself?

"Very true," he says.

"I'm here because, if you're not aware, the line to the women's bathroom is thirty people deep. I saw the guy's line. There was none. No idea what your secret is. Urinals, maybe.

But the insiders know about these bathrooms. So if you'll excuse me," she says and pushes past Finn into the bathroom.

She runs the tap and dots some cold water under her eyes, then applies blush-colored lip gloss and presses her lips together a few times. She doesn't know what to expect when she opens the door. She's fairly sure he'll be gone, back whining to Cora that they have to go. Or maybe he'll still be there. She's suddenly not sure which one she hopes for. Her nerves are taking over.

When she opens the door, he's still there. She'd be embarrassed for him if she didn't feel about him the way she did. He looked sort of pathetic, leaning on the wall, no drink, no phone. No reason to be there.

"Sorry about the other night," he says. "I just wanted to say that. I was stupid. I'm sorry."

"No need to be sorry," she says, ready to walk past him.

"You said, 'Offer's open,'" he says. Then, they just look at each other.

"I did," she finally says, and he grabs the sides of her face and kisses her, almost violently. They stumble through the bathroom door and lock it behind them. He unbuttons the first few buttons on his shirt and reaches for his back collar, pulling the shirt off in a practiced sweep. He unzips her dress. She thinks this would be much easier without so many layers of fancy clothes, but she helps him pull her tight skirt up over her hips, and he picks her up and places her onto the sink counter.

It's not a passionate, romantic encounter, and she doesn't take the photos she promised. She lets him take down his pants and push into her, desperately. She hates him for so easily betraying Cora, but she pushes this thought away. Her legs wrapped around him, her back pushed against the vanity mirror, one hand in the sink. The blitz of satisfaction feels like an electric current running through her in that moment, and it doesn't allow room for any other feelings, like remorse or shame. She hushes his grunts and moans, and the whole thing is over rather quickly.

"We've been gone too long," she says, as she hurriedly retrieves a fallen earring from the tiled floor and they check their hair and smooth out the wrinkles in their clothes.

"Go first," she says, pushing him out. "We can't go together."

"Okay, yeah," he says, rushing out the bathroom door while she waits a few minutes to leave.

They don't have time to process or talk about what just happened, but she knows one thing for sure, and she mumbles it under her breath. "He's mine now."

10

GEORGIA

I feel hungover in the morning from lack of sleep. My limbs feel heavy, and I overcompensate with coffee, which leaves me a combination of jittery but still exhausted. At night I stay up thinking of ways to kill him. I sleep in Avery's room each night, and he padlocks the door from the outside before he goes to bed. I wonder sometimes if I could make myself plunge a kitchen knife through his heart while he sleeps if I did get the opportunity. I think about poisoning him, but I have no idea how. Without a phone or computer to look up how to do it, it's a risk that could prove deadly. For me.

Every woman on *Snapped* seems to slowly poison their husband with antifreeze. We don't have antifreeze or rat poison—I've looked—but we have household cleaners and insect spray. How much would kill a person? They would have a taste, for sure. He'd know, and that would be it. I think about ambushing him when he comes in the door. I tried once. I hit him in the head with a Rawlings baseball bat, but since he's twice my size, it only enraged him and barely left more than an egg-size bump. He approaches the house with caution. He looks at the cameras and has eyes on me almost twenty-four hours a day.

When he first brought me to this house, it wasn't like this right away. He was becoming somewhat controlling, yes. But we were a pretty normal couple. I went shopping and for walks during the day while he was at work. I looked into getting a job at a hotel, something he pretended to support. I went out after he fell asleep and had a glass of wine on the porch or texted my friends back home.

He was buying time so he could set it all up. When I think about how happy I was, how blissfully unaware that life would be anything but romantic dinners, holidays, and lazy Sundays together the way it had been since we met, I feel waves of nausea like motion sickness take over. I could have gotten away if I'd had any clue—if I'd been less trusting and stupid.

He needed people to meet me and see us happy, see that I was a real person—at least a few coworkers and some family. Then, when I supposedly became ill, he had their sympathy, and it didn't seem odd that they'd never met this ill wife who never leaves the house. They'd met a happy, normal person who became ill; he crafted it carefully. With each turn, he made sure he dropped clues about my instability to make him look like the selfless, long-suffering husband. Once the groundwork had been laid, everything changed overnight. I went from giddy newlywed to this.

I'm standing at the kitchen counter with a third mug of coffee in my hand when I see a woman walking toward the house. I don't know who it is. Before I can step out from in front of the window and pretend not to be home, she sees me and waves. I don't wave back. I put my mug down and chew on my knuckle, thinking. I have to open the door now, don't I? I think about Lucas watching. No matter what he's doing, when he hears voices trigger the audio alert on his phone, he'll stop and listen. Sometimes, he might not be watching in the moment, but he'll always scan the footage later to make sure there is nothing he missed—at least the parts where voices are involved.

I don't know what she'll say. Will he be angrier if I don't answer and appear normal and friendly, or if I talk to her and say something wrong? What could she possibly want? I decide not to answer.

"Hello?" she calls. "Anyone home? It's Paula Landry from up the street. Yoo-hoo!"

I stand behind the front door in the dark entryway and wait for her to leave. Then an envelope is shoved under the door and onto my bare feet. I gasp but cover my mouth quickly so I don't give myself away. Then I hear footsteps down the porch stairs. She's leaving. I open the sheers on the front window and peek, ever so slightly through the blinds. When she's out of sight, I grab the envelope and bring it into the kitchen. There's a yellow sticky note on front that says *Dropped in our mailbox by mistake. Has your address on it.* It's addressed to me. To me! How? What could it be? My hands tremble uncontrollably. It's from the credit union I opened an account at back when I arrived, when I had my own money and never thought twice about getting a local bank account or telling Lucas about it. Why would I? I'd always been independent—always made my own way. What could it say?

I can't open it here. He'll already see that somebody dropped something off. I have to wait until Avery's daily noon nap on the porch and freeze the camera before I open it. The hours before I can see what it is are agonizing. There's no way he didn't know about this account and drain it so I wouldn't have access. There can't be money in it. So I probably shouldn't get excited. He controls everything, every other detail. It was all planned: how he's cut off my phone, access to internet, transportation, money. He forced me to sign off on everything, adding his name to my bank account to keep control of my money. He forced my signature on documents he brought home on a lot of things—I've lost track—so there is a tiny flutter of hope in my chest that maybe he didn't know about this one.

It's not like I mentioned it. He was showing signs of being a little controlling—guilting me about small stuff, having me check in and call everywhere I went, acting jealous over nothing. I thought it was him being overly protective since I was in a new country, but I guess there was a small part of me that thought I should protect my money, money I'd earned, since my world now revolved around his income, his house. It felt safe. It wasn't much, a couple thousand. God, it seems like an absolute fortune now. I need to see what the letter says. How can I hide it?

Just before noon, I place Avery in her high chair. She eats bits of banana and yogurt as she kicks her socked feet against the table. There is a mess of old mail in the wooden mail organizer on the counter. I stand near it and drop a piece of bread into the toaster. I can only work with the pieces that are lying on the countertop. I can't move anything. I see what looks like a spam offer from a car dealership. Lucas is very tidy but tends to jam junk mail into the organizer all week and then clean it out on the weekend. This is a great benefit to me right now. I make a fresh pot of tea and pour myself another cup. Then I pull out a plate from the cabinet. I place it on top of the car dealership envelope. When my toast is ready, I butter it on the plate and then pick up the plate holding the envelopes beneath it.

"I'll be right back, bug," I say and then head over to place my plate and mug on the porch table. Before I do, I make sure to say "Oops," as if I forgot something, and then I place my plate on the stand by the front door where my letter sits. I go back to the kitchen and grab a spoon, then pick up the plate with the bank letter underneath it and take it outside. I'm trembling. My knees feel like they'll buckle I'm so incredibly nervous, but I quickly go in to collect Avery and place her on a blanket on the daybed with her musical book to play with until she gets tired.

I eat my toast and wave back at Cora, who is excitedly waving my way. I pray to God she doesn't come over. I need time. After Avery is asleep, I lie down next to her and slip my hand beneath the daybed cushion, locating the small remote that allows me to freeze the camera. I can only guess that the function is working, since I am not actually looking at the surveillance screen, just a camera lens. So far, he's never seemed to think anything is off, so that's how I know it works. The heart-pounding risk each time I do it makes me ill.

I try to breathe deep and calm my nerves a minute. Then I pull the letter out of my pocket and rip it open. I press my knuckles to my mouth as I read it and then read it again. Oh, my God. I can't— Oh, my God! There's money. It's an annual statement. My pulse throbs in my ears. I recall declining to receive monthly statements to save the planet from paper waste. If I hadn't, he would have seen monthly statements come through and that would be it. My. God. He didn't find out about this account. There's twelve hundred dollars in it! It's not a passport and a plane ticket, but it could get me out. This time I wouldn't waste my time trying to set up a plan or passport first, I'd just go as far as the money could take us. Tears begin to fall, and I frantically wipe them off the bank statement and fold it up, shoving it in my bra.

This is a miracle. This is somebody watching over me. A lot of mail gets sent directly and doesn't actually get forwarded to the PO box, but he always checks the mailbox, and I'm not allowed to go near it. This feels like more than luck: it feels like salvation. I hold my head in my hands and rock back and forth, my mind racing, planning. How do I get to town? I have to.

"Oh, sweetheart, are you okay?" a voice asks, and I leap to my feet, holding my heart. "Oh, God, I'm sorry," Cora says. She puts her hand on my shoulder.

"No. It's fine. I just— You startled me," I say, and she sees Avery sleeping and then puts her finger to her lips, indicating she'll be quiet. She sits down without being asked, so I sit back down as well.

"We had the toy drive last month, and I found a box of baby toys in the garage that got left behind, so I brought little Avery this," she says, producing a plush octopus from her bag.

"Oh," I say. "That's really lovely. Thank you. She'll love it." Cora smiles, pleased with herself. I know a sane person would offer tea, and since she's showing no signs of leaving, I ask her if she'd like a cup.

"That would be great. Thanks," she says, and I remember the porch camera is frozen, and if I go inside while the surveillance shows me sleeping, I will be so incredibly screwed.

"You know what, I'm so sorry. I just used the last tea bag," I say. "I was planning to go into town and get some today." It's all I have. I don't think she believes me.

"That's okay, dear. I just wanted to make sure Avery got this is all."

I should offer her something else, but I can't, so I make conversation instead, as it's all I have to offer.

"It's nice today," I start.

And it is. It's sunny today, which is fitting because I feel light for the first time in months. It's still light-jacket weather

110

during the day and cold at night, but I know winter is coming, and I feel this rare flutter of hope expanding in my chest that maybe I'll escape before it gets here.

Cora continues making small talk about things I don't have the luxury to care about—Weight Watchers, and a new organic cat food she found to feed the neighborhood stray she's apparently named Alfalfa. Avery begins to stir. Cora puts her fingers excitedly to her lips and smiles as if she's never seen a baby before and will endure physical pain if she can't touch her.

Avery wakes happily today, blinking at us and stretching her little legs. Cora looks to me.

"You can give it to her if you want," I say, and she gives a joyful little shimmy of her shoulders, takes the stuffed octopus, and sits next to Avery on the daybed.

"Hi, sweet girl," she says softly, and Avery coos and flexes her hands, reaching for the stuffed animal.

"This is for you. What should we name him?" she says, tickling the bottom of Avery's feet. I see Cora's open bag next to her empty chair. I can feel my cheeks flush with shame at the very thought of stealing from the nicest woman on the planet. I will pay her back, though. If she knew why, she wouldn't fault me, I tell myself. I just need ten dollars to get to town. How? I can't have her go inside to get something or bring Avery in or anything. It will tip off the motion-sensor cameras inside. It would ruin everything.

"Looks like someone needs a fresh diaper. Did you tinkle? Yes, you did," she says, and it sounds a little more like she's talking to a puppy than a child, but Avery loves it. Cora doesn't even ask me: she just pulls a clean diaper out of the bag of toys and baby supplies that sit near the front door and begins to take control.

I feign cleaning up by plucking up Avery's bottle and a few toys and then sit in Cora's spot.

"You didn't have to do that," I say.

"I love helping, especially with a baby," she says, and I peer down at her bag, my heart beating so loudly I think she can hear it. She starts to tell a story about when her daughter was young, but all I hear is my pulse. I keep my eyes steadily on her back as I ever so slowly reach my hand into her bag and pull out her leather clutch.

"That was before we had mommy blogs, you know, so…" she continues. She turns slightly, looking for somewhere to chuck the dirty diaper, and I leap up, concealing the clutch.

"I'll take that!" I say and take the diaper, then quickly turn my back and pull out a twenty—that's all she has—and walk the few steps to pull a plastic bag out of the baby bag and stuff the diaper inside. I walk back to her spot, the clutch inside my cardigan, and sit back in her chair. She turns around, picking up Avery.

"Isn't that better? Yes," Cora says to her.

I can imagine I look pale as a ghost. *Shit, shit, shit.* She sits at the edge of the daybed, bouncing Avery on her lap.

"Her booties," I say, desperately hoping she turns back around and doesn't just reach down and pick them up off the deck floor where Avery must have kicked them off.

"Booties! Yes, sweetheart, it's chilly, isn't it?" She sweeps Avery up in her arms, lays her back down on the daybed, and pulls on her tiny crocheted bunny booties, and I drop the clutch back into her bag and let out the breath I was holding for so long my lungs ached.

I exhale and watch how tender she is with Avery. I think for a second that I have found someone to trust. In a wild, mad moment, I want to ask her if she could possibly watch Avery for a little bit. I've only had the camera frozen for about twenty minutes. If I could get there and back in an hour, Lucas might just think we'd taken a longer nap, and it might not raise any red flags. He hasn't noticed anything amiss yet. It could be my only shot. I could take a cab with the twenty and be much faster than a bus and much faster without Avery. It's not mad. I have to try.

"She sure likes you," I say, and Cora's eyes fill with pride or pleasure or something like that. "There's no way you'd want to watch her for me, for just a little bit, is there?" I ask, nervously.

"Of course!" she almost shouts, not missing a beat.

"I wouldn't want to impose," I say, out of obligation.

"I'd be thrilled to," she says.

"I was gonna make a quick run out now and be back in an hour," I say. Cora's face is a mix of something: surprise and disappointment, if that's possible. I can imagine she thinks I am capable of leaving the house but just don't want to do it for her, perhaps. But I really don't have time to worry about that.

"Of course," she says.

"I should just be an hour, hopefully less."

I watch Cora cross the street to her house with Avery on her hip and a giant baby bag slung over her shoulder. I hope I can trust her. I have to act fast. I need to go in the clothes I have on. First, I slide my plate with the dealership envelope under it, inside the front door, carefully, with one arm, so I'm not caught by a camera. Then, once I know Cora isn't within eyeshot, I make my way around the side of the house. I can't walk down our street and risk being spotted and having it mentioned to Lucas. I head for the small park behind the house, and when I see it's empty except for a young mom I don't recognize pushing an infant on a swing, I sprint across the park and keep running until I hit a main road.

I can't believe I'm doing this. I can't believe I left Avery. *It's okay*, I tell myself. Focus. I don't have a phone to order an Uber, and it's not the kind of city that is full of passing cabs. *I don't have time for this*, I think, as I walk backward down the

113

sidewalk, blocking the sun with my hand and searching for any sort of Lyft, cab, or Uber that might stop, but I don't see anything, so I put my thumb out. I'll probably get murdered, but I have no choice. It's the middle of the day on a busy street, so maybe I'll just get groped and not murdered.

It doesn't take long for someone to pull over. Of course it's a middle-aged man.

"Hey there," he says, pushing open the passenger door. The car is a Passat from the '90s, and he brushes empty beer cans off the seat to make room for me. He smiles at me from behind a frightening tangle of unkempt facial hair, and I notice his feet are bare. I weigh my options. Is this my only shot, or will I inevitably waste time fighting him off?

Then I see a taxi, four or five car lengths behind him, coming up to a red light. I run at it, and I throw myself in front of it as it slows. The diver honks at me and waves me out of the way, but when he stops at the light, I open the door just as he tries locking it to keep the crazy lady out, and I throw myself into the back seat.

"What the fuck are you doing, lady? I'm off duty. I'm on my lunch."

"Please. It's urgent. It's only a few miles away. Please. It's an emergency," I beg.

"Well, call the cops," he says.

"It'll take too long! Please!"

"Jeez," he says, running his hand through his hair. I look at the address on the envelope. I can't give him a bank address because he'll wonder why the bank is an emergency and maybe kick me out. I know it's at Keller and Sixth, so I ask him to drop me there. He just shakes his head and drives.

"I'm so grateful. Thank you. Thank you so much." After we drive the short distance, I ask how much.

"The meter is off. Just go," he says.

"You're a saint, really," I say with tears in my eyes and then run through the pharmacy parking lot across to the front of the bank. I try to pause before going in so I don't give away my desperation and alarm anyone. I take a couple breaths and tuck my hair behind my ears. I try to calm down before going inside. It feels so incredibly strange to be outside of the walls of that house; everything seems to move slowly, in a sort of surreal haze. I feel light-headed with adrenaline as I wait in line to speak to a teller. I. Don't. Have. Time. For. This. I think about the camera and how long I've been gone. I'm still okay, it's been less than an hour total, but I have to hurry.

When it's my turn, I approach the bank teller—a woman in her thirties with a slicked back ponytail, large hoop earrings, impractically long nails. I show her the bank statement and ask to withdraw the balance and close the account. She says the usual *We're sorry to hear that* spiel and then asks why. I say I'm moving, that it's urgent.

"Certainly. I just need your ID, and you can fill out this form."

"No, I don't— I didn't bring my ID. I thought this statement with my name on it would be enough," I say, my voice breaking. I hadn't thought about not having ID because he took mine so long ago, but I thought this would be enough. I don't know why, but I thought there was a chance.

"How do we know that's your name without ID?" she says.

"Please. Please, I beg you. I need this money. It's mine. That's me!" I yell. She raises her eyebrows at me. This can't be happening. I'm so stupid.

"I literally beg you. Woman to woman. It's urgent. I need to get away," I say, looking in her eyes, willing her to understand that I am in danger, and I think she does. She softens and swallows and purses her lips.

"I'm so very sorry," she says. "It's just not possible. I would if

I could, really," she says, and I open my mouth to scream—to throw myself onto the counter between us and wail and beg and tell her everything, but that sort of scene would mean police, and Lucas has the police in his back pocket. I can't scream. I need to get back to my baby. I can't run with no money, and I would never leave Avery behind. I feel tears flooding my eyes. The woman signals to another teller to take her spot a moment, and she comes around and helps me into a chair. She kneels next to me.

"Are you all right? Do you need help?" she asks kindly. *Yes, I need help*, I want so desperately to say, but I don't.

"I need a taxi. Please. Can you please call for me? Quickly?" She nods but lingers a moment, seeing if I might say more, then she goes behind the counter and makes a call. I see someone who looks like a manager type in a navy suit and combover eye her and furrow his brow. She quickly escorts me, the woman making a scene, out the front door.

"They'll be here soon. They said to wait out front," she says, still sympathetic but ready to be rid of the problem. I sit on a bench in front of the building and wait for the taxi. I'm too heartbroken to cry. A woman with a kid of about seven sits next to me. He carries a Happy Meal and has one hand inside of it, pulling out fries and stuffing them into his mouth. Then he drops the red box and begins to howl. His mother consoles him. She kneels to gather up what's salvageable, telling him the burger is wrapped, so it's okay. Then my cab pulls up to the curb.

She's left her purse on the bench as she helps her son. I'm a monster, he's turned me into a monster, because I grab it and tuck it into my coat before running to the cab door and letting myself in. I watch as we drive away: she hasn't noticed. I greedily pull out its contents, praying so hard there is a cell phone. There's not.

I find a gold watch. I think it might be a Gucci. I quickly put it in my bra. There's forty dollars, which I also take, and that's it. Besides a hairbrush, some makeup, a roll of Tums, Advil, hair ties, a baggie with half a browned apple, and keys. Goddamn it. I took her keys. I take her ID and shove it into my shoe. Then, I tap the driver and hand him the purse.

"Someone left this on the seat. There's a name on the credit card if you can get it back to her."

He takes it with a sort of grunt of recognition but doesn't really say anything.

I lean my head against the window and let the tears fall, blurring out the world rushing by. The world that I am no longer a part of.

11

CORA

I sit at the piano in my living room with Avery on my lap and she squeals and giggles as I take her finger and plunk out "Mary Had a Little Lamb" with it. After that, she pounds out her own tune by slapping her little hands on top of the keys, delighted with herself. I bounce her on my knee as I page through a three-ring binder of sheet music and familiarize myself with the popular songs at the piano bar.

I think about Grant in the soft candlelight the other night, and it feels so forbidden. Even my private thoughts of him make me jumpy when someone comes in the room, as if they can read my mind. I'm immediately on the defensive if someone talks to me while I'm letting my mind drift to scenarios of us alone after closing time and how it would feel to be touched by him. How can one evening with a man I've known for years stir up so much…desire? I guess that's the only way to put it. I'm ashamed of the feeling.

In all honesty, I feel like I'm behaving like a nervous maniac this last week, and I cannot imagine how Finn could not only betray me but not let on or act at all different. I haven't actually done anything wrong, and I'm sure I'm acting different. My suspicions were never based on him changing his behavior or my gut feelings; they were always things like lipsticked joints and *Drinks with C*—actual clues. If he is unfaithful, he's really good at it. But my own strange feelings over the last days have made me think that maybe he's really been honest with me. If indulging a fantasy makes me feel this much guilt, surely the act itself would cause him to change and there'd be a shift. Overcompensation, paranoia, I don't know, but something.

When Avery starts to tire of the piano and get fussy, I notice it's been almost two hours since Georgia left, much longer than I thought she'd be, so I think about Paige and how much it would cheer her up to hold this sweet baby. I put Avery's little hat and shoes on and then realize I don't have Georgia's number to tell her I'm across the street. I look for a Sharpie so I can leave a note on her door, but I can't find one, so I look through my phone for Lucas's number. It's buried there somewhere from when he moved in, and I shoot him a text telling him Georgia can pick up Avery at Paige and Grant's place when she gets back and could he please let her know as I don't have her number.

I give Avery a Chips Ahoy! cookie that she gums on as we cross the street to Paige's.

"Knock, knock," I say, as we open the wooden gate on the side of the house, and I shift Avery higher onto my hip as I walk the paving-stone pathway to the backyard.

"Hey, Cor," she says without turning around, so I sit opposite her, propping Avery on my lap. Her mouth goes slack upon seeing us. She points at Avery.

"You have a baby," she says, flatly.

"It's Georgia's little girl, Avery."

"Why do you have her?"

"I'm watching her for a bit while Georgia's out. Isn't she perfect?"

"I thought she was a hermit. Where did she go?" Paige says. I purse my lips and roll my eyes.

"That was probably just gossip we shouldn't go around spreading," I say.

"*You* told me that," Paige says.

"Well, anyway. Here," I say, putting Avery on her lap. I'm sure she'll protest and hand her back to me with a look of annoyance, but she doesn't. She holds Avery facing her and bounces her slightly. Avery smiles up at her, trying to grab the hair tie at the end of Paige's loose braid. Paige takes it out and lets her have it. On instinct, I want to pull her away, explaining that it's a choking hazard, but I don't. I watch them play together, Paige pulling it away gently with a thumb and forefinger, and Avery pulling it with all her might in a closed fist. For a moment, I think I see Paige's eyes glossy with tears. I don't know if I've done a terrible thing, bringing a child here in the space where hers no longer lives, or a good thing, making her happy in this moment.

"The ball was fun the other night. I was glad you could be there," I say.

"Yeah" is all she replies.

"So I feel like, I mean, I've been thinking about it, and maybe the whole, you know, our arrangement isn't a great idea."

"Why the change?" she asks, still fixated on playing with Avery.

"Well, you've followed him for two weeks and nothing. I think we have our answer," I say.

"Well, it's up to you, but two weeks isn't much. Just because he's not cheating today doesn't mean he hasn't and that I won't catch him if I keep looking."

"I know. I just... I feel like he's proven himself to be honest, and now I'm the bad one, not him."

"Well, look. It doesn't cost you anything unless I catch him, right? I haven't tried my last-ditch effort to trap him in something myself. Because I think we need more time—like, it can't be obvious to him—but it's your thing, so whatever you want," she says, standing, Avery on her hip. She goes to grab a blanket off the back deck and lays it out on the ground. She places Avery on top, and Christopher waddles over. Avery screeches excitedly when the dog sniffs her with his wet nose, and we both laugh. Christopher makes a few circles before lying down and resting his head on Avery's leg.

I pet his head mindlessly. Maybe it's that I want to stay in this space that's been created—a space where I have tried my hardest to find out if he's lying to me and he's been proven innocent. I want to hold it up as proof that he loves me—that I was wrong, and now I can move forward without constantly holding back from him in subtle ways every day. I can stop the second-guessing and self-loathing that comes with not feeling good enough. We can be happy.

Once upon a time, we drove straight through the night, on a whim, all the way to Teton National Park to watch the sunrise from the bed of Finn's pickup. We drank gas-station coffee and talked until our voices were hoarse. When we were just out of college, we crashed a 5K like some might crash a party. We just joined in and started running with everyone else, just for the free craft beer and party at the finish line. I watched him play Iago in Shoreside Community Theater's rendition of *Othello*, and he'd come to all my games when I joined the ladies' Foxtrot softball team. We shared a mango mousse with a chocolate heart inside on a sidewalk café in Florence, and we made love in a small rowboat on a lake I don't remember the name of when we visited his parents in Wisconsin. He bought me an engraved thimble from a little gift shop that I still have somewhere. We were in love. We were perfect. I want it back.

"I guess I'm starting to think it was a crazy idea, and I'm so glad it was you and not a private investigator. I mean, what was I thinking, right? I trust him. I shouldn't have done this. I feel...guilty."

"If you're sure, Cor. That's fine."

"I'll pay you for your time, though. Please let me," I say, but before she can answer, we hear a man's voice hollering from the front of the house.

"Georgia?" the voice yells.

"Oh, it must be Lucas," I say. "I told him we'd be here when they were ready to pick her up."

"Back here," I call. A few seconds later, Lucas appears. His face is red, and his jaw is flexed but softens as soon as he spots us, and a smile spreads across his face.

"Uh, hi there," I say. I think about the fact that it can't be later than three o'clock and he's usually still at work. I never see his car until after six or so. "You're home early," I say.

"Georgia isn't feeling well," he says.

"Oh, no, she seemed fine," I say.

"That's what happens when she tries to be brave and go out, poor thing," he says, still smiling, approaching Avery and picking her up from her blanket on the ground. She starts to cry.

"How long have you had her?" he asks, and suddenly I'm a little uncomfortable giving her to him, and I'm not sure why. It's just a sense. His body language doesn't match his smile.

"Oh, not long. Georgia's running a quick errand, I think," I say.

"Well, that was so kind of you to watch her," he says. "Wasn't it?" he asks Avery, kissing her head.

"Anytime. She was just a darling," I say.

He starts to pull his wallet out and ask how much he owes us.

"No, please. Really. We loved having her."

"Well." He smiles widely and nods. "Thanks again."

"I hope Georgia's okay!" I call as he begins to leave.

"She will be, thanks," he says and starts toward the gate. I feel a tightening in my chest, and again I'm not sure why. I know how I can read into things and attach meaning where there isn't any, so I don't let myself do that. He's never been the friendliest person. I know a lot of wealthy men in the community who have a major superiority complex because of their jobs or the senators they have dinner with. That's how it is around here, so I won't let myself continue to think the worst of everyone. He didn't do anything to merit it.

"He's definitely off," Paige says, shaking out the blanket and folding it up. "Want some tea...or a margarita?" She laughs.

"No, I better get back," I say. "Thanks, I mean, really. You were a real friend for trying. It's just all a little too much, and I need to decide to be...peaceful. Ha ha. That's too much Oprah talking, but really. Thanks," I say and squeeze her hand before I go.

As I walk back across the street to our house, I pause and look over at Georgia's. I want to stop. I want to dismiss the paranoia that always gets me in trouble, but...she should be back. He shouldn't be home. Something feels wrong.

12

GEORGIA

When I finally arrive in front of my house, I'm hopeful that everything will be okay. There's a good chance that Lucas didn't notice the video that shows Avery and me taking a two-and-a-half-hour nap. Maybe he only glanced at the screen once.

I look horrendous. I'll probably make her think I'm even stranger than she already does turning up like this. In the taxi, I tried to concentrate on thoughts of Avery and stay hopeful and calm, but as the dark thoughts crept in, I had trouble catching my breath. It seems so easy from the outside. If I heard about a woman like me, I wouldn't understand. But the town isn't big, and he's set up a trap at every corner. Everyone here looks up to him. There is not one person I can go to who he hasn't known for years.

It seemed for so long that I just couldn't figure out an obvious way to escape. But a very clever man spent a very long time setting up this world, and it's designed with no escape. And the truth is finally starting to sink in. I have no identity, no proof of who I am, and no way out. He calls me Georgia—a nickname, because my skin is pale as a Georgia peach, he said—and introduced me that way to everyone. I found it charming. But it was another setup. My name is Nicola Dawson, and I'm finally realizing that I'll never be her again.

So in the cab, I couldn't breathe. I had to go back home with no plan and no hope. Finally, seeing my distress, the cabbie pulled over. I was sitting on the curb with my head between my knees, trying to catch my breath, to pull it together, and before I knew what was happening, medics had pulled up. I had to run. I don't know which would be worse: them taking me to the hospital and Lucas finding out I'd escaped the house, or having yet another recorded incident of my instability. I just got up and ran as far as I could, and when I was blocks away from them, I tried desperately to find another cab to hail, but that just doesn't happen in a small community like this, so I walked. I ran when I had the strength, and by the time I made it the four miles home, my hair was plastered to my face with cold sweat, I'd ripped the knee of my jeans, my eyes were bloodshot and full of tears, and I had no time to care because I needed to get my baby and get home.

I run to Cora's door and ring the bell. She answers quickly and looks me up and down.

"What happened?" she asks, hand to heart.

"Car broke down. Long story. Can I get Avery? Sorry to rush, I really appreciate—"

"Oh, it's okay. Lucas picked her up a little while ago," she says, and I feel almost weightless, my knees weak, and all the blood drains from my face. Bright bursts of light flash behind my eyes, and I feel like I'll fall, like my body will give up and my heart will stop right here, but I have to think about Avery. I have to go into that house and face what's to come because Avery is there.

I back away from Cora, stumbling, then catching myself. I can't open my mouth to speak, so I just walk across the street, looking at the warm orange light glowing in the windows. It looks like a normal family lives there—like if I peer in the window, I'll see a husband watching TV with a beer, a baby at his feet playing with her shapes toy, all waiting for me to come home so we can have dinner together and talk about our day and laugh and laugh.

I stand on the porch a moment before I go in. I have the wherewithal to click the remote that freezes the porch camera. That's probably why he's come home early, but I don't know for sure. And I need it if there is the slightest chance he didn't notice it.

When I walk in the front door, I don't hear a sound. I hesitantly cross the front room and into the kitchen, where Lucas sits at the kitchen table with a lowball glass of whiskey on the rocks and a smile on his face. He lives for this. The punishment. The control.

"Where's Avery?" I ask, knowing it's a short time before the rage will surface, praying she's safe.

"Napping. Drink?" he says, the game beginning. I shake my head as tears spring to my eyes. I stand very still and watch him, waiting.

"Sit down," he says, still smiling. I slide into a chair at the opposite side of the table. The house feels cold, and all the curtains are drawn. We are sitting in the light left from the afternoon sun that shines through the middle of the curtain in a thin yellow line across the kitchen floor, a laser beam of light in the dark house.

"As you well know, you can make this easy or hard. Where. The. Fuck. Did you think you were going?"

There is, of course, no right answer to this. Almost every answer somehow turns into me being a whore and trying to turn tricks for money, which is not something out of the realm of possibility—I'd do anything to get some cash at this point—but every answer is punishable, some worse than others, and since I have money on me that he'll find, I say, "I found a necklace on the walk out front of the house, so I went to pawn it. I'd like to have money of my own." I add this last part because I've learned it somehow helps to play into the fantasy that I really am just a housewife in need of an allowance rather than a prisoner. Adding that bit makes it seem like I see myself that way.

"What don't you have that you need? I provide you with everything. You have good food, nice clothes. Look around you. How many people live in a house like this?" he asks. "Look!" He demands that I actually move my head around as if I haven't seen the inside of the house in which I have been locked for an eternity. I obey.

I see the white walls and cabinets, the white quartz countertops, the white area rug under a greige couch and love seat, the joyless, loveless space that is as sterile as a medical-office waiting room. I left my toast plate on the front hall table. That must have driven him mad. My eyes land on the French doors leading into the den. I see my reflection in a small square of glass and shudder.

He stands and walks toward me, slowly. He stands above my chair, and I hang my head.

"Stand up," he says, but he doesn't give me space to stand. I have to push my chair back and rise to my feet. And then it's there: the white-hot pain as he puts his hand around my throat and slams me up against the wall. He keeps me there by the neck while he shoves his hand into my pockets and down my bra and pulls out the forty dollars I stole from the woman at the bank and the twenty I took from Cora that I never ended up paying a cabbie with anyway. He throws it on the ground.

"This worth it?" he screams, spit landing on my face. "Sixty goddamn dollars! Because I don't sacrifice enough to give you all of this. You need this that bad, huh?"

"No," I say, dutifully.

"What?" he screams.

"No," I say, straining to breathe. He lets go of my neck, and my own hands flutter to it instinctively as I gasp for air. I lean over the chair and try hard to catch my breath before whatever comes next.

If he kills me, the fantasy he's spent so many years crafting is over. I know he doesn't want me dead, but I also know he has plans to make that happen if he needs to. His go-to plan is to make me overdose on my antidepressants so nobody would ever suspect a thing. No mess, no suspicion. That's my theory—that he doesn't want me dead—but I could be wrong. He could be grooming a younger version of me online right now, ready to off me and fly to some country to do the same to her. I really have no idea, so I don't struggle. I think of Avery, and I don't scream or cry or fight back.

When he opens the door to the basement, panic rises in my throat, my chest tightens, and my hands shake, but I won't claw at him and make him carry me down. Not this time. I need him to feel like I learned my lesson and will acquiesce to him. He makes me walk past him to go down the stairs. I take slow and careful steps as I obey his silent command. I lean against the drywall with my left shoulder and take the second step carefully, unsure of what he'll do, because I've never not fought the basement room before. And then, when I make it to the fourth stair down, I feel the blunt force of his heel between my shoulder blades and the searing burn as my breath leaves my lungs. I don't tumble, grasping the railing or searching for my bearings, I fly and land on the concrete floor with a crack that sounds like breaking bones.

He doesn't bother locking me in the cement room. He just clicks the dead bolt on the basement door above me and leaves me there. I lie still for some time in the semidarkness. There's still a square of weak light from the egress window, and I try to look down at my body before the light goes completely. I move my wrists and then I try to sit up, feeling sharp stabs of pain. When I take in a breath, it pierces my back. I broke a rib, at least one. That's okay; there is no real medical care needed for broken ribs. No crutches, no boot, no cast, just time. I get myself to my knees, and I know there will be severe bruising on the side of my face and hip where I landed, but only my right ribs seem broken.

I crawl over to a pile of dirty linens in a laundry basket, careful to take only shallow breaths. I pull them out and onto the floor so I can lie down on them. Was that the last opportunity I'll ever have to escape? He let me swing Avery at the small park behind the house a couple times a week while he watched from the window. Now that's gone—the last modicum of freedom.

The dirty mop and bleach smell coupled with the crippling pain make me crawl to the utility sink to throw up, only I can't stand, so I vomit on the cement floor near the metal drain. I think back to the last time I was sure I'd found a way out. It was after I knew he'd trapped me, but when he was still taking me out in public now and then for show, and with rules. No using the restroom. If I had to, we would leave the event, and he'd be infuriated, so I didn't drink water or anything else the whole day to ensure I didn't have to go. No leaving his side, no discussing my past, no sulking or *antisocial bullshit*. This phase only lasted a few weeks because I tried getting into someone else's Uber when he was saying his goodbyes outside a restaurant. No matter how many times I screamed at the driver to go, the guy took his time putting directions into his phone, and then it was too late: Lucas had jumped in beside me.

That's also the night I found three hundred dollars and thought it would equal freedom. In the restaurant lounge, his work was having a little cocktail party, and I was within a few feet of him all night. At one point, he got cornered in a conversation. I saw his eyes dart around for me a few times, but these were important figures in his world, and he couldn't be rude, so I slipped out of his sight and into the coat check. I dug in every pocket and handbag for cash until I came up with just over three hundred dollars. I pushed it down into my underwear and returned to the party, figuring I'd pay later, but I never did because I materialized in a group of women who were chatting near him. I inserted myself into the conversation, and after a few minutes, Lucas came over, and one of the women affectionately grabbed my arm and said, "Sorry to steal her away from you, lovebird."

This made it appear that I had been cornered by the woman and had no choice but to be polite like he'd told me to be. Mercifully, the punishment didn't happen. And I thought that money was definitely a way out, that he didn't know. I paid a guy in the neighborhood the whole amount to get me a fake passport. This was before Lucas locked me in at night. He was still pretending I had some autonomy, but there were cameras and alarms, so it was, of course, part of the game. I learned the code to the alarm and cameras over time by watching him. It took weeks before I could piece together the six-digit code, and when I did, I went to the park behind the house and gave this guy all of my money. I knew the guy from the first few months we moved here, before I realized what was happening, so I trusted him. Sort of. But it was a shot I had to take.

I wish now that I had just run. It was before Avery, so maybe I could have. Even though he said he had every resource to find me and he promised he would and then he'd kill me. But I wanted to go home, and I needed that ID. I never got it, and the guy used my money on drugs. He actually told me so. To make things worse, the coat-check man got fired for stealing, Lucas mentioned days later.

Now, lying here, unable to hold my baby, a year into this hell that has become my life, I feel like letting go. I sometimes think it would be better if I just took all the citalopram in one swallow and floated away from here in a painless, weightless sleep from which I'd never wake up.

But Avery.

Then I remember the gold watch I stole. I put it down the side of my shoe with the ID, just in case. I close my eyes and let the tears stream down and fall on my neck, the labor of the crying immediately causing severe pain in my ribs. I wince, but I focus all my thoughts on the watch that he doesn't know about and how I will sell it. I took the woman's ID. I learned the hard way that you need an ID to pawn or sell, and now I have one. She's a few years older, a few pounds heavier, but she's a brunette of average height, and it could work. It's another chance. I have to try again.

13

PAIGE

Paige wakes up earlier than usual. She takes a mug of coffee and goes out front in her robe to water her marigolds and let Christopher eat the dandelions in the garden against the house. She hears a baby crying incessantly and sees Lucas and Georgia's baby sitting in a pink mesh playpen on the porch. Usually she'd scream at any careless parents to shut their kid up the way she did at an Applebee's a few months back, as she took crayons and coloring menus away from two toddlers and shoved them in her purse, to their parents' horror. Maybe not coincidentally, that was the last time Grant tried to force her out to a restaurant.

This time, she remembers meeting little Avery and she feels something—a tightening around her heart, an ache that makes her want to run over and pick the child up—but the mother is skittish and makes Paige uneasy, so she doesn't follow her instinct. She can't quite understand why she wants to protect this baby, but she shakes it off when she sees Lucas come out onto the porch.

It's not just Lucas. She sees him slam open the screen door and hold it, impatiently, a scowl on his face, as the wife walks out very slowly. It looks like she's limping. Or something doesn't look right, anyway. She looks either really hungover or…maybe she's sick and they're hiding it, and that's why they're so odd. He gestures impatiently, angrily toward the baby, and Georgia goes to the child immediately and kisses her several times. He sees Paige watching them and waves. She doesn't wave back. Everyone is a suspect, and that weird son of a bitch isn't getting a wave from her. When he goes inside, she notices Christopher making circles, so she instructs him to poop on the Kinneys' side lawn.

"Go right there, bubs. See? Over there. Good!" she says in the high-pitched voice she uses when she talks to him, and he obeys.

She lies on the couch and watches *Dr. Phil* and *House Hunters* until noon. She remembers what seems like such a short time ago, when Caleb sat in the recliner to her right while *Dr. Phil* was on. He asked how she watched this crap. There was a woman on that episode who had put bleach in her eyes to fulfill her "lifelong dream of becoming blind."

"Who is this supposed to be helping? The show says it's trying to show a cautionary tale and help other people avoid… what, exactly? How many people want to blind themselves? It's so exploitative," he'd ranted.

Grant always joked that they should wrap up an actual soapbox and put it under the tree at Christmas so he'd have something to stand on when he argued with the news or broke down exactly why her shows were garbage. Paige smiles to herself at this, and then the familiar stinging behind her eyes threatens, so she gets up and pushes the thoughts away.

She needs a distraction, so she decides that it's time to see if the plans she has set in motion have begun to take hold. She's surprised Finn hasn't called her yet since the other night, but she knows he's pretending to be aloof for Cora's sake.

She texts him. Hey, sexy. Miss me yet? She waits ten minutes before a reply comes back.

Who is this? it reads. Is he fucking serious? Okay, it's his wife's friend, maybe he wouldn't have a reason to have her number, but she thinks he's more likely just playing a game.

Was the other night so forgettable? she texts. Now this is vague because she knows he's sleeping with a motel-hooker. She probably wouldn't have his number, though. But she can't be sure. She is sure, however, that he's sleeping with Charlotte, too, so maybe he is just biting off more than he can chew, juggling it all, forgetting who's who. He very probably has a secret phone for the exchanges with these other women. He's probably panicking that Cora will see his real phone.

She looks out the window and sees Cora and Finn raking leaves together. *Aw, how sweet.* If he left his phone on the front step next to his gardening gloves and coffee mug, Cora might have seen *the* text pop up. She didn't, but he still looks furious. How scandalous of Paige.

You can't text me like this, the message comes back. She sees him standing in the middle of the yard, looking down at his phone.

Why not? she replies. There is a long wait before she gets a response. She watches Mia come out of the house in leggings and an oversize hoodie. She goes right up to her dad, and Paige watches his face go white as he is startled by her and pushes the phone deep into his pocket. She holds her hand out and he gives her a set of keys. They say something Paige can't hear.

Then Mia goes to the car and gets in. Cora yells something to her—"Bye, honey!" it sounds like—but Mia doesn't pay her any attention. Poor Cora, Paige thinks, but only for a moment because she is distracted by Finn, who looks like a man in quite a predicament. He stabs his rake into a pile of leaves and goes to sit on the stoop and sip his travel mug of coffee.

She watches him sigh and lean his head in his hand a moment. Cora doesn't see this because she is distracted by Georgia, Paige notices. She watches Cora watch Georgia try to lean over to pick up her baby and then hold her side in pain. Then she kneels and breaks down the easy-assemble mesh sides of the playpen so she can move to Avery and be next to her. Odd, but she's not thinking of that now. She watches Finn start to text, then he looks up. His look seems far away for a moment, like he's trying to think, but instead he meets Paige's gaze from her front window. She waves at him. He looks back at Cora to make sure she doesn't see; he's stunned for a moment. Then he stands up abruptly and goes inside.

I'm not sure why you're texting me like this, the message says. Oh, she sees what he's doing. He's skilled at this. He's covering his tracks, playing stupid in case Paige were to show Cora the texts from her side of things.

Meet me to discuss if you don't want me to text you...or call you, she replies. She could be more threatening, but she should tread lightly so he doesn't back away even more. There is nothing for a good while. She watches Cora look around for him a moment, but it seems like she's not bothered that he's gone because she walks off across the street. *Dear God, I hope it's not to bother poor Georgia.*

A half hour later he replies, Wild Roast Coffee Shop at 4.

Well, well, she thinks. That sounds just perfect.

Paige slips into her soaker tub, which she has filled with scalding water and eucalyptus-scented bath salts. She takes her time shaving her legs with baby oil and thinks about what to wear.

She feels guilty about misleading Cora. She was going to try to get evidence for her, but things have changed, and now she wants more. They aren't right for each other anyway, but that part will have to wait.

When she pulls up to Wild Roast, Finn is already there, which annoys her because in some subtle way it gives him an upper hand, choosing the table, settling in with his coffee. She comes in, tossing her long, glossy hair over one shoulder and taking off her tight suede jacket to lay over the back of her chair. She hoped he would stand and help her, but he does not. She sits.

He doesn't smile or greet her; he just furrows his brow and sighs.

"So what's this about?" he asks.

"Excuse me?" she says. That was not what she was expecting.

"If I want you to stop texting, I have to meet you. Was that some kind of threat?" He leans back and folds his arms.

"Uh. Seriously? No, I was saying it would be easier to meet if you don't want Cora to see your texts. Are you at least gonna get me a coffee before you give me the third degree here?" she says, flustered, trying to take back some control.

"Yup," he says, angrily, both hands slapping on the edge of the table as he gets up.

"Skinny latte," she says with a smile, tucking her keys into her handbag and hanging it on the back of his chair. He surprises her by sitting back down a second and leaning over the table.

"This is not a thing," he says, pointing back and forth between them. "Just so we're clear." Then he stands and goes to the counter. Paige is rattled, hurt if she's honest, but she also sees an opportunity she needs to seize. She saw him open his phone at least a dozen times that night at the bar. His password is a weak swipe in the shape of an *s*. She didn't mean to see it, but it was right in front of her all night; she couldn't avoid it. Okay, fine. She meant to see it. And now, she finds, it will prove very helpful.

She checks to make sure his back is to her in the coffee line. Then she opens his phone and quickly scrolls through his contacts, taking photos of the ones she wants with her own phone. She sees a memo app, and since he has a couple people in front of him in line still, she opens it. One of them is titled *Passwords*. Yes, please. She clicks it, takes a photo of a few of them quickly, and then she turns his phone upside down on the table so he won't notice the glow of the screen if he comes back before it times out and turns off. Very interesting, she thinks. *Something I bet he wouldn't want Cora to see. She'll save her new information for a later date if she needs it.*

When he comes back, he puts her paper cup of coffee down and sits. He looks defeated and exhausted.

"I was drunk, okay? So just tell her if you're gonna tell her. Or what? What do you want, exactly?" he says.

"What makes you think I want something?" she says, countering his frustration with a calm voice. He scoffs, looks at the ceiling and then back at her.

"Then, why are we here? If you didn't want something, you'd chalk it up to a fun night, move on. Don't get Cora involved."

"Oh, so you did think it was fun," she says, smiling over her cup at him and then blowing at the hot steam.

"Games. This is what I'm talking about. It shouldn't have happened," he says, and she interrupts whatever is coming next.

"But it did," she says, not smiling anymore.

"So then, what, for God's sake, what? Get to it already. What do you want from me?"

"For a guy trying to hide a secret from his wife, you sure are coming in pretty hot at the one person you might think about being a little nicer to," she says, but he only gets more agitated.

"Because there's no point, Paige!" he shouts, and they both glance over their shoulders to make sure nobody they know could be within earshot. He lowers his voice.

"You think I didn't stay up every night since—just knowing I was fucked?" he continues. "I fucked up, I know. So just, what? What are you gonna tell her, exactly?" Desperation cracks his voice ever so slightly.

"I don't want to tell her either. Why would I want to do that?"

He doesn't respond, he just looks away from her, not buying it, waiting for the punch line.

"I can deny it, you know. You're not exactly the most stable person around," he says, but she doesn't let it get to her.

"I just want to see you. That's all," she says.

"What?" he says in an exaggerated tone, overenunciating the *t* at the end and raising his eyebrows.

"Why not? You seem like you could use somebody a little wild and…unstable. Maybe that's just…a better match for you. Look at Grant. He's the nicest guy in the world, but we outgrew each other. Can't we just have some, I don't know, fun? Dangerous fun," she adds, laughing a little. He looks at her, making eye contact. She can't read the look.

"I'm not that guy," he says. *Liar.* "So if you wanna tell her, go ahead. I'll deny it, and you'll lose a friend."

"Wow," Paige says. "You sure about that?"

"I don't know what you're trying to do here. I said no to this whole thing that night when you drove me home, and you still come back, all up to something the other night at the party. I don't trust you," he says, punctuating the last few words like he's made a good point.

"Me? I came back? I had sex with myself in that bathroom? I'm sorry. You're the one who doesn't trust *me*? Ha!" Her voice is high and pinched. This combative facade of his should signal danger and make her let it go, but she does not.

"You have no proof, so…"

"How do you know that?" she says, and he stands and shoves his phone in his pocket.

"I think we're done here," he says. He turns and walks out of the café to his car.

That's cute. He thinks we're done.

14

CORA

I almost wonder if I'm imagining it, but Finn seems so attentive the last couple days. No, I decide. It's me. I've been so busy thinking the worst, I haven't appreciated him or noticed how hard he tries.

I stand at the stove and stir up a skillet of Hamburger Helper. Finn is lying on the couch watching the news. I like the muffled sound of reporters' voices as it gets dusky outside, and the house smells like browning onions and garlic. I go to the arched opening to the family room and watch Finn a moment. I take it all in. Our family, our home. I can free myself of this paranoia and torture I put myself through. He has done nothing wrong. It's been me. And I can just stop. There is an overwhelming relief that rushes over me with this realization. I go to the fridge and pop the tops off two bottles. I sit at the end of the couch, handing him his and sipping mine. He looks quite surprised.

"Uh, thanks," he says. "Everything okay?"

"Cheers." I clink bottles.

"You're having a beer?" he asks, looking around like it's a joke and something else crazy is about to happen.

"Yeah, why not?"

"Because you...hate beer?" he says.

"Well, this one tastes like my Apple Brown Betty," I say, pleased about the sugary hard cider I found at the market. I'm making an effort, too. "We should watch that movie you've been talking about. The Bigfoot thing," I say.

"The documentary?" he asks, looking paranoid like I'm up to something, which is slightly annoying, I have to admit.

"Yeah, that. I can make popcorn."

"Okay," he says and watches me walk back to the kitchen and spoon Hamburger Helper and salad greens onto plates. I look back at him with a questioning expression and he turns away.

When I call Mia for dinner, she slinks into the room in oversize flannel pants and a clashing sweatshirt. It's like she's trying to look homeless. She has her earbuds in, and when she sits, she looks down at the plate and rolls her eyes and takes them out.

"Problem?" I say.

"Uh, no, just that I'm vegan, and I don't know why you keep trying to force me to eat tumors and hormones is all, and how is this carb fest on your Weight Watchers?"

"It's five points," I say, defensively. She picks at the salad.

"I hope you taste the animal's pain when you eat its dead body, because it's barbaric," she says.

"Please, we're eating," Finn says.

"Oh, my God! That's literally... Can I please just take a

snack to my room?" she asks, grabbing a cereal bar out of the pantry and heading down the hall before waiting for an answer. I have to admit I'm now a bit put off by the ground turkey and push it around my plate.

"I feel like I'm losing her," I say.

"Nah, she's just being a teenager," he says, looking past me to the football-game highlights on the TV across the room.

"She's been a teenager for a while, and this—" I make a circle gesture with my hand "—like, all of this, is new."

"I wouldn't worry, honey. She's a good kid, just moody. Kids are moody," he says, putting his hand on mine, and I feel my heart fill and my head feel floaty and light. I don't confide in him that I'm getting legitimately worried about how she's so withdrawn over the last months and that I think she might be doing drugs. I want the night to be special, so I change the subject as I clear the plates.

"Are you still doing your golf thing with Lucas this weekend?" I ask, scraping my uneaten turkey and noodles into the disposal.

"Uhh, no, he had to cancel," he says, cracking another beer and bringing it to the couch. I stop what I'm doing and follow him, wiping my hands on a tea towel.

"Why?" I ask or, rather, demand, considering the way it comes out. He stops midstride and turns to me.

"Wha— He didn't say. Did you wanna sub in for him, or…?"

"Ha ha," I say, abandoning my work in the kitchen and sitting next to him on the couch. Not the usual opposite sides, occupied by our phones sort of thing, but close. I pull the fleece blanket off the back of an armchair and cuddle up to him.

"I beat you at putt-putt once, so maybe I could sub in for him," I joke. "I think he's weird. For the record."

"Who?" Finn asks, oblivious.

"Lucas Kinney. Hello." Just then, there's a crash. It sounds like glass shattering, and we both jump to our feet. There's someone in the house. I hold my heart, and Finn grabs a baseball bat out of the junk closet next to the kitchen. He puts his finger to his lips for me to be quiet. The noise wasn't from upstairs, but I still fight the urge to run up and check on Mia. It came from the basement maybe, or…

"What are you gonna do with that?" I ask, my hands trembling uncontrollably, my heart pounding, thudding between my ears.

"The gun's upstairs. Shhh," he says, and we both stand still, frozen in fear, trying to hear where the noise is coming from. After a couple minutes, we don't hear anything else.

"Stay there," he instructs me.

"No way," I say and follow closely behind him as he clears the house, opening every bedroom and bathroom door with a jerk and then standing back, ready to swing at the intruder. When he swings open the door to the garage, I see the glass. His passenger window has shattered.

"Who's there?" he yells into the darkness.

"Just lock the garage door and call the police. Don't…" But he's already flipping the lights on and examining the damage. I stand in the doorframe as he carefully walks around both of our cars.

"Who's there?" he shouts again, sounding a bit comical if I'm honest, with his stupid bat. He peers inside where the glass used to be, checking for anyone in the car.

"Finn," I call, and then he opens the doors of my car with his bat overhead, but there's nobody there.

"It's clear," he says, and I race upstairs just to double-check Mia is okay. When I see her slouched on a beanbag chair, talking on the phone, I breathe a sigh of relief. I don't tell her about the noise; I just slip back downstairs and go into the garage, where Finn is googling *spontaneous glass breakage* on his phone.

"You think it broke itself?" I ask, my nerves calming a little since we checked every corner and it's clear.

"Nobody's here. The garage doors are closed. I don't know," he says.

"Maybe it was Lucas Kinney," I say.

"What?" Finn says, sharply.

"You didn't see the way he looked at me when he picked up his baby. He's not right."

"So anything that happens is his fault because you decided you don't like him. Now he's a magician?" Finn asks.

"Someone was in here," I say with certainty, and I *feel* certain. There's something left over in the air—a little trace of electricity when a person has just occupied a space. Finn shifts back and forth in a mock attempt to look for the phantom intruder. I point to the narrow window close to the ceiling of the garage. Finn laughs.

"A guy a head taller than me snuck in through that, to do what exactly?" He sits in the driver's side, avoiding the glass, and looks through the car. "I don't see anything missing."

"What if he made himself a key? Oooh, yeah, what if he let himself in just to mess with us—like our sense of safety? Did you ever see that movie, *The Strangers*? Liv Tyler and that guy from *Felicity* are in this house, right, and they are tormented by these three creepy people who just show up and scare them… and then they kill them, like for no reason, just because they can—'cause they're psychopaths. It could be like that. Who else would do this?" I ask. He goes back inside, and I follow, closing and locking the garage door behind me.

"I can't even begin to tell you how many things are wrong with that, but let's start with *How did he get a key?*" he says, retrieving his beer from the table on the side of the couch and sitting down.

"You lost your keys a few months ago. Oh, my God! We're changing the locks. Whoever found your keys, or TOOK your keys, got into the garage. Holy shit."

"Cora," he says.

"It could have been at golf or the bar. Holy shit," I say again. I get myself another beer and sit nervously, facing him cross-legged on the couch.

"Should we call the police?" I ask.

"Cora. No. Come on. You're being ridiculous. Look at this list of reasons a window can break on its own," he says, turning his phone to me. I look at the reasons: installation issues, a crack leading to spontaneous breakage, thermal stress, and a bunch of other things.

"So a freak accident is more likely? Really?" I say.

"More likely than the neighbor being a psychopath, I'd say. Wanna know who's weird? Brenda Welenski, who already has her Christmas tree up, and it's October. Why not randomly pick her to be the neighborhood stalker?" he says, and then picks up the remote and begins clicking through channels.

"Whoa. How can you just go back to normal? I think we should call the police."

"Cor, come on."

"Then, change the locks. We have to change the locks. We should have when you lost the keys to begin with," I say, increasingly irritated.

"Fine, I will," he says.

"Tomorrow," I insist.

"Okay. Look. Nothing was taken, so I think we should relax," he says, and I reluctantly agree, but he didn't see the scary way Lucas looked, and the strange way he's been behaving when I catch glimpses of him. No, I don't think I will ignore this.

Finn goes to bed early because he has an early morning, but I stay downstairs, light a fire in the fireplace and wrap myself in a blanket on the couch. I'm feeling creeped out, so I get back up and turn off the living-room light so nobody can see in. I stand at the glass sliding door and think about it supposedly spontaneously shattering in the middle of the night. I look to Paige's house, and all the windows are dark. I look to Georgia's and see lights on and movement. Just Lucas sitting at the table in the front room hunched over a pile of papers and his laptop. I wonder what would happen if I went over and knocked—brought a bottle of wine, said I just wanted to visit?

I unplug my iPad from where it sits on the side table and curl back up in my blanket and open Google.

Lucas Kinney, I type. A ton of stuff comes up because of his job. I wouldn't exactly call him a public figure in this size of town, but there is plenty to see about him on his various promotions, his history as a prosecutor, his profile on LinkedIn, articles he's written about boring legal stuff. I do learn his middle name from a few of these sites. Cameron. That narrows things down a good bit.

After close to an hour of reading uninteresting bits about him, I decide I've earned a handful of BBQ Pringles, so I'm about to close down my iPad and go to bed when I see something. A wedding announcement. Lucas Kinney and Caterina Cattaneo, July 12, 2009. I zoom in on the photo of Lucas, who looks relatively the same, and a small-framed dark-haired woman with huge brown eyes and an expression of elation. Huh. So he was married before.

When I look up Caterina Cattaneo, nothing else comes up except a handful of Facebook profiles. It's not hard to match her photo to her Facebook profile. When I click on it, it looks like it's private. Hmm. I wonder if *Caterina Kinney* will produce anything further, so I search the name, then quickly decide to try to narrow it down and type *Lucas and Caterina Kinney*, and then I see something very unexpected. Her obituary. I feel a hot rush of adrenaline shoot through me as I click on it. It doesn't say how she died, just information about how she was a beloved daughter and friend, stuff about the service, and that she's survived by her husband, Lucas Kinney. I click out of it and search *Caterina Kinney death.*

I skim unrelated headlines and find an article. She drowned. *St. Joseph County Coroner Mike Sanchez said the cause of death is listed as undetermined after an autopsy.* Oh, my God. Poor Caterina! My eyes fill, and I think about how young she was. Twenty-four, the article says.

Police were called to the home at about 6:15 p.m. Monday on a report of a possible drowning. Officers found the woman in the backyard pool. Her husband was visibly distressed. There has been no sign of foul play.

His wife died in an undetermined drowning. I want to call Paige immediately. She was there when he came over. She saw his eyes go dark. I can ask her what she uses to spy on the neighbors. Then I stop myself. No, she already thinks I'm crazy for following Finn and finding nothing. I need to do this myself.

I get on Amazon and look up surveillance cameras. Just like that, I have hundreds of options. Night vision and pairs with my phone? Yes, please. Thirty-four dollars. Click. Lucas better watch himself. Cora's got nothin' but time on her hands for a charitable cause.

15

GEORGIA

When he lets me out the next morning, the only reason I know I'm free is because I hear the click of the door unlocking. It doesn't open, just a small click in the quiet darkness. The only time he's left me down there for more than a day was months ago. It was two days, and I learned later he took Avery to a public day care while he went to work. He doesn't want to have to do that—he doesn't want to display any out-of-the-ordinary behavior, so one night is usually it.

When I climb the stairs, I ignore my pain and hunger. In the night I peed in the floor drain by the utility sink and drank water by putting my mouth under the tap so I didn't give him the satisfaction of running in desperation to the bathroom or for a bottle of water.

When I reach the top of the stairs and go into the kitchen, he's sitting, one leg crossed over the other, reading the paper and blowing on a travel mug of coffee. I ask where Avery is. He stands up, irritated, like I'm putting him out, and opens the door to the front porch. I walk slowly outside to find her playing happily in her playpen. She loves to be outside. Even in cooler weather, it's the only thing that keeps me functioning—that small sample of a world outside. So we're always out here. I go to pick her up, forgetting momentarily about my broken ribs. I wince and rest my hands on my knees for a minute, hunched over, trying hard to breathe through it.

Her playpen has mesh sides with pink plastic anchors; I easily remove the mesh side so it collapses so I can sit next to her and hold her to me.

After I hear Lucas slam the door and watch his car drive off, I remember the gold watch in my shoe. I don't know where he's going, since it's late in the morning on a weekend so not work. I have to be careful, because he could come back anytime, and he's always watching. Even more carefully after yesterday.

I spent hours last night thinking of where to hide it, and then I recalled a quarter-size tear in the vinyl cushion of one of the porch chairs. I leave the ID where it is, but I slip the small metal watch out of my shoe and into my hand and eye the chair. I don't look up at the camera. It's not a time we would take a nap, so I can't freeze it, and I'm still not sure he didn't find out about that. It would be like him to wait so he could punish me again. My only choice is to do it anyway and be careful. I sit in the chair. Avery giggles at me in her fuzzy ladybug sweater and matching little hat. I smile back at her and slowly run my hands down the sides of the chair until my fingers find the hole on the right side. It's smaller than I thought.

With one hand, I tear it a little wider so the watch can fit, then I push the watch inside the cushion bit by tiny bit, moving as little as possible so it will appear as if I'm just sitting, if not a bit nervously, because why wouldn't I be?

It's almost all the way in, and I see Cora walking right up the drive toward me. Son of a bitch. I'm still in yesterday's clothes. This is his fault. This is his goddamn fault if she sees the state I'm in. He put Avery outside. He didn't wait till I got cleaned up because he was too angry to act like an adult.

I push the watch all the way in and then have no plan, so I sit frozen a moment, thinking about how I could possibly explain away the fact that I am not only the horror show who showed up at her door yesterday but also have a bruised and scraped face. Goddamn it. It doesn't matter if it's his fault: it's now my responsibility to clean up his mess or repeat last night, or worse.

"Georgia, morning!" she says. And then she sees it all. She takes in my injury and dirty clothes, the dark lines under my eyes, the makeup I'm sure is smeared. "Honey, are you okay?"

"Cora, morning. Yeah. I'm so sorry about yesterday," I say, imagining the ping notification Lucas is getting right now from his voice-detection alerts, listening to every word— if not right now, reviewing it later. I have to be careful. I'm desperate to have a hot shower and eat something, but now I have to put on an improv show, and I'm just so not up for it.

"Don't be sorry. I'm so sorry if there was a mix-up. Your husband didn't seem happy about me having Avery," she says. Then looks me up and down again and adds, "You don't look okay. Can I help?"

"Oh, no. And no, he wasn't unhappy about you having her, it was just that— Well, I mentioned about my car…"

"It broke down," she confirms.

"Yeah, well, I mean, I was hit—rear-ended pretty bad, which is…which is why it broke down. The airbags went, all of that, so I think he was just really worried. He didn't know what was going on is all," I say, emphatically. I hope he's listening, because I could win an Emmy for this.

"Ah," she says. Okay, maybe not. Maybe she's not buying it. I look down at myself. My clothes are soiled, my hair is still wild and frizzy. I have cuts on my face, and I can feel the dots of dried blood, cuts from my fall that haven't yet been attended to.

"I was so worked up when I got home, I took a Xanax and fell asleep on the couch like this. I was just about to get in the shower, actually," I say. Not a bad performance. The women around here love their Xanax and lorazepam, but is it believable I came to her house in the late afternoon and am just now getting it together? I don't know, but I did the best I could. He can't be angry about that.

"Oh, sweetheart, I'm so sorry. Can I help you out today?" she asks so kindly I almost want to cry.

"Oh, no, no, I'm much better now," I say, going to Avery and bending to pick her up. It feels like my rib cage pierces all the way through my lungs as I try to lift her, and I cry out and breathe as slowly as I can to alleviate the pain.

"Oh, my goodness," she says. "You really hurt yourself. Let me get her."

"No, I'm really fine," I say, because I have no choice. If she comes into that house, I'm so fucked. I don't even know what he'd do. I feel the cold sweat bead across my back and between my breasts as I grit through the unbearable pain and pick up Avery. I clench my teeth and hold back tears.

"Well, you just let me know if you ever want me to watch her again. She was an angel. Or any—anything you need," she says uncertainly.

"That's so lovely, and again, I'm so sorry. I must look a fright. It was a rough night, that's all. Thank you so much for checking in, though. Really," I say.

"Of course," she says, and I can tell she wants to talk more, but I smile and wave Avery's hand goodbye to her, and we go inside. I set Avery in her high chair and force myself not to scream at the pain in my side as I do. I know she can't be too far away yet. In fact, when I peer out the window, she's standing on the sidewalk, looking at the house.

Cora, Cora, I think to myself. *Please God, don't get involved.*

I close the curtain and take out a box of cereal. I pour a pile of Cheerios onto Avery's chair tray and make myself a bowl. I start a pot of coffee and sit at the table, moving careful spoonfuls into my mouth until the coffeepot fills. I stand at the sink and drink down three large glasses of water to try and rehydrate before pouring a glorious cup of black coffee.

I prepare myself for the pain this time before I lift Avery from her high chair. It doesn't matter if I deepen the fracture with each lift, I will have to keep doing it multiple times a day, so I brace myself. I hold my breath and move her, painfully, so indescribably painfully, to her carrier in front of the TV. I put on a sexist princess show and take my coffee into the bathroom.

The thin, black flakes of dried blood fall onto the white porcelain floor of the shower as I stand under the hot water, taking deep breaths, forcing myself to stay hopeful that there is a way out.

I realize, as I rub shampoo into my hair and let the fruit-scented foam run down my body, that I have no idea how dangerous Lucas could be outside this relationship. What else does he get away with because of his status? Is Cora in danger? He would never do anything overtly, he couldn't take that risk, but is she too close after he found Avery with her, after that conversation on the porch? The truth is, I just don't know what he'd do given the opportunity. Frame her for something? Plant something? I don't know how to protect her.

After I dry off, I slip on jeans and a loose jumper and go into the living room to watch the rest of *Sleeping Beauty* with Avery. She looks like a perfectly normal and happy baby, cooing to colorful animated movies and surrounded by expensive toys. How much of what she's seen at this young age will she remember? How long until he punishes her for acting out? Maybe he never would. He says he never would, but how do I know?

I go to the kitchen and sit at the table with a mug of coffee. I think about the frozen camera out front. Does he know? Did he get tipped off when trying to figure out how I got away? I walk outside and try to appear as if I'm not up to anything. I sit on the edge of the daybed, and with one hand, I try to carefully pull out the small remote I keep under the mattress. It's a subtle move. Practiced and slow, but this time, I don't feel anything. It's gone. He's figured it out. He's got me. I don't react.

I go back inside and pour a fresh cup of coffee into a *Best Mom* mug Lucas bought me when I first got pregnant, and then I sit on the stool at the kitchen island. My decision is made. I'm just gonna go.

I may never have this chance again. In college, my friend Kelsey got a Gucci watch for her birthday that looked like the one I stole. It was thirteen hundred dollars. She told everyone, because she couldn't believe her boyfriend would spend so much on her. I haven't seen any in this style less than five or six hundred, so worst-case scenario, I get three hundred dollars at the pawn shop. That's enough for a bus ticket two states away, and extra for a cheap room and food for a week or so. I now have someone's ID I can use to pawn. I cannot pass up making my move now.

I'll have to steal something else once I get somewhere, maybe, and feel terrible about that, but I am keeping a mental log and I will return what I can. I'll return this woman's ID and pay for her watch. I will pay it forward, I will do whatever, but right now, I need to protect my baby.

If I walk out of the house right in front of the camera, he will notice quickly. He can be home in twenty minutes. I'll do it Friday. It will give me a couple days to sneak a duffel bag and a few changes of clothes into the laundry basket. If the video shows me dumping a pile of laundry into the washer, he might not notice me stuff some into a cloth bag. I can do it down inside the washer. There is only one camera in the basement, and it's not aimed at the washer and dryer, but I'll still hide it just to be extra careful. I can put Avery's baby tote on the porch in the morning when I bring her out for coffee, pretend to do laundry, retrieve my duffel bag, and walk out the front door. Her stroller, rarely used, has been stored in the corner of the porch next to oversize potted plants for ages. I can take that, too. I'll need help. I'll need Cora.

16

PAIGE

Why is Grant here on a Wednesday? Paige watches out the window as he uses a leaf blower on the lawn. He looks like a Ghostbuster with the contraption strapped to his back, and there will be more leaves in an hour, so what's the point? There are a few things she'd better get out of view before he comes in, which he will, for coffee or just to insist she take out the recycling more often or tidy up the mugs lying all around the house.

She doesn't feel one bit bad about smashing Finn Holmon's car window. She's no stranger to sneaking into the neighbors' garages. She's quite good at it, actually. She saw Finn with the hatch of his SUV open after he pulled into the garage. He stood a moment with his head bent down, looking at his phone, texting, probably with one of his bimbos because he looked around in a covert, guilty way for a moment. She saw his laptop bag propped up next to his golf clubs in the back of his car. Distracted by his phone, he shut the hatch without taking the laptop bag and closed the garage door. She was sure he'd left it in there unwittingly, but it turns out he must have gone back out to get it between the late afternoon and her break-in, because it wasn't there. That was a disappointment, but when she saw his day planner sitting on the passenger seat, she knew she needed it. Who locks their doors inside their locked garage? She certainly doesn't, and she didn't expect his to be locked. That's his fault: she did what she had to do. She spotted a nearby fire extinguisher, grabbed it, and hit the heavy bottom of it against his window. She swiped the planner as quickly as she could, then hoisted herself back up on their recycling bin, slipped out the slim window she'd come in, and dropped back down onto the HVAC unit outside. They should really be more careful. Anyone could have broken in like that.

The planner is now sitting on her coffee table because she isn't finished paging through it. He will be out of the office for a lunch meeting tomorrow. Good to know.

She takes the planner and brings it into the bedroom where a cardboard box sits with Finn's name written on it in Sharpie. He *will* pay attention to her. It might just take some time. She drops the planner on top of the photos of him with the hooker and him with Charlotte in the hallway at the ball. She's also printed out his passwords and contacts and has kept the rose he gave her at the bar. She pulls it out and smells it, even though it's long dead and the petals are dried and brittle. She wraps the flower in a small towel to make sure it doesn't get broken inside the box, then she shoves all of it into her wardrobe and goes back into the kitchen to put on a pot of coffee.

"Why the hell don't you have gloves on?" she asks Grant when he comes into the kitchen, rubbing his hands together.

The weather dropped last night, and it's starting to feel like winter. He shrugs and pours a cup of coffee.

"Well, for God's sake, you'll lose a finger to frostbite," she says and goes to the hall closet, where she pulls out a plastic storage container of winter accessories and drags it into the kitchen. She sits next to him at the table and starts to pull out mismatched gloves and mittens.

"I bought you Isotoners once. Where are those?" she asks.

"That was fifteen years ago," he says.

"Yeah, so they should be here." She pulls out a tangle of scarves and unknots them. "Ohh, I've been looking for this one," she says, coiling a chunky knit scarf around her neck, and keeps searching. She sees him smiling at her.

"What?" she says.

"Nothing. You're cute." He sips his coffee and keeps the amused look on his face.

"I'm a middle-aged woman. I assure you I'm not cute," she says and then presents him with a pair of brown leather Isotoners she pulls from the bottom of the bin.

"Would you look at that," he says, taking the gloves and trying them on for size. He flexes his fingers and keeps them on as he drinks his coffee. "Thanks."

"Need a hat?" she says, plucking a tragic brown ski cap from the pile.

"Absolutely."

She puts it on his head, and she laughs at how ridiculous he looks, but he leaves it on and does a little dance.

"You're laughing," he says, sitting back down. She responds by stopping. "It's nice to see. You seem...happier lately."

"I don't know about that," she says.

"I do." He smiles. Then he gets up and brings his mug to the sink. He rinses the dirty dishes that are piled up and starts to load the dishwasher.

"You don't have to do that," she says, pushing scarves and woolen hats back into the storage bin.

"Someone does," he jokes, but she doesn't appreciate the passive judgment. He picks up on her irritation.

"It's a lot for one person," he continues, looking out the window rather than at her. "The yard is a lot by itself. The gutters need cleaning."

"I can hire a service for that," she says flatly.

"The air filters need changing, the crack in the bathroom tile needs replacing—"

"What's your point?" she says. He's quiet for a while as he finishes loading the dishes and pushing the racks in, closing the dishwasher and starting it. He wipes his hands with a dish towel and turns, leaning against the counter. Paige is trying to sit on the plastic cover of the storage bin to force it shut.

"The point is maybe I should stay a few nights a week."

"You want to come back?" she asks. "I thought we talked about this."

"I'm just saying a few nights a week. To help out," he says, a note of hurt in his voice. She thinks about it a minute.

"It's your house, too. So I guess you should do what you want," she says, giving up on the bin and sitting at the table. He purses his lips and nods slowly.

"What?" she says.

"When *you* want me to, you let me know," he says. He could say this coldly, but he doesn't. He could let the sting of rejection cause him to storm out, or give up on her, or lash out, or a variety of other very human reactions to her constant difficult behavior, but he never does. He goes to her, kisses the top of her head, and lets himself out.

She feels sick. She wishes she could change how she feels. She trades her coffee for a glass of wine and sits in the front window seat with Christopher, who makes six circles before he lies down on the pillow at her feet. All she can think about is Finn, and it's not fair to Grant, it's not fair to anyone—this obsession that nobody would understand. She hates Cora being a victim of this, but she feels like she can't stop what's started.

The next day, she walks around the house nervously tidying up, thinking about how to best pull off what she plans to do. She can't get caught, so she'll need some backup stories to weasel out of the situation if she does. She really can't think of one single explanation, so she can't get caught.

She decides that the wig from her Marilyn Monroe Halloween costume would be a decent disguise: the opposite of her long dark hair, and she'll wear her reading glasses and some dark lipstick. Nobody would recognize her if they looked on a security camera or even ran into her. She finds these items and stuffs them into a messenger bag and goes.

His lunch meeting is from one to two o'clock, and she hates waiting around all day. It was fine when she slept the day away for all those months. Now, though, she has a renewed purpose, and she wants to just get moving. She stops at City Blooms for a mixed bouquet of mostly lilies and baby's breath, and then she drives to his office building and looks for his car in the parking lot. The lunch is at Grimaldi's, so he'll have to drive there. It's a few miles away. She parks in the back of the lot and waits. When she sees him come out of the revolving front door, he's with Charlotte. They don't touch one another. She's on her phone, and he's slipping his suit coat on.

So that's his lunch meeting. She should change plans and follow him, ruin the lunch, walk right in as if it's a coincidence and sit at the table next to them to see how he fumbles his way out of it. But her work here is more important. She watches them get into Charlotte's car. Thank God she was watching the door and not just his car. She hadn't considered he wouldn't drive. When he gets in the passenger side of Charlotte's Tahoe (which is far too large for her itty-bitty frame), Paige notices him glance around. Hmm. She watches a moment longer and sees Charlotte kiss him. This goes on for some time until they part, her giggling, it looks like. Both of them looking around the lot for one more check that nobody is out there. Paige ducks farther down in her car. Then Charlotte buckles her seat belt, and they pull away.

So you think I'm just gonna let that happen, huh? Paige thinks. Then she picks up the large bouquet she purchased with a glittery helium balloon (last-minute buy) wrapped around the pretty foil paper and bouncing behind her as she walks up to the building.

On the fourth floor, she finds the name of his company in fancy stencil across two glass doors. She sees the receptionist through the glass and knows that the young woman with a bouncy bob and oversize false eyelashes will tell her to leave the flowers with her and she'll make sure he gets them, but she can't do that. In the outside hall, there are two leather chairs with a low table in front and a spread of popular magazines lying across them. She has to wait until Eyelash Girl leaves the desk. It's the only way. She does her cell-phone move and holds it up to her ear, pretending to be engaged in a conversation so she doesn't look suspicious just standing there nervously. Instead she looks like someone who got interrupted and will continue her business in a moment. She passes the door and sits in one of the chairs, just out of sight, and waits.

It takes forty-five godforsaken minutes before the receptionist leaves her desk. Paige doubts Finn will return from his so-called lunch meeting in an hour, but she hurries anyway. She walks right past the desk and scans the row of office doors for his name. There are a few people in a meeting at a table in the center of the office—a modern, open-concept arrangement. One of them smiles and lights up upon seeing her—assuming all the romance and surprise that must be attached to the gift, no doubt. If someone let Paige back here, it must be okay, so nobody seems to bat an eye. She spots his door and slips inside. His laptop sits open and plugged in, but the screen has timed out and is dark. No matter—that's what his list of passwords are for. She pulls the power cord from the wall, slips that along with the laptop into her messenger bag and zips it closed, then she leaves the flowers where the computer used to be and walks out.

"Hey!" a voice calls. She walks faster. "Hey, ma'am." It's the receptionist, walking toward her, holding five reams of printer paper and headed back to the front desk. "You can't be back here."

"Oh, sorry. I'm just— I was delivering flowers. They told me to go on back," I say authoritatively.

"Who? I would be the only one to do that, and I didn't," she says, probably making a scene to cover her ass so everyone knows this was not her oversight.

"Someone did. Otherwise I would have left them up front, wouldn't I? This is wasting my time for my next delivery, so…" and then she walks out the front doors, not waiting for any further response.

She glances around as she walks swiftly to get to her car to make sure she doesn't pass Finn on his way in. She takes great pleasure imagining him reading the card. She wasn't going to leave one, originally. She was just going to use the flowers to get in. Then, the more she thought of how delicious it would be to confuse him and maybe expedite a breakup, the more certain she was that it was the right thing to do.

Finn, I bet you thought these were from Charlotte, but they're not. I'm on to you, it reads. She thought that was just enough for him to question her about them and become the right amount of paranoid and miserable.

Before she gets in her car, she thinks of another opportunity she hadn't anticipated because she assumed he'd be driving to his lunch meeting. She clicks her car key out of its plastic fob, holds it in her fist, and ever so subtly runs it down the length of his precious Range Rover as she walks past, gets in her own car, and drives home.

17

CORA

When I get my Amazon package in the mail, I'm practically giddy as I rip open the bubble envelope and pull out my very tiny spy camera. It's not marketed as a spy camera, but from the size of it, what else would it be for? Now, I know the only place I can safely put this is on their tree in the backyard. When Lucas is at work, Georgia is often out front. Now that it's gotten cold, that might change, though. Hmm. Still, I can't do it at night when he's home. It could backfire in a big way.

Their house backs onto a small park. I'll just stroll through the park, walk close to their fence, and clip it to a tree branch. It looks like an old iPod Nano with a tiny clip in back. Easy, though I know it's not the best place to put it because what will I see in the backyard? But there are sliding glass doors off the deck into the kitchen, and maybe they don't keep their blinds closed all the time. But even if it produces nothing, it's a good test. I can familiarize myself with the phone app and at least it's a start. Maybe I can make a bolder move if this tester works.

I shakily shove the camera back into its packaging when I hear the garage door open. Finn is home hours early. I hide the package in the cabinet under the sink and pretend I didn't almost get caught plotting to commit a criminal offense, but he can always tell when I'm hiding something. Damn it. If he did see it, he'd think I was spying on him, no doubt. What is he doing home? When he walks through the garage door into the kitchen, I can tell something's wrong.

"Hey, you're home early," I say, peering into the garage behind him. "Got the window fixed? Good. I was worried about you freezing to death this morning."

"Just cut the shit, okay," he says, and I feel my heart speed up and a tingling heat spread across my chest. I can feel the blotchy red anger rash materialize without even looking.

"Excuse me?" I say, steadying myself against the counter so I don't scream. So I don't pull out my hair and scream at the top of my lungs, *What the fuck did I do now? I thought things were finally so good!*

"A blonde woman showed up at my office today," he says, nostrils flared. He pulls a fifth of bourbon from the cabinet and takes a glass from the dry bar next to the fridge.

"Okay," I say, impatiently.

"My colleagues gave me a description that sounded a lot like you," he says, pouring his drink and turning to me.

"Why would I be at your work?" I ask, genuinely confused. I didn't do anything. How is this possible? How are we having this same, tired conversation when I didn't actually do anything this time? He just shrugs in an exaggerated gesture.

"Well, it wasn't me! What did they say? They described *me*?" I'm already yelling.

"They said a blonde with a sort of bob haircut came in and dropped off flowers." He looks at me with his eyes bugged out and an exasperated expression, like that's the whole story, like I should confess.

"So, short blond hair, that's all you have? And you're mad that you think I brought you flowers?"

"Come on. Just— Don't. I'm so sick of this, Cora, goddamn it. I am so tired of defending myself to you all the time."

"What the hell? First off, I wasn't there. I don't have a clue what you're talking about!"

"You didn't add a nasty message in the card? Who else would do that?"

"That's a great question!" I say with a raised voice.

"So the card says, *I'm on to you*. Well, I happen to know a blonde who knows where I work who always seems to think she's on to me. Who the fuck else could it be, Cora?"

I don't say anything. I force myself to stay angry instead of crying. I will not let him get the better of me.

"So cut the whole act, and give me back my laptop," he says, sitting down at the kitchen island with his drink. He runs a frustrated hand through his hair and makes a grunting noise. I am absolutely disgusted with him. Who the hell is *on to him*? If he even knew how much he was giving himself away right now by accusing me. This one time, he's wrong. It wasn't me.

"Give *what* back?" I say in a forced calm voice. "Now there's a missing laptop? The story just gets better and better. Please tell me what else I did while I was on my mission to ruin your life. Sounds like I had a busy morning!"

He puts his head in his hands, then slowly lifts his head, taking his time to be dramatic, then he sips his drink.

"I work in goddamn cyber security. Do you know how it looks that I got my computer stolen? Do you know the sensitive shit that's on there? I could be fired. I'm…fucked! Because why this time? What now? What are you *on to*? You know what? I don't even… I don't even know anymore," he says, and I feel my heart breaking with each word he utters. Tears spring to my eyes, and I turn to the sink so he can't see them.

"Don't know what?" I ask.

"You need help," he says, and then I hear him get up and he's about to walk away and leave it like this, leave me confused and devastated, just to make sure he has the upper hand in the situation. No.

"When exactly was I at your office?" I ask, blotting my tears with a paper towel before I turn back to him.

"Just don't," he dismisses me.

"*When* do you say I was at your office today?" I practically scream. I do scream. My throat hurts from the effort, and he stops in his tracks and turns around, shocked. Then he almost dismisses me again.

"Because I was out all day," I say, pulling my purse from the kitchen stool and grabbing a handful of receipts from my billfold. "Ten fifteen, coffee with Janine Watkins at Wild Roast. Eleven twenty, a parking-meter printout." I slam each receipt in front of him, and I gain confidence with each piece of evidence. "Eleven forty-five, Deluxe Nail Salon. Twelve thirty, lunch at Perry's Steak House with Amy Patecki about the next Meals on Wheels event. One thirty, gas at Conoco. Two o'clock, last-minute stop for chicken and salad mix for dinner. And now it's—what?—two thirty? When, exactly, did I have time to bring you flowers and steal your laptop?" I say, throwing the receipts in his face and watching them flutter to the ground. I keep every one of them for write-offs for my charity work. I don't use all of them at tax time because I don't nitpick a cup of coffee here or a mile of gas there—it's charity after all. I just know I'm supposed to keep them, so I meticulously do. They finally came in handy.

After what seems like an eternity of deafening silence in the room, he finally says, "You spend too much money," and walks out. Raw anger heats my blood, and I shake with rage. My hands tremble so violently I can barely pick up the strewn receipts, so I don't. I leave them for him to deal with. It's hours before I have to be at the restaurant to play the piano, but I am not going to stay in this house until then. I am not going to follow him and plead my innocence. Instead, I'll go spend some more money. That's what I will do.

I'm not dressed for the piano bar, but I won't go upstairs to get clothes. He is expecting me to stay and to apologize and cook dinner and tiptoe around his mood, but instead I'm gonna go buy a new dress and shoes for tonight, then get to the restaurant by six and treat myself to a long, slow dinner with appetizers, pasta, and dessert. And wine. Then I'll play vintage jazz in front of a nice group of folks who actually appreciate me. That's what I'll do instead. Fuck him.

A couple hours later, after I picked up a cornflower-blue, A-line dress that I wear out of the store and a pair of glittery Louboutin stilettos, I still have a little time to kill, so I go to Glow Up Day Spa and get my hair done. I decide that it's time for a change. I've always kept my hair above the shoulders and wavy, and I'm not sure why: I just got stuck in a comfortable style. So I feel completely out of my element when I ask for extensions and platinum highlights. No, I remember why now. Finn once said he liked shorter hair. That's why I never changed it.

When it's done, I barely recognize myself. I examine my reflection in the mirror. I could almost pass for a curvier Reese Witherspoon, I decide, delighted. I turn sideways, and then back again, several times. I don't look like the Stay Puft Marshmallow Man in a housecoat who flipped a table on one of Finn's bitches and cried and apologized for months after.

I look like Cora. A woman with movie-star hair and a nice rack who gives an extra-generous tip just because she can.

Grant is surprised to see me at Moretti's so early. He makes a pretend big deal of me eating there and tells the staff to take extra-good care of me because I'm their star musician. He compliments my new hair and says it suits me just fine before disappearing back to manage the kitchen.

I eat crusty bruschetta drizzled in olive oil and Parmesan cheese, compliments of Grant, who stops by my table now and then with a white napkin draped over his wrist and a bottle of red wine he refills my glass with. I don't take out my phone to see if Finn tried to reach me or even to entertain myself. I just take in the Tommy Dorsey piping softly through the speakers and the din of quiet conversations at the candlelit tables around me and enjoy the moment. I don't let myself worry about anything else. I order artichoke and tomato panzanella and a pineapple semifreddo for dessert. I don't feel one bit guilty.

I play the piano for a couple hours. A portly man with a pockmarked face gets drunk and sings "My Funny Valentine" four times. A young couple put a twenty in the tip jar on the piano and sing "Every Time We Say Goodbye" horribly off-key, but mostly I just play old classics as background music for the bar. Then, as if the day hadn't been unexpected enough, Grant takes the microphone. He asks if I know "In the Wee Small Hours of the Morning." I say of course I do, and I think he's joking, but he stays standing there in front of the piano with the mic, and when I play, he starts to sing. All of the chatty couples at booths and the patrons bellied up to the bar all stop and listen. He has a lovely, euphonious voice, and I'm completely taken aback. He's a shy singer who doesn't try to make eye contact with anyone or put on a show, and when the song is over, the place erupts with applause. The off-key couple, a little tipsy, even give him a standing ovation and shove more money into the tip jar.

After everyone is gone for the night except a few kitchen staff taking inventory in the back, I linger. I think maybe Grant has taken the back staircase up to his room and I've missed him, but then he appears from the swinging kitchen door with a couple glasses of wine in hand.

"May I join you?" he asks. I slide over on the piano bench, allowing him to sit down.

"Thanks," I say, taking the glass of wine. "Nobody told me you were putting out a record." I hold my glass up to clink. "You were...really good."

He clinks back but gives me a dismissive gesture.

"Do you always sing? Is that why piano-bar nights are so popular?" I ask, and I think I see him blush.

"No. That's the only song I know," he says, and I laugh.

"That seems like a random song to be the only one you know," I say.

"When Caleb was little there was a movie we watched, I don't remember the name, but that song was in it, and when I put him to bed that night, it was the first song that came to mind when he told me to sing to him like Mommy does. She was working, so I sang him that. Then he always asked for it," he says, and I don't know what to say. The fact that he's talking about Caleb at all is a big deal, and I fear saying the wrong thing back after this vulnerability he's shown.

"He was a musician, right?" I ask, hoping it's okay to ask.

"He played in a band. I mean, they weren't good." We both laugh quietly. "He was studying journalism, of all things. Third year of college, and he loved it."

"Oh, really? That's what I did before. I was a reporter. In Tampa. 'Bay News 9,'" I say. I know Paige probably mentioned Caleb's major. I remember him changing it a few times, and it's not the kind of thing you pay that much attention to at the time, so I guess I'd forgotten.

"I didn't know that," Grant says. "I could see it, though. You have a camera-friendly face." He smiles and looks down at the piano keys. "He wanted to be an investigative journalist. At least, for six months that was the plan. It might have changed again in due course." He puts down his glass and pokes absently at a couple piano keys.

"I can teach you how to play it, if you want," I say, and he laughs.

"You make it look pretty easy, I'll give you that, but I can pretty close to guarantee you that I would be terrible."

"Not possible. Look." I put his finger on middle C, and I guide him, singing the simple notes. "C, D, E, E, *hours of the morning*. C, D, E, *wide world is fast asleep*."

He opens his mouth in mock surprise, pleased with himself, and repeats the notes on his own, making a few mistakes, but still looking at the notes like they're magic when they come out as the tune he recognizes.

"You're a musical prodigy, I bet, with a voice like that," I say.

"You're very generous," he says. We both give a short, nervous sort of laugh. I look up at him, and I don't know who kisses who. We move in to each other at the same time. It's not the passionate, against-the-wall, clothes-ripping sort of thing I had let myself fantasize about a few times until my guilt shut it down. It's impossibly soft and tender. Like two people who love each other rather than unfaithful spouses in the throes of a heated affair. He holds the back of my head, and my hands run down his back and then up through his hair, and then, as if we're both struck by some simultaneous realization, it stops as mutually as it started. I think. Except that I didn't want it to stop.

"I'm sorry," he says.

"No, no. I'm sorry," I say, fixing my unfamiliar hair, which feels twisted and wild.

"We can't," he says, with a sad longing I know very well. There is silence for a minute.

"I know," I reluctantly agree. Then I stand, and he plucks my coat from the old-timey, tree-shaped coatrack near the door and helps me on with it. When I open the door the wind whips fallen leaves inside the entrance, and I hold my skirt down and yelp. Then he leans in and kisses my cheek and whispers, "I'll probably regret it for the rest of my life, though." I look him in the eye and squeeze his hand. For the umpteenth time today, I'm about to cry, but again I do not.

I drive in the quiet dark until I get to our street. It's very late, and the houses are all dark, even mine. I feel a little like a woman with nothing to lose, so when I see Alfalfa, stalking through the Kinneys' lawn, I decide that could be my reason for being there if I get caught. It's too cold for the cat to be out, so I stop to collect him.

I retrieve the camera from where I left it. I think it will blend right in with the front-yard tree I clip it to. Maybe it will see inside some of these front windows and show me who the real Lucas is. Maybe not, of course. It could be just filming the side of the house for all I know, but it's worth a shot.

18

GEORGIA

On Friday morning, I set my plan in motion. I've placed the duffel bag at the bottom of the laundry basket, and each time I pick up Lucas's discarded clothes from the night before, which he always leaves for me, I drop in things, little by little, like a toothbrush and socks into the duffle bag. My plan can only work if Cora is home, so I find myself peering out the window every few minutes making sure her car is still there.

I look at Avery's diaper bag and stroller in the corner of the porch as if they are in danger of being stolen. They're there. They're fine. *Breathe.* Avery eats a big breakfast of yogurt and pancakes I cut into little seahorse shapes with a cookie cutter because she adores it. She gums on the tail of her blueberry pancake, and she's so happy and perfect, and I need this to work. Dear God, I need this to work.

After I clear away her food, I give her a toy and hope it

interests her long enough for me to go down and empty the laundry from the dryer into the basket with my duffel bag in it. I make myself walk slowly down the stairs, my heart beating in my throat when the sight of the cement room and the smell of the mop hits me. I try to breathe and keep my mind focused on the plan. I pull out the laundry, dump it on top of my bag and carry it upstairs.

It's all ready. As soon as I see Cora outside, I have to make my move. I have to grab the bag, take the stroller down the five stairs from the porch to the street, and I have to quickly stuff her baby bag in the back, then put her into it and go.

Another painful hour and a half has gone by, and I am afraid she might stay in today. She never stays in. She's in and out all day. Like nothing I've ever seen before. I tell myself it's okay. It's not a magic day, I have everything in place, I can wait until Monday if I have to. It's still all safe in my head. He can't read my mind. *Breathe.*

It's 11:42, and I wait outside. I'm sitting on the porch chairs even though it's freezing. I have on a down coat, and Avery is wrapped up in a blanket. I feel for the rip in the chair and find the ID and watch with my fingers and very carefully work the items out until I feel them in the palm of my hand. I hold them tightly and watch her house, and then finally, I see someone come out the door and her taillights blink with the click of her key fob. For a minute I don't recognize Cora. Her hair is different and she looks…different, but it's definitely her.

"Cora," I call, and she looks to me, quite surprised, but smiles and waves from her driveway. I can't imagine she thought I'd invite conversation as I never have before, so she leaves it at a wave, unlike her, and starts to get into the car. My heart is beating so hard, I can see it through my coat. My hands shake so it's hard to grip the stroller handle. My breath is shallow and painful, and I think I might collapse with panic. I don't have time to hesitate. I have to use every second. I have to go.

"Cora," I say again. She stops and turns.

"Hi." She smiles, but her eyes don't match her face. She looks sad, distracted.

"I'm so sorry, I still don't have a car and something sort of urgent has come up. Is there any way you could take us to town if you're going that way?" I ask, so desperate I hear the quiver in my voice. I know she may say she's in a hurry, she's late, and to get an Uber. But her face changes. She smiles, and her eyes wake up.

"Of course, sweetheart. I'm happy to," she says. "Oh, wait." She stops.

"What?" I ask. Oh, my God, there is no turning back now. What?

"I don't have a car seat," she says.

"Oh, ours is in my car at the shop, but it's okay this one time. If it weren't urgent, I wouldn't—"

She interrupts me, opening the garage.

"I know we have one in here. Maybe two!" She giggles and starts rummaging through shelves of toolboxes, a wheelie cooler, bikes, old sporting equipment. I think my heart might cave in. I don't have time.

"I am waiting on grandkids… Well, not waiting, but she's off to college in a year and a half, so it's not too far off. I kept all of her old toys, too. Hmmm. Hold on, I know it's in here somewhere," she says, and I look back at our house, and I know the cameras can't see me now. They only display all the rooms of an empty house with an escaped prisoner. It's been at least five minutes. If he saw me leave right away. I have fifteen minutes max. If not, there is still precious little time. I don't let on. I can't, of course. I look at the ground and shake my leg, nervously.

"Ah. I knew I'd find it," she says and leans into the back seat. "Now, let's see if I remember how to do this part," she says, and all I can do is nod gratefully. She finally buckles the car seat into place, and I put Avery inside. She seems thrilled by the adventure. I get into the passenger seat, and Cora backs out. I feel like I can't swallow, I can't catch my breath, but she doesn't notice. She's telling me a story about car seats and manufacturer recalls and how they made things better back in the old days.

And then just like that, she clicks her blinker on, and we make a left, and I see our house in the rearview mirror, and I wonder if it could really be the last time I ever see that absolute hell again.

"So where do you need to go?" she asks, headed in the general direction of the main shops and restaurants. I don't have an address, and I can't tell her I'm going to a pawn shop.

"Uh, you know, I'm meeting a friend. And it's right by Spirit Pawn…uh, that Mediterranean café," I say.

"Ephesus!" she says.

"Yeah, that's it," I say, looking back at Avery's amazed face at a rare car ride. The delicious coastal air spills into the car from the cracked windows, and the western juniper are rich and green, and I could cry at the sight of something as simple as the shops and restaurants along the roadside.

"I hope your friend is okay," Cora says.

"I'm sorry?"

"You said it was urgent. I hope everything is okay. I'm here if you need anything," she says, taking her eyes off the road for a moment to give me a reassuring smile.

"That's— Cora, this is so nice of you, and that's— Just thank you so much for being so kind to me," I say, feeling the slightest sense of relief with each passing mile, but knowing the hardest part is in front of me. I wish I could pay her back.

When she drops me off, I unbuckle Avery, take the stroller out of the boot of Cora's car, and sit her inside. It all seems to be taking an eternity, and now I actually have to go inside the Mediterranean restaurant because she thinks that's where I'm meeting some friend in peril.

"Thank you, thank you so much again," I say, standing at her window.

"Do you wanna put my number in your phone in case you need a ride back?" she asks. I want to tell her I'm never coming back, but of course I don't, and I can't tell her that I am the only person on the planet without a phone, so I don't take her number either.

"Oh, my friend will take me, but thanks."

"Okay, good luck, then. Bye-bye, Avery." She waves and then pulls away. I lean down to fuss with Avery's safety belt and shoes, so I can wait until her car is out of sight and not, in fact, go inside the restaurant. When I'm certain she's gone, I hike the bags up over my shoulder and walk as quickly as I can to the pawn shop across the parking lot.

Inside, a man I can smell from across the store sits on a stool behind a glass display case. His girth spills out from beneath his anime T-shirt, and he doesn't look up when the bell above the front door chimes as we enter. I don't waste time. I walk up to the glass counter and stand in front of him. I clear my throat, and he looks up.

"Yes?" he says very formally. "How may I help you?" I pull the watch out of my pocket and slide it across the glass.

"I'd like to sell this," I say, and he picks up the watch and examines it in the light.

"It's Gucci," I point out.

"I can read," he says, but not in a snarky tone. He just sounds like he talks to everyone that way. He peers down at me and lifts an eyebrow.

"Where did you get this?" he asks.

"Uh, I don't remember. Why?"

"Well, I hope it wasn't a gift from your husband or anything because it's a fake." He hands it back to me. "Sorry."

"No. No! It's not. It can't be!" I yell, then quickly lower my tone. "Please. Look again. Please."

"I've been doing this for twenty-seven years. I assure you it's an obvious knockoff. It's not worth anything."

"It has to be. It *has* to be worth something. Anything. Ten dollars. Anything," I plead, and now the other employee and the two other shoppers have stopped to look at me but have quickly looked away.

"I'm sorry, but it's not even worth that. I wish I could help," he says, and everything becomes blurry, and the man looks like he's moving in slow motion. My knees feel like they'll buckle. I can't go back. This can't be happening.

"No. Check again. You're wrong. You have to be wrong!" I scream.

"Ma'am. Please. You're making a scene. I'm very sorry I can't—" and then I stop listening. Everything sounds muffled. An older man is standing with another employee a few feet away. He's looking at me with pity. The other employee has pulled a velvet tray full of jewelry for sale and is showing the items to the patron. There are mostly rings in the tray. I see a tiny white tag on a diamond solitaire ring that reads *$1,300*. I feel pinpricks of heat climb my spine. I look at Avery, who's just happy to be looking around at all the shiny items. And what else can I do? I lunge at the velvet tray, grab the ring, and run.

I run out the door, pushing her stroller ahead of me. Avery begins to cry at the jolt and my panic and the men yelling to stop me. It's pathetic. Alone, I could have outrun them, but I wasn't thinking. I wasn't considering the bumpy, rock-studded concrete in the parking lot that would slow down the wheels of her stroller. I didn't think through opening the door and maneuvering out two bags and a stroller. I didn't think about anything, I just run, and I am caught before I get out of the parking lot.

The police are called.

They try to make me stay where I am until the police come, but I say it's too cold for the baby and walk back inside, forcing them to follow me. Two male officers arrive twenty minutes later. Of course they're male. And they know exactly who my husband is, but today, according to my ID, I'm not Georgia Kinney, I'm June Barrett, thirty-one years old. People don't report IDs stolen, do they? They just replace them, especially since the purse was returned. I guess I'll be finding out the hard way.

I hear the anime T-shirt man explain in dramatic detail exactly what happened, but I don't say anything. I sit on the orange plastic chair near the front window and feed Avery goldfish crackers as I push her back and forth in her stroller trying to calm her.

After a few minutes, one of the officers comes over to me, and gently explains that the shop wants to press charges and so he will be forced to arrest me. I look over at the shop employee, who shrugs.

"It's all on camera. What do you want me to do? I could lose my job," he says.

"I have a baby!" I yell back at him. "You psychopath!" I expected to get a citation maybe, but I never thought they would arrest me. I stand and have the urge to run. I almost do it, but it would be so absurd and comical at this point. I'm a trapped animal. Again.

"Ma'am," Officer McAllen says, "we'll do our best to let you make some calls and find someone to pick up your little girl. We're not taking her to jail." He laughs at his own joke, and I think I stammer, or at least open my mouth to say something that doesn't come out.

"Jail," I repeat. And then I'm in the back of a cop car being transported to the police station with Avery. On the way, the officer explains that bail should only be a few hundred if it's my first arrest and there are no red flags that I won't show up for my court date. The urge to throw up increases with every word he says. Money, court, jail.

"Can you pull over?" I blurt.

"I'm afraid I can't do—"

"I'm gonna throw up!" I yell through the plexiglass dividing us, and he quickly pulls over and clicks my door unlocked. I lean out and vomit until my insides ache. He doesn't say anything to me. When my eyes are bloodshot from the effort of heaving, I close the door, and he pulls back into the lane and keeps going.

At the station, they are nice enough to let me sit in a holding room with Avery while they run my driver's license. Thank God June Barrett has a clean record. When I explain that I don't have any money on me and I'm not married (of course they don't see a ring because I'm not allowed to wear one; Lucas knows I'd try to sell it) they don't exactly take pity on me but I can tell they are just trying to get me out of here with a slap on the wrist and a court date.

"What happens if I don't have anyone to come for me?" I ask, starting to panic again.

"We'd have to keep you until your arraignment, which will probably be Monday since it's after noon on a Friday."

"And Avery? What will you do with her?" I say, tears filling my eyes. He stops tapping on his computer and leans back.

"I'm afraid we'd have to call child welfare if there is nobody who can pick her up," he says, and I wonder what the charge would be for lunging across the desk and stabbing out the eyes of a police officer for even suggesting separating us.

"There is one person I could try," I say instead. "I don't have her number, though. Cora. Cora Holmon, and I have her address!" The officer pushes a pad of paper and short pencil across the table toward me.

"Write it all down, and I'll have someone try to track her down for you," he says. I write it down, and he walks out of the room, leaving Avery and me alone together. I want to pick her up and hold her to me, but my ribs can only take so much pain, so I sit on the floor next to her and kiss her hands and tell her everything will be okay.

19

PAIGE

Finn's laptop proves very useful. There are emails going back a year that Paige screenshots, emails to herself, and prints. She drops them into her box labeled *Finn* inside the bedroom wardrobe. She doesn't want to keep the laptop, she just wants to get what she needs off it. So she will drop it off at his front door. If he were to start pointing fingers at her, the last thing she needs is to be in possession of stolen property. She doesn't think he really could without exposing himself, but maybe the secrets on his computer are worth the risk, she's not sure, so she cleans it with a disinfectant wipe.

Both his and Cora's cars are gone, so on her way out to go and visit Charlotte, she leaves it on their doorstep. It wasn't hard to find pathetic, sickly sweet emails and Facebook messages between Finn and Charlotte. It's like he wants to get caught. She doesn't know why Cora finds it so hard to gather what she herself did, easily, in just days. Finn makes Cora feel like she's the paranoid one and leads her down dead ends, that's probably why.

It's a Friday afternoon, and Charlotte is out of the office all day, according to their exchanges. Paige has emailed Charlotte from Finn's account asking her to meet him at Milio's for lunch and adding that it's urgent. Charlotte agrees, asking if everything is okay. Paige assures her that it is but to please just be there at twelve thirty.

Paige has taken a lot of steps to get what she wants, but this will set in motion something nobody is expecting. She doesn't bother changing out of leggings and a sweater. She wraps an infinity scarf around her neck, pushes her feet into knee-high flat boots, and rehearses one more time what she'll say before she leaves the house to meet Charlotte.

Before she goes, she applies some ChapStick. It's gotten so cold and dry outside. She feeds Christopher a pocket biscuit and tells him he's a good boy, pulls on a coat, and looks herself in the hall mirror before she walks out and says, "This is it. Don't fuck it up."

When she pulls into Milio's, she looks around the front window and tries to spot Charlotte, and there she sits, nervous as anything, waiting for her lover to find out what his cryptic message was. She holds a cup of coffee and taps her fingers on the table. Paige would almost feel sorry for her, but she doesn't. The tramp knows Finn is married, so she deserves no sympathy.

Of course, the woman has no idea who she is when Paige enters the restaurant, so she's jarred when Paige sits right down across from her in a two-top table and stares her down, saying nothing.

"Uh, hello. I think you might have the wrong table?"

"Don't remember me, Char?" Paige asks, pronouncing it again as in *charbroil*.

"I'm sorry, who are you?" she asks, leaning back and twisting her pretty hair with the fingers of both hands. On guard, but not full-on defensive yet.

"Oh, right. You were pretty drunk. We met at the trashy charity ball. You remember. A couple weeks ago," she says, and she can see the woman put together the mispronunciation of her name with this rude stranger at her table.

"Oh, yeah, I do remember you. But, uh, I'm meeting someone, so it was nice to see you, but..."

"You're meeting me," Paige says. Char laughs a humorless laugh and reasserts herself.

"I can assure you I'm not, so if you'll excuse me."

"Finn's not coming," she says.

"Uh, I'm sorry, wh..."

"You should be sorry," Paige says, "but that's not why I'm here. Your affair with Finn..." she starts, but Charlotte begins her protest earlier than Paige anticipated.

"My what?" You're..." She starts to fuss with her things like she's getting up to leave.

"Oh, for fuck's sake. I do not have time for the theatrics," Paige says, pulling printed-out transcripts of their texts and emails and a photo of them embracing at the ball, and places them on the table in front of her.

"I..." is all that comes out of Charlotte's mouth.

"Please. Go on. You what?" she asks.

"What is this? What do you want?"

"You know he's married, right?" Paige says, and Charlotte doesn't answer but looks away and gives an exaggerated sigh.

"Right. Of course you do, because I was there when you were introduced to his wife," Paige says.

"I think you should leave," Char says.

"So all I want from you is to know how long it's been going on."

"Why would I tell you that? I'm leaving. I'm calling Finn, and you can deal with him," she says, pulling on her coat and scooting out of the booth.

"No, I don't think that's how this is gonna go. Your husband is Anthony Cohen," Paige says, and the woman sits back down, and her eyes gloss over like she's about to cry, but she doesn't say anything.

"When I say I've seen all your messages and emails with him, I mean *all*. So if you don't want me to talk, you'll tell me. How. Long?" Paige says, and waits for a response, unsure if the woman will burst into tears and storm out to call Finn or what, exactly. Her pulse races. She needs to know.

"Almost two years," Charlotte finally says with a defeated look. She takes a tissue from her purse and dots her eyes. "Why are you doing this? Why do you care?"

"Were you with him January 17 last year?" Paige asks.

"How would I remember that? Why?"

"Because I think he killed my son. In fact, I'm pretty sure of it. The only reason I'd go near the son of a bitch with a ten-foot pole is to get the information I need. And I need this. I think he was in a car, pulling onto our street at ten thirty on the night of January 17, and his calendar says he was meeting with *C*. Was that you? Or was that my son, Caleb? Because I have other reasons to believe it might have been my son. You have to know something," she says, her voice breaking.

"You think he's gay," Charlotte says. Paige responds by slamming her hand down on the table, folks around them turning to look.

"Do you have any way to remember if you were with him?" Paige hisses, and Charlotte fumbles with her phone and opens her calendar. She scrolls months of pages to find last January.

"I was in Denver for a work thing that weekend," she says. Paige grabs her hand and closes her eyes. She doesn't thank her or explain further, she just quickly lets go and says, "When you see Finn, I highly recommend you leave him. You owe his wife an apology, but since she'll never get that, you should know that he's probably dangerous. I don't need to hurt you or ruin your marriage. I don't care enough because I don't even know you, so I have no plans to tell anyone about this, but you'll do a few things for me in return." Paige stops and waits for a response.

Charlotte nods. "Of course," she says, but her words barely come out as her voice cracks. She clears her throat. "Of course, anything."

"First, do not tell him you saw me. Do not mention my son. If I find out that you did, I'll go to your husband with these photos. So deal with your own shit, and keep my name out of it. Yeah?" Paige says. "Also, cut it off with him. Now. He's not yours. He has a family, and he's a fuckface. If you're gonna cheat, trade up."

Charlotte nods vigorously and gathers her things. She stands up and leaves as quickly as she can without causing a scene.

Paige is surprised at how long it's been going on. Certainly the other women Cora was worried about were valid concerns. It's impressive how he's done this for so long without Cora actually getting proof. She decides to follow Charlotte. If it's been a two-year relationship, if she thinks he's possibly a killer and she has just been threatened—warned to cut things off with him—she'd have questions. Where else would she go but straight to him for answers?

As she drives she thinks about how she assumed it would be easier to get close to Finn the way Charlotte has—easier to get information out of him without breaking windows and stealing laptops—but she couldn't get close. It's only because she was too much of a risk for Finn, being so close to Cora. That, she's sure of. She thought about using Charlotte to somehow get him talking about that night or why he has Caleb's number in his phone and a history of text exchanges with him. Then, she'd threaten to reveal the affair if she didn't get the information Paige needed. But there are a few things wrong with that. It would take too long, and she doesn't know if she can trust Charlotte, despite what the woman has to lose. Plus, Finn might get suspicious, and she needs to build her body of evidence before that could happen. Anyway, she really has everything she needs at this point. She's almost ready to make her move.

Before she does, though, it would tickle her to see him get a small taste of his own medicine on Cora's behalf. She signals right and pulls into the parking lot of Finn's office building. She parks close to where she did last time she was here and watches the door. After five minutes she sees Char pull in. Of course she does. A few minutes after that, Finn comes out the front doors with a scrunched-up forehead, looking around until he spots Char's car. She gets out, and they are talking. There are no dramatic hand gestures or yelling. She has kept her side of deal, it looks like, and has not confronted him about Paige or her threats or accusations he's dangerous. She might have, but Paige had to take that chance. She had to know who *C* was. Those texts tell her he knew Caleb more than a grown-ass man should know the teenage kid next door. Yes, he was twenty-two when he died, but those texts show that they had communicated for a few years. Cryptic texts. She can't figure that part of this puzzle out yet, but she needed to eliminate a part of the equation, and she has.

Finn reaches his arm out to touch Char's shoulder, and she pulls away. It's the body language that tells Paige what she needs to know. She's ending it, and he's not letting that happen. She's calm and sad-looking. He's desperate but trying to stay subtle about it in the middle of his work parking lot. She can't hear the words, but he's practically begging. That's clear. Charlotte's hands go up in front of her, an I'm-done-with-this gesture. She backs away; he moves to her. She gets in her car and shuts the door. He calls after her, tries to block her driving away for a minute and even knocks on her window. She looks away. He gives up. She drives off. He punches a brick column in front of the building and walks inside with bloody knuckles.

"Well, then," Paige says out loud and then drives away herself. That was slightly satisfying, but now she's ready to nail him to the wall. Before she goes to the cops, she needs to show Cora all the evidence. She needs to tell her everything. She's so sorry to betray her dear friend, but it was the only way.

20

CORA

Finn is acting like a moody teenager. I think he's actually pouting, and I have no idea why. It's Friday afternoon, and he's supposed to be leaving from his office for a weekend trip for work. Now he's suddenly home early and has let me know the trip has been canceled but he's going out for drinks with his coworker Buddy LaFond tonight.

We've barely said a word to each other for a couple days, and now I see his missing laptop is sitting on the counter. That's curious, isn't it? I unload a bag of groceries and realize I forgot coconut milk for the curry I was going to make for Mia and me tonight.

"Holy shit. Your hair," Mia says, coming into the kitchen in her perpetual pajamalike outfit. She was at a friend's overnight, so she hasn't seen it.

"Yeah, I thought it was time for a change," I say.

"Daaang. You never let me get extensions," she whines.

"When you can pay for them yourself, you can get ten-foot-long hair if you want."

"I like it. It's, like, so blond. You look like the chick from *Game of Thrones* if she were old," she says, then grabs an apple from the fridge.

"Thanks," I say, patting my hair, and she bounces off to her room. She seemed almost…like her old self instead of a gloomy recluse for a minute there. I put bran flakes and peanut butter into cupboards with a lighter heart.

My phone rings for the second time today with a number I don't recognize. There was no message after the first call, so I don't answer because it's spam as far as I'm concerned.

Finn comes into the kitchen. He opens the fridge, and again, like a teenager, he stands hunched in front of it, looking for a snack.

"Your missing laptop reappeared," I say, against my better judgment, but I am starting to really not care anymore.

"Yeah. Wonder how that happened," he says, curtly. I stop in midreach from the counter to slide a box of pasta on a shelf, and my back tenses, and I freeze a moment. I should just leave the room and avoid a repeat of yesterday. I should sit and explain in all sincerity that I promise I had nothing to do with it, but instead I say, "Maybe you lent it to one of your girlfriends and forgot."

I can feel an electricity in the air—a palpable tension all around me. Then I hear the cover of his laptop slam shut.

"Are we doing this again? Cora, fucking really? *Really?* I am not in the mood for this bullshit today," he hollers, and I shush him and look down the hall, making sure Mia doesn't overhear.

"Why are you in such a foul mood?" I ask, because even in one of these old infidelity arguments, he never raises his voice when Mia is home. That's an unspoken rule, so something is going on with him.

"How would you feel," he says, "if I were constantly accusing you of something you weren't doing? Oh, and who's the new Barbie hair for? Some drunk guy at the piano bar who comes in to see you?"

"What?" I say.

"Ya like that? You're just out in the world, working, minding your business, and you're constantly hounded, doubted, accused. We've been over this too many times. I'm done," he says, stuffing his computer into its cover.

"Done with what?" I ask, calmly.

"This conversation. Don't—don't do that—twist my words, make it seem like I meant…"

"I just asked a question for clarification," I say.

"This is what you do. You're manipulative, but you think you're this innocent, put-upon wife. I don't buy the act. In fact, I'm pretty sick of it. You need help, Cora. You should go see whoever it was you saw last time you spun out like this."

"Dr. Higgins," I offer.

"Yes," he says, not even really paying attention anymore, but looking at his phone.

"Ah. Maybe I do need to talk to someone," I say, but he doesn't hear. His fingers are furiously texting, and then he announces he's meeting Buddy.

"It's four o'clock. I thought you were getting drinks later tonight," I say, and he sighs and goes to pick up his coat where he's tossed it over the side of the couch.

"This is exactly what I'm talking about" is all he says before I hear his footsteps down the hall and the garage door opening. I sit down on a kitchen stool and bury my face in my hands.

"Mom," I hear a small voice say. I look up, and Mia stands

in the arched entry into the kitchen with her hands lost inside her sweatshirt sleeves, looking like a little girl.

"Honey, hi. Are you okay?" I ask, and she runs over and wraps her arms around me.

"Oh, sweetheart, what? What's wrong?" I ask, pulling out of the hug to look at her. There are tears in her eyes.

"He was so mean to you."

"Oh, baby. I'm so sorry you had to overhear that. No, no. He's just, yes, he's being a bit of a…"

"Dick," she supplies.

"He's under a lot of stress, and things just boiled over today. I am so sorry that we let our stupid argument affect you. That's not okay. Everything is fine," I reassure her.

"Okay," she says. "And for the record, I still like your hair. It's not Barbie. It's cool," she says. My heart swells with love for her. My little empath girl who tries to be so hard for the world around her.

"I like it, too," I say, and I can tell it's a rare moment where she wants more from me. She doesn't want to run to her room or go out with a friend. She wants her mom.

"I have triple ripple fudge I hid in the back of the freezer if you want," I suggest.

"Does it have a fur coat of freezer burn on it?" she asks.

"Possibly."

She shrugs, and we sit on stools at the kitchen island as the sky gets dusky with streaky pinks and reds. She sits cross-legged, and we eat right from the half-gallon container with two spoons.

"Are you gonna, like, get divorced?" she asks, and I feel a nausea like motion sickness move through me.

"Nooo," I say, a knee-jerk response. Then, after a minute or so I add, "How would you feel if we did?"

Mia doesn't rush to tears or look shocked. All of a sudden

she looks like a kid who knows so much more than I ever gave her credit for.

"I wanna tell you something," she says. Every part of me tenses. It's the sentence and tone together a mother doesn't want to hear because it could be any horrible thing that comes next. She looks down and taps her spoon on the counter, nervously.

"You're always asking, like all the time, what's wrong with me lately. But, like, for a year. Not that it's, like, your business, but things…I don't know, changed for me…then. Whenever. I just mean, that pot you found, back in January and I said it was a friend's. It kind of was. Someone did give it to me, but the point is, the joint a few weeks ago, it really wasn't mine. Like, I get why you'd say what you said to Dad is all I mean. I've thought the same thing a couple times…just had a feeling," she says. I don't ask her for more information. I don't ask her what she means. My heart suddenly breaks at the thought that she has to worry about who Finn is fucking. It infuriates me. But my only worry is about her now.

"Who gave you the joint?" I ask.

"That's the thing. It's, like, I'm afraid to make you guys mad, but, Mom, for God's sake. I'll be a legal adult in, like, a few months, so it's not a big thing."

"Okay, true, so what's 'not a big thing,' then?"

"So Caleb Moretti, he gave me that joint back in January. Well, he gave a lot of people more than joints. He was kind of the guy to go to for that sort of thing…" she says, and I don't want to stop her, but I'm so absolutely shocked, my hand flutters to my heart. Paige thinks her son was a dean's-list college student with a Boy Scout background, impressive volunteering record, and zero flaws. He cannot have been the neighborhood drug dealer.

"What? What do you mean the guy to go to?" I say, louder than I meant to.

"Mom," she sighs.

"No, I just— I'm just a little— Caleb? I don't— So, what— so what are you saying, exactly?"

"Well, Caleb said Dad bought stuff from him sometimes, so when you found that joint in the laundry, I'm just saying that I would tell you if it were mine. It wasn't. That's all, so…" and I want to find Finn and press my fingers into his throat until he stops breathing for allowing her to know this about him—to worry, to carry this around—but I can't. More than that, I want to take the burden of knowing this away from her.

"So wait, then. What did you mean when you said I've been asking what's wrong— I still don't know what's been wrong," I say, thinking there is more. She shifts in her stool and puts her spoon down.

"I really liked him. I know. I *know* he was older," she says, and I swallow down the words *Five years older!* instead of screaming them. Fine, five years means nothing at my age, but teenager versus full-grown man does make a difference, and the thought of it makes my cheeks burn red, but I keep calm.

"So you were…dating him?" I ask.

"No! I mean…no. We were close. Friends," she says, shyly.

"Why didn't I know this?" I ask, because I feel like I have known Paige my whole life and that our kids grew up together, but really, if I think about it, she only moved in ten years ago. This would make Mia seven and Caleb twelve. Caleb went to private school. We are more backyard-wine and book-club friends than family-barbecue types. I guess, when I think about it, they knew each other very little before they were pseudoadults. Just bikes-in-the-neighborhood sort of acquaintances with a giant age gap separating them.

"For God's sake, Mom! Nothing ever happened. He didn't like me back."

"Oh, thank God," I can't help but blurt out.

"Okay, really?" she says.

"No. Sorry. It's just… So you're telling me he was a drug dealer. Is that what you're saying?"

"Oh, big-time," she says and sees my mouth gaping. "But he was like this really amazing soul, y'know? Like you could tell all the drug stuff wasn't really him," she says.

"So you were not seeing him, though," I try to confirm.

"No, I sorta wanted to, but he was seeing someone else, but, I mean, since he died, I just—I don't know, haven't been myself. I feel…guilty. I don't know," she says, and I can feel her pushing back, her defenses coming up.

"Why? Why would you feel that way?" I ask, confused.

"I don't *know*. I just, I miss him is all. I wish I could have helped him," she says, and then the tears come. I'm suspended in this surreal moment of being horrified that Paige doesn't know her son was a drug dealer and that my daughter maybe almost dated him…and also want to save this moment with her head on my shoulder. I wipe the tears from under her eyes with a swipe of my thumbs and look her in the eye.

"I'm so sorry I didn't know and you were dealing with this all by yourself. He was your friend, and I didn't know that, and you've been feeling a lot of grief ever since," I say. Sometimes I hear Dr. Higgins when I recite these active learning tools I have come to know. "You couldn't have fixed him, though, and it wasn't your job."

"I know," she says, looking down at her hands. "We used to go sit in the swings in the park behind the Kinneys' house at night sometimes and, I don't know, just talk. A lot. I still just can't believe what happened to him," she says, trying to compose herself now. So this is why she changed overnight. She was in love with a guy who didn't love her back, and then was killed, and I don't know what else… Did she do more drugs than she's letting on? I just thought she was getting to the I-hate-my-parents stage, even though she was never that person, and all the while, she's been grieving. I feel like the worst mother in the world.

"Anyway, it's fine. I just thought you should know…about the joint," she says, standing and going to the fridge to pull out a soda. Then she's shuffling to her room, already with phone in hand, looking through TikTok.

My phone rings again. It's that same number. I pick it up this time, my frustration fueling me.

"Yes?" I snap. "What? I don't know a June Barrett. I think you have the wrong person," I say.

"She's absolutely insistent that you know her and that you're the only person who can help her. Very insistent. She has a baby, Avery, and says you'll pick her up. Is there any way you could just come down and help sort this out?" the man's voice says. Avery? Oh, my God. What in the hell is going on?

"Okay, yeah. I'll be right there," I say and hang up the phone. Is this a joke, maybe? Does this have something to do with Finn? I'm so utterly confused. In a fog over everything that has happened in the last two days, I grab my bag and get in my car to go bail some stranger who knows my name out of jail.

21

GEORGIA

When Cora walks into the holding room and sees me, her face goes completely blank. Confusion is an enormous understatement.

"Geor—June!" she says, catching on quickly, seeing what I need without understanding anything else that's happening. They tell her the bond amount and ask if she's willing to take me home. She quickly and emphatically agrees, practically opening her purse to get her wallet out before they're finished. She doesn't ask why I'm there. She just helps me.

Thirty minutes and some paperwork later, and I'm in her car with Avery asleep in the car seat that is still strapped into the back, driving back to that house. She lets the silence sit in the air until I'm ready to speak.

"Thank you. Thank you so much," I say, my voice breaking. "I'm so sorry to involve you and have you do so much for me…"

"It's absolutely no problem. Are you all right?"

"No. I'm not. I can't… Please, I can't go back," I say, and I begin to sob. I cry so hard I can barely catch my breath and Cora pulls to the side of County Road 8 and tries her best to calm me. I can't even speak to tell her anything else. I'm just choking on my own sobs as I try to keep them quiet and not wake up Avery, but I can barely breathe.

"Shhh, it's gonna be okay," she says, taking my hands, rubbing my back. "Oh, sweetheart." Her eyes well with tears, too. "What in the world is going on?"

After I get myself under control, I still have trouble breathing as the crying remains like hiccuped spasms in my chest. My face is hot, my eyes burn. I try to tell her.

"I have to get out of here. I can't go back. It's not safe," I manage, looking at Avery and back to Cora.

"He's hurting you. I knew it," she says.

"It's more than that."

"What? What's he done, what do you mean?" she asks, and I have no choice now but to trust her, to tell her everything. I cannot go back this time.

"He's holding me there. He won't let me leave," I say, and I see the realization of it all hit her—why I never go anywhere and don't socialize or drive or anything—that I'm not a recluse, I'm a prisoner.

"But…last week, you went to town," she says, clearly second-guessing what she had just put together. I explain the frozen camera and my attempt to get to the bank and escape. I explain the other escapes, and how I got the ID off someone on a park bench and the times before that, but I always get caught. And when I finish, I see her face, and I've never seen that look on anyone's face before. It's shock and horror, but still confusion as to how it's possible he could be holding me prisoner in plain sight. Her face is white and frightened.

"Why didn't you tell the police? When you were there? We have to go to the police," she says, ready to pull out and turn the car around.

"No, stop. Please. I know. I know it sounds like it should be that easy," I say. "He's a judge. It's his word against mine. I called them once, and he had a good laugh with them about how unstable I was. He has set me up as an unhinged, depressed person. There are medical records, prescriptions, the police report when I lost it and they found me to be the volatile one. They would have no evidence that what I'm saying is true. Just a respected man's word against mine. Zero evidence. They'll send me home with him, and he will kill me. I have to get out—get far away—but I don't have any money or documents. I have nowhere to go. He's made sure of that." I tremble and bury my face in my hands. Cora turns up the heat in the car and grabs a folded-up blanket from the back and puts it around my shoulders.

"Okay, listen. We're gonna get you out. Let me help you," she says, and I look up at her, blinking, unbelieving.

"You'll help me? You won't call the police?"

"No, you can stay with me."

"I can't. Your family will know and I can't— Someone will tell...they'll slip or they'll act nervous. The police might come by asking about me— Avery will— I can't risk that."

"We have a mother-in-law unit by the pool in back of the house," she says. "Nobody has stepped foot in there in I don't know how long. You can stay there. It's far enough away from the house, you won't be heard. Finn and Mia don't have to know."

"He'll be across the street." My hands are shaking so violently that she has to take them in hers again and hold them on my lap.

"This is why it will work. If he's looking for you, he would never look there. Right? He'll think you're running as far away as you can. It's just until we make a plan. I can pull out some money. We can find you a safe way to do this."

I throw my arms around her neck and just let myself completely break down. I thank her so many times I'm sick of my own voice. I can't believe it. I knew it would take making a friend to get help, someone who I could trust and not a stranger who would call someone or tell someone and get me killed. He made sure I never got close enough to anyone for that to happen. The camera glitch might be the only reason I'm here, that we were able to talk. Her persistence in making sure I felt cared for, even though I never returned the kindness, is the reason I'm here. Can this really be happening?

When she begins to drive again, I feel sick the closer we get to that house.

"Do you think he's reported you missing yet?" she asks.

"I've thought a lot about that," I say, "and I don't know. Do they really make you wait twenty-four hours to report? I don't know. If he did, did I make it out of there with seconds left before the cops figured out the missing person was June/Georgia? Maybe he won't report it at all. He said if I ever got away he'd spend the rest of his life hunting me down, if that's what it took, and he'd kill me."

"I can't believe all this time you were just right there and I didn't know..." she says, and as we pull onto our road, she gasps and makes a sharp left. I look behind and see a cop car outside of our house.

"Okay, don't panic," she says.

"Oh, my God, oh, my God," I say, starting to rock back and forth, my eyes blurring with fear. She stops the car.

"Get out," she says.

"What?" For a split second, I think I've been tricked, that she is part of this thing with Lucas. Then, she opens the hatch.

"Here's what we do. There are blankets in the back. Do not wake Avery up. Lay her in the back, and lie next to her. I'll cover you up. When we pull in, I'll park in the back drive. I will go out front to ask what's going on so you can sneak into the guesthouse. Got it?" she asks, and I nod, jumping out and unstrapping Avery gently from her car seat. Cora pulls a key off her ring of keys and hands it to me.

"This is to the room," she says. I take it and shove it into my pocket. As I lay Avery down in the back, I watch Cora pull out the car seat and toss it next to somebody's garbage can in the alley. I would never have thought of that. Her grace in a crisis is really something to behold. She covers us up.

"Don't worry. There is no reason for them to look for you in my car. You're not a criminal. This will be fine," she says. But I don't feel like anything will be fine ever again. As she drives the few short blocks, I can hear my heart beating. I try to hold very still and take deep breaths.

"Shit," I hear her say. "Okay, the cop just waved me over before I could turn into the back. Do not panic."

I suppress a whimper as I hear her roll down the window.

"Oh, my goodness, what's all this?" she asks so calmly it's hard to believe. I feel bile rise in my throat. Avery pushes against me, making a small sound—the tiny whine that happens just before she lets out a wail. Hot tears spring to my eyes, and I can hear my own heartbeat in my ears.

"Sorry to bother you, ma'am, but we're looking for a missing person. Do you live here?"

"Yes, right there. Who's missing?" she asks.

"Your neighbor, it looks like. Georgia Kinney. Do you know her well?"

"Oh, that's terrible. No, not very well. How long has she been gone?"

"Just a few hours, but…"

"A few hours? How is that missing? You had me worried."

I put my hand over Avery's mouth before she gives us away. My tears are hot on my cheeks as I push away the overwhelming feeling of guilt—that I'm hurting her, that I'm a terrible mother—as I keep her quiet.

"Look, her husband is certain something is very wrong, and he's someone who wouldn't overreact to this sort of thing, and we're taking it seriously and don't want to lose time."

"Well, I will definitely keep a lookout and ask around," I say.

"Thanks. We might have more questions later on," he adds.

"Of course. You know where I am," she says, and I hear the window close. I feel the car pull into the alley and I exhale, taking my hand away from Avery's hot, angry little face. She howls and cries in overwhelmed hiccups. I kiss her over and over and tell her it's okay as Cora pulls into the back driveway and parks. I dig in my bag for some candy to distract her and she takes it with wide eyes and calms down a little bit.

"It's to the left on the other side of the pool. Go. When they leave, I'll come out to check on you," she says, and then she gets out, clicks open the hatch ever so slightly, and when I hear her footsteps disappear and the back door open and close, I slide out the back and hike my bags over my shoulder. I pick Avery up as gently as I can, and I try to steady my shaking knees as I walk the short path to the guesthouse. I let myself in and lay Avery down on the bed.

It's a tidy little space with a kitchenette and full bathroom. The bed is covered with fuzzy pillows and a fluffy down comforter, and no matter how in danger I still am, I have never understood the feeling of safety as acutely as I do now. I've never felt overwhelming relief the way I do right now. I lie down next to Avery, and my mind reels with all of the scenarios where he finds me. Could he suspect Cora of helping me, after finding Avery there that one time?

When I hear the click of the door, I leap to my feet and feel like my heart will explode. But it's just Cora. She comes with sandwiches and bottled water. I cross the room to leave Avery sleeping, and we sit at the small table near the kitchenette. She pushes a notepad at me.

"Make me a list of whatever you need for a few days. We have plenty of food, but we'll need diapers and any other things for Avery you can think of, toiletries, whatever. Finn is gone for the night, and Mia lives in her room, glued to her phone, so don't worry. I'll be careful."

"I can't believe what you're doing for me. I really can't ever thank you enough. I'll never forget it," I say.

"It's what anyone would do," she says simply, but it's not.

"Look, I was actually getting a little bit worried about you..."

"Me?" Cora says, hand to her chest.

"You kept coming over. Lucas noticed. I don't know what he is capable of outside that house. I could be paranoid. But he's well connected and always tells me he could kill someone and make it look like an accident," I say, fearing she might change her mind, but I need to tell her everything.

"Oh, if he came for me, I'd blow his head off," she says matter-of-factly, and I can't help but let a small laugh escape my mouth. "And so can you," she says, unlocking a cabinet and indicating the gun inside. She hands me the key. "And there is an alarm on this guest house. My mom used to visit and insisted on it because she was afraid of her own shadow. Keep the blinds shut. You'll be okay, and I can certainly handle myself," she says.

"I can see that," I say with a smile.

"You're not alone now. We're gonna get the stuff you need immediately, and we'll sit down and work out a plan. We need to get you a phone tonight so you can call me if you need me. I'll do that now." She stands and goes to the door. She turns and points to the wall cabinets.

"Oh, and Georgia…"

I look up from Avery and back to her.

"Extra blankets are there. There's cable, remote is there, and most importantly, there is wine in the minifridge."

I stand up and walk over to her.

"Thank you. My real name is Nicola, by the way. Nicola Dawson," I say and hold my hand out to formally meet her.

"I'm sorry?" Cora says, tilting her head in confusion. "Wha— I don't…"

"I'm not Georgia. He wanted to make sure my family couldn't find me, no one I loved could trace me, so…"

Cora closes her eyes and shakes her head, a compassionate and empathetic gesture, and then takes me in her arms and hugs me tight. "Oh, sweet girl. I'm so sorry." She holds me for a long time and then says, "Nicola, I'll be back soon."

22

PAIGE

Paige waits for over an hour for Cora to get home. She periodically peers out the front window to see if her car appears in the drive and wonders where she is. When she sees Cora pull around back, she finds it odd. She pulls on a coat and picks up the box with Finn's name on it with all of the things she's collected from him inside it and walks over to Cora's. She doesn't see the lights on inside by the time she reaches the house, so she walks around back.

Cora is standing at the open hatch of her car unloading a bunch of bags.

"You bought diapers?" she asks, and Cora screams and drops the bag in her hand, whipping around in horror.

"Jesus!" She has to lean her hands on her knees to steady herself. "What the hell? You almost gave me a heart attack," she says, panting for breath.

"Sorry. I saw you drive up. You said Finn was out of town and we should do wine tonight. I was supposed to come over like an hour ago," Paige says.

"Oh, God. Sorry. His trip got canceled and then I guess I forgot."

"Anything I should know?" Paige says, eyeing the box of diapers.

"Ha. No, just a charity-drive thing. Come on in. I'll get this stuff later," Cora says, quickly closing the hatch and leading Paige inside.

"Wait, if Finn ended up staying home, we can reschedule."

"Oh, he went out," she says, and they go inside. Cora pulls a bottle of white out of the fridge and grabs two glasses. Paige thinks she seems nervous, like she's working hard to act normal. But she still has to do what she came to do. She watches Cora anxiously move around the kitchen, plugging in her phone, searching for something in the snack cupboard and then finally noticing the box Paige is carrying.

"What's all that?" she asks.

"Is Mia home?" Paige asks, and Cora looks a bit confused.

"No, she went to a friend's. What's up?"

"I have to talk to you about something, and it's—I don't really even know where to begin, but you need to know and there's—"

"What?" Cora cuts her off. "You found something. With Finn, you ended up finding something," she says, her face draining of color. Paige doesn't know if that's the place to begin, but she answers anyway.

"I did. I'm sorry."

Cora stands, a blank look on her face, pours a glass of wine, and goes to sit on the couch. After a minute, Paige follows.

"There's a little more to it, and I need you to hear me out." She puts the box on the coffee table and takes out the photos. First the hooker, then the one of Charlotte and Finn close but not too close at the ball, and then the printouts of the emails between them that fill in any gaps the photos don't show. Cora looks at them. She picks up the stack of emails and pages through with a numb look in her eye. She doesn't cry. She sets them down.

"Well, I guess I already knew, didn't I? Of course he's cheating."

"I'm so sorry, Cor," Paige says.

"Don't be. You saved me my house and a lot of money. I don't care anymore. I don't have any tears left for him. I don't know how to feel right now," Cora says, but Paige knows how this goes—she's just in shock. It hasn't sunk in fully. She definitely cares.

"I even asked Char to have coffee. I thought we'd be friends," Cora says, her voice hollow and even. Then she lets out a short, humorless laugh, takes a sip of her wine, and then goes back to the counter and brings over the bottle. She stares out the window to the blackness outside and doesn't speak. Paige has to press on.

"The thing is, the more I followed him and dug into his life, the more I found—and not just this."

Cora turns back to look at Paige, who is sitting across from her on an armchair.

"What? What else could there possibly be?"

"I'm sorry. Okay, I just— I didn't tell you what I was doing because I wanted to know for sure. I owe it to Caleb to…"

"Oh, Jesus. Paige. No. Come on. I can't possibly listen to this right now. I'm sorry. I'm not— I care, it's just, we've been over everyone in the neighborhood, and if you are gonna tell me that now you are back to suspecting Finn, it's probably not the best time. Please. I can't really take any more today."

"I know, but you have the right to know who he really

is, and I have proof. And before I go to the police with it, I thought it was only fair to tell you," Paige says, and Cora sighs and leans back in her chair with her wine.

"He told the police he'd only ever said hello to Caleb at the most, like when you two were over at our house for dinner or something. He said he'd have no reason talk to him or have his number. But Caleb's number is in his phone records."

"How in the hell do you have his phone records?"

"I stole his laptop, and I have his passwords," Paige says, and Cora's eyes expand and her mouth opens, but no words come out. "I'm sorry," Paige continues, "but I had to know. I did want to help you, too, but I just had this nagging...hunch. And then something he said made all the pieces fall into place. I ran into him when I was following him, and we chatted, and I don't remember what we were even talking about—it was at that bar—but he said 'Daymmn' like, instead of just saying *damn*, he said it in this very distinct way—a far-too-young-for-him, frat-boy sort of way... You know what I mean, right?"

"Yes, I do know," she says, somewhat defensively, Paige thinks, but she's listening, at least. They've both made fun of how annoying he is when he talks like that.

"So I remembered—like, that word hit me—a few days before Caleb died, he was arguing with someone outside. It wasn't anything extreme, just raised voices. I thought it was with a friend. I remember hearing that 'Daymmn' so distinctly. It was a short disagreement, and when I looked outside, Caleb was already in his car going wherever, and I saw a guy walking away... He was wearing a UMass ball cap backward. And you'd say, so what? A ton of kids go to UMass, but this was a '90s-style cap with the lacrosse sticks crossing the logo, and I still didn't think anything of it then—like, it didn't register until I saw him at the bar and he had it on—

the same, old-school UMass cap backward. That was him arguing with Caleb."

"I am not putting together whatever you're trying to say," Cora says, but Paige goes on.

"Why would they have reason to talk at all, let alone argue? Finn is a grown man. And twenty-two or not, Caleb is still the neighbors' kid. He said they never talked, but Finn has called him, there's records of it, and they argued. Why?" Paige says, becoming more agitated.

Cora seems calmer than Paige thought upon learning this. She puts her wineglass down and leans her elbows on her knees, clasping her hands together.

"Look, I think maybe this can be explained," Cora says.

"Please, explain it, then." Paige crosses her arms and waits.

"Mia told me something earlier that I didn't know, that Finn bought pot from Caleb. Maybe that's why they talked. I mean, that has to be it. I don't think it's more sinister than that."

"What? No. I don't accept that. Caleb wouldn't do that—he was on the dean's list. He was... You know what, then why did Finn lie over something like *pot* when the police were talking to everyone? We're talking about murder, and he'd lie and risk getting caught looking really suspicious over... pot?" Paige says, knowing Cora hates it when she says *murder* because the police have ruled it an accident.

"I'm sure he didn't think he'd be investigated for anyone to unpack it any further, so he probably just covered his ass without thinking," Cora says.

"Why are you defending him? After what I just showed you, it's hard to understand how you're not at least entertaining that he might be someone with secrets," she says.

"Okay," Cora says. "Is that all there is?"

"No," Paige says.

"So, what, then?"

"Well," Paige continues, "it's funny how Finn is in cyber security and knows a thing or two about surveillance, and the cameras at the entrance to the community weren't working."

"They weren't working for weeks. The HOA sent a notice," Cora says, but Paige goes on.

"He got his car fixed the day after the hit-and-run. I stole his files. There's an invoice," Paige says, handing Cora a copy. "Front-bumper damage," she points out. Again, Cora doesn't look shocked the way Paige expected.

"Paige. God, I can see how you think— No, Mia hit a pole in the Trader Joe's parking lot that weekend. That's all this was. I think you're—"

"Yeah, I remember you telling me that. But is she telling the truth?"

"Really?" Cora says. "You don't think you're taking this too far now?"

"She has one of those kids' debit cards where you guys can monitor the account and put money in. It's called Greenlight, right? Well, the next day, five hundred dollars is transferred into her Greenlight account. Did you give her that much money for anything?" Paige asks, and for the first time, Cora looks horrified.

"Oh, my God." She takes the printout, and Paige knows she cannot believe the intrusion into her personal life even though it was about Finn and not her, but what she's looking at is suddenly too disturbing for her to worry about that now.

"I didn't know about this."

"Is it possible he wanted her to take the fall for the car and he paid her off? And I'm *not* saying Mia knew anything, of course..."

"Of course not, she was out on a date that night. I..."

"Right, but maybe it was a way Finn could cover up the

repair. He could use Mia without her even knowing. Look." She hands her Finn's day planner.

"Jesus, Paige. How the fuck did you get all of this stuff?"

"Just look. January 17. It says *Drinks with C.* I thought it was Charlotte, so I met with her, but she was out of town that weekend. I think it was Caleb."

"But why? Why would he have any reason to— I need a minute. This is nuts. Why?"

"Here's why. Here's the whole goddamn thing. Caleb saw Finn getting a blow job in his car down somewhere at the edge of the neighborhood. He must have told Finn he knew about it, and Finn must have tried to pay him to keep him quiet like he did to Mia. Caleb received a thousand dollars through Venmo the day before he died. We never knew from who. The police think it was an accident. They never investigated this. Guess where it came from?" Paige says.

"No, please. Oh, my God," Cora says, burying her head in her hands as Paige smacks down another page of Finn's bank records. Cora stands. She waves her hand in front of her face and tries to catch her breath.

"If I take this to the police, it's more than enough for an arrest. Look what Finn had to lose if he were caught…"

"I know," Cora practically whispers. "I just can't take any more. I can't hear one more thing. Jesus Christ!"

"Okay," Paige says, packing the things back into her box. Cora walks to her wineglass on the coffee table and downs her drink in one long gulp and then walks over and looks out the French doors to the backyard. After several minutes, she says, "Let me talk to him before you report all this. I need to hear it from him, to see if he's lying."

Paige doesn't want to say that she's been pretty lousy for a long time at telling when he's lying.

"Of course," she says instead. "Ask him about his alibi. He

says he got home at ten that night, and you couldn't verify it because you were asleep, but he was out for drinks with Lucas Kinney, and his wife confirms Lucas was home at that time. Seems like she'll say whatever he wants, so maybe talk to her," Paige says, and after a couple minutes, Cora turns.

"Did you do all this spying on everyone, or just Finn?" she asks, and Paige isn't sure why that matters, considering. Cora knows she spies on everyone, but not to what extent.

"I just kept finding more on him, so I stopped needing to look at other people."

"What about Lucas Kinney? He was with Finn that night. What if he's involved? Did you go to these lengths to look at him?"

"Sort of. For a while. I dropped a recording device in his briefcase last month but I couldn't retrieve it again."

"What?"

"Yeah, it wasn't easy with this fucker either. I had to follow him to work and spend half the day in the cafeteria hoping he'd eat there for lunch, which he did not. But he did go to the Starbucks, and I had to cut in line to get behind him and drop it in. I had a whole spiel ready about what a coincidence it was seeing him here and how my CPA's office is on the sixth floor, but he didn't even notice me. Shocker, right? That guy's so in his own creepy world."

"Jesus," Cora says.

"I got a little dirt on a lot of people, but he was harder because he's so private and closed off. It's not easy unless you get close to a person and have a place to start, so nothing really."

"If you could get that recording device back, could you still recover what's on it?" Cora asks.

"Yeah, but I don't think I need it anymore. You think... what? That he was involved, too?"

"I don't know what I think. I just need a little time." Cora looks out the window again. She looks small and ghostly, like someone who's lost everything in a matter of moments, which is exactly what she is. The seething anger Paige came into this with is making way for something else: absolute heartbreak for Cora.

"I'm so sorry, and I'm sorry I lied to you, but this was the only way."

"No," Cora says sharply, and Paige is taken aback a moment. Then Cora turns to her. "You're not the one who needs to be sorry." Cora embraces Paige and lets the tears flow as she holds on to her friend.

23

NICOLA

When Cora comes back, she looks like a different person. She's clearly been crying and looks exhausted. She holds a couple oversize bags and enters the side door quietly. I've kept the lights off and sit in front of the small, gas fireplace with Avery playing on a blanket. I hop up to help her with the bags.

"Sorry, that took a lot longer than I thought," she says, pulling items out of the bags. Granola bars, coffee, bread, peanut butter, fruit.

"Wow. You didn't have to do all this. You've done enough already."

"You need to eat. And here. This is a pay-as-you-go phone. I put my number in it for you, so if you need me, you can call." She seems anxious now instead of steady and calm. She goes to the fridge and pulls out a bottle of wine.

"It's a wine kind of night for me. Want to join me?" she asks. Something's happened, I can tell.

"Sure," I say, taking a glass she's already poured for me even though I don't want it. She sits on the blanket next to the fire, and her face changes when she focuses on Avery.

"Look at this sweet girl," she says, swinging Avery's little feet and pretending to gobble up her pink booties. Avery giggles. I sit cross-legged next to them.

"Have the police come back to talk to you?" I ask, treading lightly, not sure why she's upset.

"No. I think you're as safe as you can be here. He's having them officially search for you, it looks like," she says, and I put my glass down and nervously fidget, kneading my fingers in my palms.

"There is no scenario in which we will let him take you back. I don't care who he is," she says, and I love her for this, but I don't think she understands the reach of his influence. Or that he really would just kill me if that's what it came to.

"Did you know he was married before?" she asks.

"What?" I say, but I mean, I don't know why that would surprise me, really. It doesn't, in fact. I don't care anything about him or his life before me. "No. Why?"

"It could be relevant."

"What do you mean? To what?"

"Well, here's the thing. I need you to trust me, to hear me when I tell you this."

"Of course I trust you. How could I not?" I say, no idea where this is going.

"His first wife died," she says. "She drowned in their pool. Years ago."

I feel immediately nauseous: my head is light and dizzy.

"It was an undetermined cause, but, of course, he was there,

214

and they bought his story. I don't know if it was investigated or if it's important. Maybe it's irrelevant, but…"

"It's not," I say quietly.

"So look, I know the last thing you want here is to tell anyone else…"

"No! Please. I can't even believe *you* know— I can't— This is getting… Oh, my God…" I trail off, not knowing how to handle any of this.

"But here's the thing. Paige can help us. I know you don't know her well, but we need her. This is where the *trust me* part comes in."

"Why do we need her? The more people know, the more risk. Please," I say, feeling totally without control over my own fate right now.

"Because last month, she dropped a recording device in Lucas's work bag. It's tiny, and it records one hundred and ninety-two hours of audio."

"What? Wait. It recorded audio in our house?" I ask, baffled by this. "Wha- Why?"

"This could be everything we need. You gotta hear me out. Do you know this bag he uses for work—a briefcase-type bag?"

"Yeah, but…" I can't complete a thought in my mind that comes out as anything but an incoherent stutter.

"She did it, not knowing what she'd get. Does he bring his bag home at night usually?" she asks.

"Yeah. It's always on the table in the front hall or in his office. But wait, stop. I don't understand. Why would she do that?"

"Let's just say, we have found Lucas to be…off? Suspicious. I thought something was going on myself," she says.

I feel a flood of gratitude. She was trying to save me even before I knew it.

"I actually clipped a camera to your front tree to see what he was up to," she says, and a sudden laugh escapes me as I cover my mouth. I'm just so shocked someone was looking out for me. Someone cares that this has happened. But just as quickly, my eyes fill with grateful tears, and I blink them back.

"I can't believe that," I say, smiling a genuine smile for the first time in as long as I can remember.

"So if you can, trust her, because I trust her with my life, and I know you can. We can try to get the recorder. She says it's voice-activated, so it doesn't just run all the time. It recorded the audio whenever you spoke. Do you think, with one hundred and ninety-two hours of speaking, we'll hear what we need, what you've described?" she asks, pouring another glass of wine. She's thought this through in such a short time, and I'm trying to keep up.

"But why does that matter? I thought we were going to get me and Avery as far away as possible?" I ask, feeling very uneasy that the plan seems to be changing.

"Yes. And we will, but what if we don't have to?" she asks.

"We do have to! What do you mean?" I begin to panic. "Oh, my God, I can't— This has to work. I have to go. I thought you—"

"Honey, no. I'm sorry. This isn't meant to scare you. I will help you. I absolutely promise. All I mean is, you say it's his word against yours, and his status, all of that. If there is concrete proof of abuse, he can go away, and you don't have to run and look over your shoulder the rest of your life. That recording will back you up," she says, putting her glass down and shifting toward me as she speaks.

I just want her to drive me to the airport, but I have no documents. I want her to drive me at least five states away, but I have no money or job or ID. I mean, I need her. I have to listen.

"What if he just gets a slap on the wrist and gets out and finds me?" I say, smoothing Avery's thin wisps of baby hair behind her ears nervously.

"Well, think about it. He'll at least be arrested. It will at least buy time to get you back to the UK, and probably an order for your documents to be searched for…legal help to get your stuff sorted out. Plus, if they find it to be true, that he's kept you there, that he's stolen your identity from you…I think it will be more than a slap on the wrist. I get that you need the proof and not just your word, but I mean, with that proof, you're so much safer. Long term." She's so sure and emphatic, I want to trust her.

But Paige. I just can't bear having her involved. It's too much. But I find that I really have little choice. What she says makes sense. I'll need a little time to put together a plan. Getting away is even harder now that I'm being looked for.

"You're absolutely positive that Paige won't tell anyone? At all. You're sure it's safe," I plead.

"Paige can keep a secret like you wouldn't believe."

"Okay," I say. And I want to say a thousand more times *Are we safe? Are you sure? Please let us be safe. I can't take any more.* But this is where I am now, and I have to trust these women. They're all I have.

"She's in the house. But don't worry. I have not told her you're here. She came over for another…issue, and there is nothing I can do about that right this minute, so let's figure out how to keep you safe. That's what I can do," she says, and I nod.

When Cora goes inside to talk to Paige, they are a long time. I know it's a lot to explain, and the thought of Cora being wrong about her and this blowing up makes me ill. I go to the sink and think I'll throw up, but I don't. I just lean over it and run the cold water and press it to my cheeks. He's only a couple houses away. He's so close, I hear my blood pumping between my ears. I feel as caged as ever.

When they come through the door, the sound of it clicking open again makes me jump. Paige looks like she's seen a ghost upon looking at me.

"Hi," she says with a reserved wave. She stays across the room, giving me my space, probably, but she acts as though she's talking to an unstable person or a rabid dog—someone who could attack without warning. I don't know how Cora told it, or if she added that I'm leery of letting Paige get involved.

"Hi," I say, moving back down to Avery, a natural instinct to protect her. I have barely spoken to anyone in so long until very recently, and it feels so foreign to be in the company of anyone but Lucas.

"Georgia, I can't…" Paige starts to say but doesn't seem to have the words. Cora steps in.

"Her name is Nicola."

"Jesus," Paige says, understanding the implication. "What a—what a fucking monster that guy is… I'm so sorry we didn't know what was happening," she says. "I don't even—"

But I interrupt her. "You can't tell anyone I'm here," I say, needing to hear it, feeling overwhelmed with how dangerous this is.

"No. God. Of course not. We're gonna take that son of a bitch down," Paige says.

"How? Because I'm sorry, I don't mean to sound ungrateful, but I don't think you understand. I know about this recorder thing, but there's no way to get it. I think we should forget that, and I should just go."

"Paige says she's willing to…break in," Cora says.

"Sneak in," Paige corrects her.

"Sneak in and get it," Cora finishes. I look at them a moment and see that they're serious.

"That's— No. That's crazy. That's... Do you have any idea how dangerous that is?" I say in disbelief.

"I mean, if you have the alarm code, I could get in. Sort of disguise myself from the cameras. I do it all the time," Paige says, and I look to Cora, who nervously smiles.

"Like a ski mask? Are we in a movie? This is outrageous. You'll get killed," I say.

"It's more of a hoodie and glasses sort of getup, and I think you're underestimating how often I've done this sort of thing. I'm quick with the pepper spray, too," she says, miming pulling it out of a holster on her hip like a gun. "I pepper-spray practically everyone," she says, and I'm sure my mouth is open but empty for words. I look to Cora again, but she just shrugs a timid agreement and nods.

"Like handsy men at the bar," she explains. "The mailman when I thought he was peeping. The drunk guy that got too close in line at the CVS."

"Don't you get arrested?" I ask, stunned at this strange new addition to my nightmare.

"Oh, yeah. The point is I can protect myself. I can weasel through small spaces, and I know where to look in his giant briefcase with all the pockets since I put it there," she says, and Avery suddenly begins to get fussy and cry in little intermittent bursts.

Paige tends to her, seemingly on autopilot, without a thought, still totally engaged in our conversation, but shifting Avery onto her lap and cooing at her. I just watch, because I was sure a full-blown sob was coming and she just stopped when Paige picked her up. Their interaction is strangely magical.

"We'll stay on a call with her the whole time she's in there,"

Cora adds. "She's the best person to do this." I look back and forth between them. I don't know if I have found true friends or if they are both absolutely nuts.

"But why would you? You don't even know me."

"After hearing what you've been through, I think anyone would do the same," she says, and I involuntarily scoff at this. We clearly don't know the same people, and if these two think this is just what a friend does, I wish I could stay here forever and be their friend. They're very lucky.

"What if he wakes up? What if he catches you? I can't let you do that. No. No way."

"I already told you," she says, and she makes the ridiculous pepper-spray gun-holster gesture again, and in any other circumstance this would be hilarious. But it's life-and-death, so it's not at all funny.

"Plus, the cops are used to reports of me in people's garages and cars and so they'll think I'm trying to help find you. Like a vigilante. I'm the only one who can get away with it, I'm telling you."

"Should I ask why you are always breaking into people's property?" I say.

"A story for another time," Cora says, but Paige keeps talking.

"I'm sure you heard about my son, Caleb," she says, and Cora shifts and gives her a look.

"Maybe now is not the time," Cora starts to say.

"It's just a question," Paige says, as she looks back to me.

"Yeah, of course," I say. "I saw him around."

"So then, maybe you remember that the hit-and-run happened at around ten thirty on the night of January 17, and the police talked to you and Lucas. He said he was home at ten. You were his alibi."

"Paige." Cora tries to stop her for some reason. But Paige isn't even slightly deterred.

"*But* now that I know what I know about you, he probably made you say anything he wanted. Do you remember? Do you remember when he came home?" Her body language has changed, and I feel like I have somehow gone from victim to perpetrator in a matter of seconds.

"It was a long time ago. So much has happened that I don't…" I'm not sure how my sentence will end because I do remember. I remember Lucas was home late because I got home late and was worried he'd be upset, but thankfully, he wasn't there yet. This was when I was pregnant. It was one of the last times I ever left the house. This was still the short time frame when I wasn't captive. I went out, I shopped, I started to meet new friends and get coffee. I took a yoga class. It was when he was still grooming me, and I had no idea. But I can't say this because I don't know what she wants from me. I need help. I can't have her change her mind or give up on me. Why is she asking this?

"I don't remember," I say, and then Paige's phone pings, and she gently places Avery on the blanket and pulls it out of her pocket.

"It's Grant. He's saying, *Turn on the news. Did you know the neighbor lady, Georgia, has gone missing?*" She looks up at us.

Cora goes to the TV and flips channels until she finds a local news station. The three of us stand in front of it and watch a grieving Lucas put on an act in front of the camera. A photo of me is displayed on one half of the screen. It's a photo from my time in France. I am tanned and smiling and unrecognizable. I see a woman with eyes full of life and naive hope. I see the person I was before my whole life was stolen from me. Cora and Paige look to me and back to the TV and then back to me.

"How can this be on the news if you've only been gone seven hours?" Cora wonders.

"Because he's Lucas Kinney," I say flatly, the reality of it all sinking in. I turn it off. I can't watch it anymore. "I'm gonna get her to sleep," I say, picking Avery up and bringing her over to the bed. I want them to give me some time to take all of this in. I need to be alone.

"Of course," Cora says.

"So we'll meet back here tomorrow," Paige says. "Late. To make sure the bastard is sound asleep." It's not a question; it's a plan.

"'Night," she says then, like she's simply making coffee plans with us tomorrow, and then she leaves. And that's that.

24

CORA

When I hear Nicola click the lock shut after I leave, and I know they are safe and the alarm is on, I walk back to the house, and it's dark and silent. Mia is staying at her friend's house, and Finn isn't home yet. I feel like I've been physically beaten. My nerve endings are full of electricity, and my exhaustion is mixed with rage and sadness, and I don't know what to do with myself. I walk across the living room, moonlit from the large glass doors, and I pick up a velvet throw pillow from the couch and scream into it until my lungs ache.

I think about waiting up for Finn, and being perched at the kitchen island with all of the photos of his sins spread across the Carrara marble, but I'm not capable of any more talking or crying. I can't listen to one more lie from his mouth or think about whichever of his women he's with tonight. I also can't bear the thought of him slipping into bed beside me at three in the morning with her body fluids all over him, masked only by a squirt of his cologne and my fatigue.

No, I pour a large glass of water and swallow a couple Advil to help prevent the hangover I'm sure to have after all of the wine I've consumed, and I pad along the upstairs hallway to the guest room, where I pull down the plush duvet we picked out together with his parents' visits in mind: white, when I suggested a heather gray. I slip into the sheets and stare up at the swirling ceiling fan. I turned it on out of habit, even though I hate having a fan on when it's cold out. But Finn always wants the air moving, even in subzero weather. I stare at the blur of the blades and wonder how someone's life can completely implode in less than twenty-four hours.

I hate him. I hate myself for believing him all those countless times he said he'd never even look at another woman because I was all he needed and family was everything. It was what I desperately wanted to hear, and he said the right things with such conviction, so I lied to myself. I lied to myself even though I knew. And now I've wasted years and years of my life. If I let myself think too long about that, about living a complete lie for two decades, I feel like it could literally kill me. Every beach vacation, every Christmas morning, every cocktail party where we danced together, every special candlelit dinner, it was all a front. It was a show.

I let the images of him with other women play over and over in my head until I finally submit to my exhaustion, and when I wake up, it's to the sound of Finn trying to creep in at 2:47. I think about what the me of even just yesterday would do. I would tread carefully, because he'd say he was out with (insert guy-friend's name) and they just shot pool or hung out at the bar at the golf club or whatever, and I would do something pathetic like try to get close to him in bed and see if I could smell anything incriminating, try to ask specific questions that sound like I'm interested in his night but are meant to catch him in a contradiction. He's always seen through it.

Tonight, though, I think about how great it would feel to tie a garbage bag over his face and watch him suffocate in his drunken stupor. Instead, I run over the details in my mind of how exactly I will confront him with all that I know. A time when he is sober and I have more time to think about how to respond to any of the ways he might try to lie his way out of it.

I don't fall back asleep. I feel like shit. I have a wine hangover, and I've barely slept, but by four thirty, I give up trying and go down to the kitchen to make coffee. Mia shouldn't be back until noon, so I do exactly what I've spent the last few hours thinking about. I make a big breakfast of scrambled eggs, bacon, blueberry pancakes, and rye toast with orange marmalade. I pour myself a mimosa for some hair of the dog, and it does help make me feel a little better. I bring a plate out to Nicola and tell her I'll be back later when Finn leaves.

Then, by nine twenty, the smells of frying bacon and brewing coffee have finally drawn Finn downstairs to the kitchen. He comes in in sweats and socks and kisses me on the cheek as he passes me and goes to pour a cup of coffee. Only, I know that it's the last time he'll ever kiss me on the cheek or sit in this kitchen while I make breakfast. It's the last time I'll ever make him coffee and the absolute last time I'll ever give him a fake smile when behind it is years of mounting resentment.

"How was your night?" he asks, sitting down at the kitchen island. On top of his breakfast plate is a stack of the photos and email printouts that Paige let me keep, explaining that she has plenty of copies. I see the panic in his eyes immediately. He goes white. He stands and puts his mug down. He has no idea what to do.

"What the fuck?" he says. Well, I guess that's a start. What else can he really say?

"Yeah, that's a good question. What the fuck?" I say, grateful now for the sleepless night, for the time I've had to calm myself and mentally prepare, maybe even accept reality instead of finding this out myself and losing my shit in the moment.

"The hooker is the most interesting part to me," I say very calmly. "I mean, I always knew you were fucking colleagues. You were good at lying, but I knew. But hookers. Hmmm. So you'll just fuck anyone. It's not even about an affair with someone you care for, it's just you sticking your dick in anything."

He looks like he'll storm out of the room for a moment. Then he sits on the island stool and stares down for a long time at the photo on the top of the pile, the hooker photo. I'm sure he's thinking very hard of any possible way to explain it, but there is none.

"I don't know what to say," he says.

"That's it? Really? 'Cause I'd suggest you say something," I say, still calm.

"What do you want from me? Men like sex, Cora. It's not like you're ever in the mood. You—" And I stop him right there.

"Wrong. Try starting over with a version that doesn't blame me for you sleeping with hookers and coworkers and lying to me for years."

"People cheat. All the time. Okay, this isn't, like, mind-blowing. It happens every day, so fine. It's all there. What can I say? You—"

"*Eh!*" I make a loud, throaty noise and hold up my palm. "Don't say one more word that includes blaming me. I refuse to hear it. I did everything you asked. I gave up a career, for God's sake. I offered couples counseling the last time I knew you were cheating, but you made me feel crazy and told me I needed counseling on my own. I planned date nights, I bought lingerie I was not comfortable wearing because you liked it.

226

I turned a blind eye. I was made a fool of by you and all your little girlfriends snickering behind my back. And worst of all, I wasted all these years on a total fraud, so if you open your mouth one more goddamn time to find a way to make this my fault, I swear to God, not only will I take pleasure in taking all of your money, I will fucking smother you in your sleep!" I say or, more like, scream by the end of it.

He has never seen me like this before, I know. His eyes are wide, and he looks like a little boy, sitting on his stool, looking up at me.

"Before you go and pack your bags and call whoever you were with last night to go and stay with them, I just want to make sure you know that this, *all this*—" I pick up the stack of photos and printed emails and throw them at his chest, and they fall onto the floor in a scattered mess "—is really the least of your concern. In fact, I don't even care about this," I say.

"Yeah, it looks like you don't care," he says, trying to get the upper hand. Then he tries to take back his smirk and shitty comment and softens. "Look, you have every right to be like this."

"Oh, thanks for the permission, but I don't need it."

"But people get through this sort of thing, Cora. I've obviously been—"

"A scheming psychopath." I finish his sentence. He sighs. He tried to act like he's being reasonable and I'm being outrageous.

"I've made a lot of mistakes. A lot, I know. I got away with it, and it—maybe it was exciting to—I don't know. I just— That doesn't mean I don't love you, okay? Christ." He's red and flustered. He stands and then sits again. He tightens his facial features and presses his fingers into his eyes, then makes an exasperated sound. "All of this," he says as he gestures lazily to the scattered evidence, "it looks bad. I know that, but it didn't have anything to do with love. It was just sex, just midlife-crisis stupidity. I still lo—"

"Do not say you still love me, or I will literally scream at the top of my lungs until the neighbors call the police. Midlife crisis, huh? Like that's an excuse, anyway. And also the first time I knew this happened was fifteen years ago. You were in your late twenties. I wasn't wrong. This is just who you are. You're a liar and a manipulator, and guess what, I'm an idiot for letting it happen, but I'll say it again. I don't care. It's over. We're over. What I do care about is this," I say, showing him the bank statement that shows the money he put into Mia's account.

"Do you wanna tell me what this is?" I ask. He looks over the bank statement. "And this," I tap my finger on the thousand-dollar transfer that he does not know that I know was to Caleb.

"Why do you have my bank records? This isn't our joint account. This is my private account! I don't have to answer to you about anything." He pushes it away.

"Oh, a second ago, you still loved me and people work these things out, but now you don't have to answer to me about matters concerning our daughter?"

"Why do you have this?" he repeats, a muscle in his jaw twitching.

"Paige followed you. Did you really think she was obsessed with you? She told me you might actually be stupid enough to think that, but she was just trying to get all this, and you fell for it. You really can't help yourself, can you? Even with my closest friend."

"Jesus Christ." He stands up. He goes to a laundry basket full of clean laundry I was planning to fold yesterday before my life crumbled, and he pulls on a white T-shirt as he starts to head out of the room.

"You want me out, I'm out."

"Paige is going to the police, so before you go you might want to listen," I say to his back.

He turns and laughs. "I know you wish it were, Cora, but last I checked, infidelity isn't a criminal offense."

"You transferred a thousand dollars to Caleb the day before he died. You have his number in your phone, and there are calls between you. You argued in his driveway. You have a meeting with him marked in your day planner, and you got the car fixed right after the hit-and-run. Is that enough probable cause for you?" I say, feeling like a lawyer on a bad court drama, but I have gone over these words in my head all night, and I need to see his face. I need an explanation. He turns, and his shoulders drop. He lets out a loud puff of breath and shakes his head in disbelief.

"Are you out of your mind? Mia hit a pole with the car at—"

"That's the story. Did you pay her to say that?"

"Oh, my God. Are you— Ask her! What is the matter with you? This is why Paige has been all over me, to string together all this…bullshit to try to…I don't even know what! This is— I got the car fixed for Mia. End of story!" he screams so loud, I'm sure Nicola can hear. I hope the other neighbors can't, but I don't tell him to keep his voice down. In fact, I meet his volume.

"End of story? How about the part where you give a thousand dollars to a kid you say you've never talked to and who's now dead? How about that?" I scream back. He takes an exaggerated breath and lets it out slowly, as if I'm some unreasonable, nagging wife—an annoyance to be dealt with. He walks past me and sits on the couch in the living room. I follow him and stand in the arched doorframe, waiting for him to say something.

"That can all be explained," he says, very quietly now.

"Good, because Paige is taking this all to the police. That's not a threat from me. I had nothing to do with this. She brought it all to me. So if you can explain, you probably should, because she's going either way."

"She's trying to point to me as a murderer because I talked to Caleb?" he says defiantly. I see that he's trying to make his tone sound dismissive, but it makes him sound scared.

"He saw you in a car with some woman. Getting a blow job. When I told Paige about our prenup, she thought you paid him off to stay quiet 'cause you had a lot to lose. Motive. Then all of this," I say, sitting across from him. His head is in his hands, and he's just slowly shaking it back and forth. When he lifts his head, I think I see tears in his eyes. I think I hear him whisper, *This is not happening*, but he's mumbling, and his eyes are wild.

"He sold pot," he says. "I bought… I had his number for when I wanted a little… It wasn't a big deal. Just a bit of fun now and then. That's it. God, just fucking pot. And yes, fine. Mia saw me stash something in the garage and said she wouldn't say anything. I did not ask her to hide it from you. She just said it wasn't a biggie, and so yeah, whatever. I gave her some money… I appreciated her being cool about it. That's it. But Paige going to the cops, that's so—" He slams his hand on the coffee table. "That's so Paige is what it is. She points the finger at everyone. She won't be taken seriously. It's ridiculous!"

"So when she does, and she will, you're going to tell them that you bought a thousand dollars' worth of pot from him. Um, really?" I say, feeling outside of my body somehow because this is all so surreal.

"Okay, Cora. You wanna know? Fine. I got some harder stuff."

"Harder like what? Now you're a crackhead. Seems fitting, as nothing surprises me anymore."

"No. It was coke a couple of times. God, you act like nobody can have a little fun now and then, like it's some—"

"Crime!" I finish whatever he was gonna say. "'Cause it is! So you smoked a thousand dollars' worth of coke by yourself?"

"Jesus." He shakes his head and rolls his eyes. "You don't smoke coke."

"Oh, that's the part you're grabbing on to. You're finding an opportunity to correct me rather than telling me what the actual fuck you were doing with a *thousand* dollars' worth—"

"Okay. Just stop! Yes, fine. God! I'm a piece of shit, fine. I was hanging out with a woman, and she liked the recreational—ugh!—it was just a couple times. I—" He tries to explain, and I just start laughing. I can't even believe how much more absurd this gets with every new thing I learn about him.

"Must be with the hooker. Don't see Charlotte as the type," I say, and I don't even know how I'm still talking about this. I should be banging my head against the wall and pulling my hair out at this point because this is just so outrageous. He doesn't say anything, but the look on his face does.

"Oh. I see." And I do, I get it, and I hate that it stings so bad. "A different woman altogether. You literally just have a completely other life. A double fucking life I never saw all these years," I say, fully defeated, and I sit back down on the couch and stare at the plush white area rug under my feet.

"You have to believe me. Yes, I got the stuff from Caleb, but so did a lot of people. Just ask around. It was harmless. Yes, we had a minor tiff after I paid him and he didn't deliver when I needed him."

"Oh, you had your date waiting, and you couldn't get your coke for her. You had to wait on your predinner coke-snorting. How could he? Do you realize that I had to just say a sentence like that because of you? You disgust me."

"Cora, you have to believe me."

"No. Actually, I don't."

"Fine, I'll get out, and yes, I deserve you hating me, but come on. You know I didn't have anything to do with Caleb. What you're saying is crazy."

"Do you think *crazy* is the word you want to use? Remember all the other times you said that? And I was right each time. I don't even know who you are, so no, I don't know if you're lying about this like you have lied about everything else in your life," I say and start to walk away. I don't know where to go. I just suddenly want this over.

"Cora! Stop. It was just silly drugs. It was a bad decision, I get it, but you're talking about— Why would you think I would want to harm him?" he pleads.

"I already told you. Good luck with the police. I hope you can keep your lies straight," I say, and I walk outside and get in my car and drive off because I don't know what else to do and I can't hear him say one more thing ever again.

I call Paige as I drive and tell her to go ahead and turn him in.

25

PAIGE

Paige didn't know what to expect when she brought her pile of evidence to the police station. She knows they think she's unstable at this point and knew it would prove difficult for them to take her seriously, but what she handed them was more than enough, she thought. No matter what they think of her, there is a mountain of undeniable evidence.

The guy who originally investigated the case, if you can call it that, liked to remind her of the fact she was well aware of already: he was never looking for a killer with motive, he was looking for some intoxicated person or someone texting and driving who hit Caleb by accident. The crime to him was fleeing the scene, not murder, but now she had a thing or two to say to him. So when the woman at the front desk offered for her to talk to one of the available officers, she said she'd wait for Detective Denning. And she waited nearly three hours rather than making an appointment or talking to someone else.

She sat in a stiff metal chair, hugging her box to her chest. This was it. This was her time. She'd wait forever if she had to, but she would be listened to. When Denning finally arrived, she scrambled to her feet before he could walk past her. She saw the woman at the desk point and say something to him. He turned to see Paige, and she was sure he stifled an eye roll. His shoulders dropped, and he looked like he was ready to make an excuse as to why he didn't have time to talk to her right now, but Paige approached him. The woman told him how long she'd been waiting, so he reluctantly made a gesture with his head for her to follow him back to his office.

She's been in his office before. She'd showed up all the time for the first few months, bullied her way back to see him and bordered on verbally abusing the staff. She understands why he's reluctant to talk to her, but she thinks he should have done more. She tried to understand the logic when everyone reiterated the things the detective said. *It's very hard to solve this sort of thing, no camera, no witnesses, no suspects. A freak accident with an irresponsible or maybe drunk and unaware driver, but you can't order search warrants and phone records for every neighbor you don't like.* Fine. That all might be true, but now he has to listen. Her hunch was right.

"Good to see you again, Mrs. Moretti," he says, and she knows that of course he doesn't mean it, but she doesn't care.

"What have we got this time?" he asks with nothing but placating skepticism in his voice.

"Proof," she says. She takes out the photos that prove Finn's affair and explains the prenup Finn and Cora had and how that gives him a motive since Caleb caught him cheating. She shows him the money transfer, phone records, all of it, and then sits down across from him and watches him, her eyes darting from his face to the contents he's paging through to see if she can read him. After what seems like an eternity, he finally takes his glasses off and puts down the last of the pages from the stack and looks at her. Is the look he gives her dismissive? Impressed? She can't tell. His features are always arranged in the same unreadable way, no matter what the situation.

"I'll have him come down and talk to us," he says. She wants to give him an exasperated sigh and explain it all again. *How can you just have a casual chat? You should arrest him immediately.* But she stands and thanks him instead because it's a lot further than she's ever gotten, and his willingness to look into this at all, after so many attempts on her part, is a big deal, she knows. She tells him to keep the box because she has copies of everything, and then she sees herself out. She feels the corners of her mouth creep up into something resembling a smile as she walks to her car. She's going to get justice, finally. For Caleb. That's all she wants.

She wants to call Grant on her way home and tell him, but she doesn't because he doesn't need another disappointment if, for any reason, it doesn't turn out the way she thinks it will, the way she knows it has to. She visualizes it, though: telling him that they are finally free of some of the weight of it. Her obsession and his depression that butt up against each other in the worst possible way and keep them apart don't have to control them forever. She thinks of holding him, crying with him, finally feeling a sense of closure, and she doesn't swallow back the tears that prick her eyes. She lets them fall as she drives to meet Cora and Nicola to help give another bastard what's coming to him.

26

PAIGE

At ten o'clock the women meet, and it feels riskier now that Finn is home in the main house only fifty feet away. Cora repeats herself, saying that nobody ever comes out to the mother-in-law unit—haven't maybe for years, so they should be safe—but the more she says it, the more Paige thinks she's trying to convince herself it's true. She can only pray it is.

Paige wears black yoga pants and a black hoodie. She has pepper spray in a hot-pink cartridge that wraps around her wrist on a Velcro band and looks idiotic. When she pulls out an old knit ski mask, Nicola gasps.

"I thought you said a hoodie and glasses. Are you going to wear that? You look like you're going to murder someone," she says.

"Eh, yeah, I did say that, but then I remembered what you

said about how many cameras were in there. Can't be too careful."

"God," Nicola says, "I don't know about this, it's—"

"Fucking nuts," Cora says.

"Yes," Nicola says.

"Yep," Paige agrees. "So where is your sketch, then?" she asks, and Nicola goes to the piece of printer paper on the small table. They all sit down, and Nicola shows Paige the rough drawing she's made that shows the layout of the house.

"So remember, I have a camera on the front of the house," Cora says before they dive in. Paige furrows her brow and looks to Cora in confusion.

"You what?"

"What?" Cora asks.

"Nothing," Paige says.

"Yeah, so when I drove in a few hours ago, the front curtains were open. Let's see," Cora says, opening an app on her tablet and propping it against a glass on the table so everyone can see. It's a live-stream video of the front of Lucas's house.

"It's after ten, so if that's when he usually goes to bed, hopefully we get lucky and they stay open so we can at least get eyes on you when you're on the main floor."

"Look at you, MacGyver," Paige says, laughing.

"Who?" Nicola asks.

"She's young," Paige says to Cora, trying to share a conspiratorial look, but Cora is too focused and on edge.

"But if his wife is missing, he's not gonna just keep a regular schedule, is he? What if he's up all night working on finding her?" Cora asks.

"I doubt it," Nicola says. "He doesn't actually care like a normal person in that situation. He's pissed, not distraught. If he thinks the police are on it, I think he'll get his beauty sleep." Cora puts her hand on Nicola's shoulder and gives it a squeeze, a quiet apology for all she's been through.

"Anyway, we'll be on FaceTime. We have a plan. You can see behind me, I can tuck my phone around corners. I'll have earbuds in so you can talk to me. It'll be a piece of cake," Paige says, then turns her attention to the sketch.

"So the alarm pad is next to the door to the left?" she confirms.

"Yeah," Nicola says, pointing at the paper and tracing the path Paige should take with her finger. "Once you open the door you have thirty seconds to put in the code. Which is?"

"Eight-nine-eight-three-two-five," Paige says.

"Eight-nine-eight-five-two-three," Nicola corrects.

"Oh, my God. We're screwed before we even get inside!" Cora says, getting obviously more anxious the closer they get to doing this. She grabs a pen and then grabs Paige's hand. "Say it again, please?"

"Eight-nine-eight-five-two-three," Nicola repeats, and Cora writes it across Paige's palm. Paige lets her because she has a point.

"So," Nicola continues, "if the bag is anywhere but his office, it will be right there on the table by the front door. Otherwise, there are two staircases. Maybe go up the front so we can see you on the camera."

"Yes," Cora adds.

"And then, take a right at the top of the stairs. His office is the second door on the left. It's usually on the floor next to his desk or hanging on the doorknob," she says.

"Okay," Paige says.

"Are you sure you wanna do this?" Nicola asks, pain in her voice. "I'm so sorry. I just— I can't believe you guys are helping me like this."

"I'm sure," Paige says. For the next hour and a half, they sit

238

quietly together. Avery has been sleeping since eight, Finn is watching a game in the media-room inside, and Mia is doing homework. They've kept the lights off since dusk so no attention is drawn to them, and all they can do is wait, alone together, in the tense, airless room they've created with their collective anxiety.

Just before midnight, they swing into action. Cora's camera caught Lucas walking up the stairs at 10:14, and he hasn't come back down, so he likely went to bed. They've given it a lot of cushion time before making their move. Paige has her phone in one hand and her ski mask tucked into the waist of her pants just in case she's spotted before she makes it across the street. She won't put it on yet.

Cora tries to hug Paige at the door as she exits, but Paige brushes her off and tells her not to jinx it, and then she's off. Nicola and Cora sit looking at the camera feed on her tablet and are also connected to Paige via FaceTime. Paige unzips her hoodie a bit to prop her phone inside her sports bra, so the camera can stay on and show Cora and Nicola her path as she walks through the house. She's more anxious than she thought she'd be when she arrives at Lucas's front door. Yes, she's done things like this, but to folks like Steve Wilkers with the spare tire around his middle who couldn't be bothered to get off the couch if the house were on fire, not to a known psychopath who just might kill her for sport. It's all hitting her as she uses Nicola's key and, as quietly and slowly as she can, turns the lock and opens the door.

"Eight-nine-eight-five-two-three, eight-nine-eight-five-two-three, eight-nine-eight-five-two-three," she repeats, mouthing the numbers silently as she punches them into the keypad. Then she ducks. As she crouches down on the floor in front of the closed front door, she pulls on her black ski mask she found in the tub of winter clothes when she was looking for Grant's Isotoners. Her mind drifts to Grant for a brief moment, in the kitchen in that ugly brown hat she pulled out. Then she quickly dismisses the memory that has no business showing up right now and refocuses.

She couldn't risk putting the mask on outside in case anyone happened to glance out their window, and she knows from Nicola that the porch camera only faces in to keep tabs on her, not the neighbors, so now, ducked down inside this house, pulling on a ski mask of all things suddenly strikes Paige as being deranged. But she's in now. No time for doubts.

She stays crouched on the floor for a few minutes, hearing only the sound of her own breath.

"Are you okay?" She hears the loud whisper of Cora's voice in her earbuds. She puts her thumb in front of her chest to show the camera a thumbs-up and then slowly stands. She takes her shoes off at the door so she can tiptoe, sock-footed and silent, to the curved staircase in the middle of the room.

She holds the railing and walks so softly up the stairs she can't even hear her own footsteps. When she reaches the top, she stops and listens. She hears flutes and trickling water. It sounds like the meditation music they play at the foot spa. She guesses it's a sleep aid, but how would Nicola know since she is locked in a different room at night? She doesn't stop to ask the women. She presses on and thinks this is a good thing because it's less likely he'll hear anything. Then she hears a voice and stays frozen, her heart speeding up.

"I am a smart and powerful man. Happiness is a choice, not a condition. I choose to be happy." At first, she turns to scurry back down the stairs, but then she quickly realizes that it, too, is a recording.

Oh, gross, he's listening to self-help mantras in his sleep. What a tool, she thinks, but again, this is good. She has to creep past his open bedroom door. She first takes her phone from her bra and stretches her hand ever so slightly around the corner so the camera catches what's inside.

"He's asleep," Cora's voice comes through her earbuds. "What's he listening to?" she asks then. "Sorry. Shhh. I know, I'll— Sorry."

Paige walks softly past the bedroom door and comes to the second door on the left, which is closed. She has to open it soundlessly. She steadies her breath and turns the knob very slowly, but it still makes a loud click when it opens.

"Shit," she whispers and then cups her mouth. She didn't mean to say that out loud. She slips inside the office and takes long, quiet strides to the open closet and then stands inside of it in case the noise woke Lucas up. She waits.

"What are you doing?" Cora's voice asks. Paige turns the camera around to her face and puts her finger to her mouth, telling Cora to shush. Then she turns the camera to show her the messenger bag on the floor next to his desk. Paige remembers slipping the recorder into a small tear in the lining, which will make it more difficult to get out, but after a minute of standing still and not hearing movement, she goes to the bag and slips her hand inside, feeling for the tear. She finds it.

Her palms are slick with nervous sweat and trembling a little bit as she feels around in the bag lining for the small metal square. She has to make the tear bigger in order to get her wrist through, but she tries to rip it quietly. Then, her fingertips feel what she's looking for, and she pulls it out. She shows it to the camera and hears them cheer through her earbuds. That was loud: they suck at this. If she were closer to him, that could have been a problem. She doesn't bother shushing them. She slips the recorder in her bra and wishes she had thought to wear something with pockets, and then she pads gently to the office door and waits and listens again.

There is still mostly silence, with the whisper of the trickling stream and mantras coming from his room, but she doesn't hear any creaks or footsteps, so she starts to creep down the hall. And then she hears a toilet flush, and she freezes. She hears Cora and Nicola gasp.

She doesn't know whether to run or stay still in the hall— both feel dangerous—but before she has time to decide, she sees it. His frame in the doorway. A black silhouette, backlit by the bathroom light. He steps out of the shadow and stares right at her. She screams and tries to run past him. She takes advantage of his moment of shock and slips by, but he's right behind her. She hears him say, "What the fuck?" and "Who are you?" as she tries to outrun him down the upstairs hall. She can see the staircase. If she could just get herself down the stairs, she might be okay.

But she feels him grab her shirt from behind, and it stops her cold. Her shirt chokes her around the neck with a violent yank of his hand, and she falls to the ground.

Paige can hear the unhelpful instructions in her ear from Cora and Nicola telling her to run, as if she's not trying. He's so much bigger than her that she doesn't know what her next move should be. She scrambles to her knees and starts to crawl away, desperately trying to catch her breath.

"Who the fuck are you? Hey! Hey! What are doing here?" he demands, following her. Easily only a few steps behind her. There is nowhere for her to run.

"What do you want?" he says, his face red and spit flying from his mouth. He grabs her off the floor by her hair, and her earbuds rip out and catch in his grip. She lets out a howl and kicks at him. She swings at his face with her nails to prevent him from taking off her mask, but she can't make contact. He's too strong, and he keeps her at arm's length with his fist still holding her hair. Then she kicks him between the legs as hard as she can, and when he doubles over, screaming "Bitch!" at her, she runs past him and down the stairs. It doesn't stop him. He muscles through the pain and follows her down. She sees the door, she races in that direction, but he catches her near the bottom of the stairs. Again, he pulls her hair, and she wrenches backward and falls the last few stairs until she lies flat on the marble-tiled floor.

She's glad the earbuds were ripped out because the constant screaming on the other end was only distracting. She feels for the pepper spray around her wrist and holds it in her palm. She feels the thrashing pain up the side of her leg where her pants were torn and the skin was scraped off as she hit the sharp edge of each stair. She feels a bump forming on her head where it hit the ground, but even though she can get up, she stays still a moment. He'll think he has her.

She doesn't feel him looming over her. In fact, he's not near her. He's across the front room, fumbling in a locked drawer. And then she realizes it: she should have run. He pulls out a small revolver and comes over to her, pointing it at her forehead. She lost her chance.

"I have every right to kill an intruder," he says, a coldness in his eyes that makes her shudder, that makes her feel like he hopes that's how this goes down because he wanted to be forced to use his gun. She suppresses a whimper. She uses one hand and her heel to try and push herself backward, away from him across the floor.

"Don't even think about moving." he says and stares at her, waiting for something. "Say something, goddamn it! Is this about Georgia?" he says, leaning over, getting close to her face. He searches her eyes, trying to identify her behind the misshapen ski mask, but before he can grab it off her, she takes her shot. She aims the pepper spray in his eyes and hits him with it. He involuntarily drops the gun as his hands fly up to his face.

This time, he can't see to stop her. She pushes herself up onto her hands and knees, painfully but quickly, and lunges for the front door. She pulls it open with shaking hands, leaving her shoes behind as she runs down the front steps and sprints when she hits the footpath in front of the house.

She doesn't think it's safe to run back to Cora and Nicola in case any eyes are on her, so she runs to her own home. She slips herself between the bushes and the siding of her house, ducks into the shadows, and takes off the mask as fast as she's able. Once she reaches the back garden, she pushes herself inside her back door to safety. She locks it behind her and turns off the lights, praying there was no way he was able to see well enough to track her.

She pulls out her phone, knowing Cora and Nicola will be in full panic. The FaceTime session has been ended somewhere amid the struggle, so she texts Cora.

I got out. I'm home. Not safe to come there now, but I got it. Will bring it over tomorrow.

She doesn't wait for a response, and she doesn't have the energy to explain any further. They know she's safe and out, and so she turns her phone volume down and goes upstairs, even though she can already picture the hundred texts and missed calls she'll wake up to. She didn't expect this to happen. She just can't explain right now. She has no energy left. She makes a small slit with her fingers in the bedroom drapes so she can look down at the Kinneys' house. The lights are still on. The front door is closed, though. She left it open. She sees him close the front blinds and turn out the lights and she exhales.

She runs a scalding-hot bath and lowers her aching body into the water. Her nerve endings are still filled with electricity, and she tries to take a few deep breaths and calm down. She thinks again of Grant. Wishing he were here right now—a thought that hadn't crossed her mind in a long time. She wishes he were waiting outside the door with a cup of tea and her robe and that she could hold him as long as she wanted, for years if that's what it took until everything was better. But she's pushed him so far away, she doesn't even know him anymore.

Then she thinks of Caleb. She thinks of him most of the time, but after what she's just been through, she sees what she has imagined his last moments to be with fresh eyes. Did he feel that same terror? Did he think he was going to die alone? Her poor baby. She would do anything in the whole world to take that pain away from him, to have it be her who died that night.

"My baby," she whispers into the dark emptiness around her and then leans her head against the porcelain edge of the tub and lets out a wail, and then the sobs come in waves she can't control. It should have been her.

27

CORA

Finn comes out of the downstairs guest room with a towel around his waist and a toothbrush hanging out of his mouth. I sip my morning coffee and watch as he huffs down the hall, swearing under his breath. He goes to the master bedroom for a change of clothes. The police have asked him to come down and answer a few questions, and he's absolutely livid.

He hasn't spoken to me since I confronted him, and the childishness of that and the speed with which decades of marriage can disintegrate are appalling. He blames me for finding out rather than blaming himself for the sin. I don't know why I always thought that if I caught him, he'd cry and beg me to stay. That we'd go into couples counseling and he'd change his ways, and maybe that would have happened if he was caught in a one-night stand that supposedly meant nothing, but the amount of evidence I presented him with—I guess he knows that there is nothing he can say to change it.

Not that he'd beg and cry for me. He'd be upset about the money he'd lose because of the prenup, but he'd pretend he was upset about losing me. I've woken up, and he can tell, so instead, he's acting like a petulant child, and it actually tickles me to see him squirm.

I don't think he's a killer, though. No matter how shocking Paige's evidence is, deep down I have to believe that he made a series of bad choices, just like he did with me. But ultimately, the money transfer, the texts, all of that was based on a stupid, drug-related relationship. I've realized that I don't know him very well at all, so maybe I'm wrong, but I can't let myself believe it.

I'm edgy and fidgety until he leaves the house. His presence is agitating, and the weight of all that is to come with divorce lawyers and legal battles is exhausting to even think about. So I try not to. I try to stay in the moment and take it in steps. They will question him; they will release him. He'll blame me for all the humiliation. Then what? He goes to a hotel? Stop. I need to let it go right now. I dump the last bit of my coffee into the sink. I don't need to be any more jittery. Then I put together breakfast to take out to Nicola.

A couple hours later, I'm stopped in my tracks by the ping of my phone and a text from Paige.

Get Nicola and Avery out of the house! Now! And all their things!

"Holy shit!" I mutter to myself, leaping up from my seat on the sofa and rushing to gather my coat and keys. I don't ask why; I just spring into action.

Nicola jumps and clutches her chest when I barge into the guesthouse.

"I'm sorry! But there's no time. We gotta go right now," I say, running around the space, pushing baby clothes and toiletries into a pillowcase I tear off the pillow on the bed. Nicola doesn't ask why. We just move.

"Hide in the back of the car, like before. I'll get the rest," I say, handing her the keys, and she nods and quickly picks up Avery and goes out to the car. I throw everything I see into the pillowcase and a few reusable bags I'd used to bring her food. Contact lenses, makeup, shoes, plastic baby books, even open water bottles and the dirty dishes in the sink. It can't look like anyone has been here. I don't know why I'm doing this, so I don't know how much time I have, but the adrenaline fuels me, and I toss the bags into the back hatch next to Nicola and the baby.

"What's happened?" she asks, once we are out of the space.

"I don't know yet, but let's go," I say, covering her and the bags with fleece blankets and rushing to the driver's side. I pull out carefully, and as soon as I make it off our street, I feel a flood of relief. I keep driving and call Paige.

"Paige," I say when she answers.

"Are you out?" she says, urgently.

"Yes, we're all in the car, and I'm driving. What the hell happened?"

"There's a search warrant for your house."

"What?" I ask. My chest tightens, and I feel suddenly lightheaded.

"You should all come here. If they search the house, they'll definitely search that mother-in-law unit and find her," Paige says, but I cut her off.

"Wait. Back up. Why are they searching my house?"

"Finn," she says. "They arrested him. He called to tell me because you won't answer his calls."

"He called you?"

"I'm pretty sure I was his last choice. He said as few words as possible and hung up on me, but ultimately, the message is to tell you to pick up the goddamn phone. But right now, Cor, just get out of there."

"No. What—oh, my God. But...a warrant?"

"He said he didn't know Caleb well. Caleb has never been in his car or house, but I guess with everything we gave them, they thought they had enough evidence to think Finn was lying, because they issued a search warrant for both house and car. Just get here. She can stay with me," Paige says and hangs up.

There is just no way. This can't be happening. He's a total fraud, but not a murderer. I feel sick. I pull up behind Paige's house. She opens the garage for me to pull in so we can get Nicola in through the attached door to the house without her being seen.

Once we're all inside, Paige takes Avery and sits with her on the couch while we bring Nicola's squashed belongings into the back guest bedroom. When we return to the living room, I'm surprised to see the way Paige seems to change around the baby. I know she lived for her son, but I didn't know her when he was small, and she doesn't exactly exude a maternal, nurturing side in general, so the way her face changes with Avery is remarkable. She looks like the woman I knew before Caleb died, and even in the midst of all of this crisis, it's heartening to see, even for a minute.

"I don't know when they'll search, but you can't take any chances."

"Thank you," Nicola says, obviously shaken.

"I would have come by earlier this morning, but the police had a few more questions. But that's for you," Paige says, nodding toward the kitchen. The tiny recording device is connected to a laptop on the kitchen table across the room.

"I only listened to a few minutes to make sure it worked. I don't need to invade your privacy, so you can take a listen, and if you find what we need, just mark down the time on the recording," she says, and Nicola gives a hesitant nod. She stands and walks slowly to the laptop as if it could hurt her. She sits in the chair in front of it and lets out a long, forced breath to prepare herself. Paige follows her in with the baby on her hip. She hands her the connected headphones.

"It's just Play and Stop here. And you can fast-forward if you want to skim, and since you don't want to take a hundred and ninety-two hours to do this, I'd try skimming it first."

"Okay," Nicola says, putting the headphones on and staring at the screen, which is nothing but squiggly audio lines that look like a heart EKG.

My phone buzzes. It's a local number calling. It's probably the police station. They would have taken Finn's phone. Do they really only let you make one call, or is that a TV-show thing? I don't know, but I don't care, and I don't want to hear what he has to say, so I push Ignore.

Yes, I do care. As soon as I have tapped the dismissal, I feel tears climb my throat. This man I have loved for years and years is in jail, and I am cutting off his lifeline by ignoring him. It's not fair. I should get to hate him right now and not feel sorry for him. But he has friends, and he has family, I decide. I'm not his safety net anymore. Then I stand and go to the stove and heat water for tea while Paige finds a bright cartoon with colorful ponies that spark Avery's interest. And we wait.

An hour later, Paige and I watch police pull up to my house. Mia is at the library researching a school project, and I hadn't thought about someone needing to be there. Did Finn give them keys? Would they break down the door?

"Go," she says, and I grab a cup of coffee to try to look casual. I walk out Paige's front door and attempt to walk slowly. I don't know why I think appearing normal when the police are at my house to search it is the right strategy, but I have never experienced this before. I walk up to the front door where three officers are standing.

"Hey there, officers." My God, why am I talking like this?

"Is this your property? Are you Mrs. Holmon?" asks the officer with a cliché buzz cut and *Top Gun* sunglasses.

"Yes, what can I do for you?" I ask, not knowing if I am supposed to feign surprise.

"We have a warrant to search the property," he says, looking not at me but down at a clipboard. He shows me a sheet of paper that I glance at. I see one officer already behind the house, poking around in the yard. I know we left in plenty of time, but it still makes my heart quicken thinking about what might have happened if Finn hadn't called Paige.

"Ah, okay. So, do I let you in or…" I have no idea what I'm supposed to do or say.

"That would make it easier on us all, yeah," says the older cop, who has a beer belly and a graying goatee. And I realize that, in my haste, I hadn't even locked the door. I turn the knob, push it open, and stand aside. I don't follow them in. I sit in a rocker recliner on the porch, watching them come in and out.

My home was a sanctuary at one time. When we first got married, I remember feeling like I was living a fairy tale in this big house. Over the years, it became more my own with each room I painted, each carefully placed piece of artwork on the wall, every candle or lamp for which I found a perfect spot. The kitchen I designed when we remodeled. And, especially, every milestone Mia has had. Her soccer trophies that line the mantel, her junior-high dance where she's pictured in braces standing next to her date, Johnny Algers, in front of the piano, the Christmases she's buried in wrapping paper at the base of the tree. Now, it all feels violated. My husband has become a stranger, a foe, overnight, and now strangers are invading our safe space like it's a crime scene.

They don't take much for all the mess and chaos they cause. Just his precious laptop he accused me of stealing. They already have the files, day planner, and his phone, I'm sure. They don't tell me if they found anything else they were looking for, and I don't ask. After less than two hours, they are driving away.

When I go back to Paige's, she is alone with Avery, feeding her graham crackers on the floor of the living room. Nicola isn't there.

"What happened? Where is she?" I ask.

"Lying down in the guest room," Paige says, wiping crumbs from Avery's cheek with her finger and stroking her wispy hair.

"Did she find it?" I ask, and Paige just nods. A solemn, sad gesture.

"God," I say, closing my eyes and shaking my head. "She had you listen, I take it," I say, and Paige nods. No further elaboration needed. I've already heard all the stories. I don't want to hear them again on the recording. It's too much.

"Did they find anything at your house?" Paige asks.

"I don't know," I say. "Is she gonna be okay?"

"I don't know."

We sit quietly in the living room, playing with Avery and finding kids' shows for her until night falls. Then I go to the kitchen and take out a packet of instant rice and put it in the microwave. I find some chicken and heat up a pan to fry it. Nobody has spoken in hours. Nicola is still in bed. It feels like the world has stopped. In the dark kitchen, I make up a few plates and bring them to the table. Paige wakes Nicola up, and we sit around the table, Paige still with Avery attached to her lap. Nobody eats.

"I think we should bring this to the police tomorrow," Paige says.

"I can take it," I say. "They don't have to know where Nicola and Avery are."

"I should take it," Paige says. "They already know why I would have found it, that I gather dirt on all the neighbors. Now they are actually taking me seriously."

"Yeah, that makes sense, I guess. And she should stay here, probably. Safer not to move her," I say.

"So you're better off here tonight, okay?" she says to Nicola, probably so it doesn't seem like we're talking about her like she's not in the room, which we have been.

"Okay," she says. She looks smaller and completely defeated now. How could anyone blame her? She stares at a photo of Caleb on the wall, and everything feels so hopeless. The room feels void of oxygen.

"We need them to investigate and find her documents, to prove it without any doubt. Will this audio do that?" I ask, since I'm the only one who hasn't heard it. Nicola drops her head. I look to Paige. She nods.

"Yeah. It will."

Before I go home, I help Nicola tuck Avery into the makeshift crib we've made out of couch pillows, and then I squeeze her hand.

"You got him. We're almost there. You don't have to worry anymore," I say, but even though she nods in agreement, she looks more distraught than the moment she told me everything.

"Good night," I say and walk out Paige's back door, taking

the long way around the block back to my house just to be safe, again feeling like I've been beaten up by the day.

When I walk in the back door, the place is a mess. It's not like you see on TV where it looks like the place has been robbed and ransacked exactly, but they certainly don't close cupboards and drawers behind them. I muster the energy to clean it up before Mia gets home, then I pour a large glass of red wine, and before I can sit down, she is bounding in the door.

"Oh, hey, Mom." She grabs a backpack and stuffs her iPad and makeup that was sitting on an end table into it. "Bye!"

"Wait! You just walked in the door. Where are you going this late?"

"Mom. It's like ten? And I'm staying at Chelsea's tonight. I just have to get my things. You said."

"I did?"

"And where's Dad?" she asks. The question feels like a punch. I've been so immersed in it all, I haven't had time to really remember how much this is going to destroy her. It's not the time now, though.

"Uh…he's out."

"'Kay. Bye?" she says.

"Fine. Go."

I'm too exhausted to argue. I have no idea if I said it was okay or not, and it's not worth the energy to challenge it. I don't know if she should be here, anyway. She grabs her things and runs out to her friend's car. I don't know if I should tell her anything. Isn't it better she just thinks he's a selfish bastard who does recreational drugs with other women, not possibly a murderer? I don't think I should tell her the truth. Not yet.

I walk past her room. All the lights are on, the TV is on, and the floor is covered in makeup pallets and clothes, her school bag upside down with books piled around it. A blow-dryer, still plugged in, sits in a pile of cheap silver bangles, tangled in necklace chains and hair bands. I ache with exhaustion, but I go in and turn off her TV and unplug the still-hot dryer. I turn off the lamp next to her bed, and before I leave, I notice her open laptop on her desk. She just left, so it hasn't timed out yet. I go to close the lid, and if I'm being honest, take a quick glance at her desktop while I have the rare opportunity.

I almost click the computer shut, but then a folder catches my eye. I can't make sense of it. It says *Caleb*. Right there on her screen, a tiny yellow folder icon with his name on it. What the hell could that be? Photos from when she had a crush on him, probably. I quickly swipe my finger across the mouse pad to keep the desktop alive. I stare at the icon, weighing the invasion of privacy against my instinct to protect her, if she's somehow mixed up in this, if she's protecting Finn, maybe. Oh, God.

I click it open quickly, looking over my shoulder, even though I'd hear her if she'd come back inside. When I open it, I see it's a video. I feel sweat bead on my forehead, and my heart is hammering. I click Play.

I think my heart stops momentarily when I see it. I fight the blur of tears that obscures my vision. How can this be? Why does she have this?

It's Caleb. He's lying on the ground by the entrance to the neighborhood. It's dark. He's hurt. Who's recording this?

He's lying still but breathing. Then I hear Mia's voice. This just cannot be what I'm seeing.

"Oh, my God!" Mia's voice says. "Call— Oh, my— Jesus, call for help." And then sirens are heard in the background.

"Let's get outta here!" a male voice says, but who is it?

"What?" I watch Mia step into the frame of the camera and kneel next to Caleb. The arm of the man she's with pulls her away, but I still can't tell who it is.

"Help is coming. We can't be here," the man says, and then the video stops. Pinpricks of heat climb my spine, and I play it again. I can't understand it. What does this mean? She was there and never told anyone. Why? Why would she keep this a secret when it looks like she tried to help? Dear God, is Mia involved in this? Is she a murderer? Is that what's been wrong with her all this time? I want to throw up. I stand up and try to steady my breath. I run my hands through my hair. I tremble. What does this mean? Mia hit Caleb? That doesn't make sense. She seems like she's trying to help. Something isn't right.

I watch it a third time. Then again. By the sixth time I watch, I see something that changes everything. I email the video to myself. I cannot believe what I have seen. It's not Finn. Finn didn't kill Caleb.

28

NICOLA

When I hear the rap on the door, I'm sure that it's Lucas, that he's found me. Before I can rush to Avery and pick her up and try to run, I see it's Cora—the second time today she's almost given me a heart attack. She lets herself in, and I sit at the edge of the bed and bend over, holding my chest, trying to regain my composure. My ribs ache, as I try to calm and slow my breath.

"I'm sorry. God. I didn't mean to— I'm sorry, I wouldn't have done that if it wasn't an emergency," she says.

"Oh, my God. What? What's going on? How did you even get in here?" I say in a loud whisper, so as not to wake Avery.

"I have a spare key to Paige's house. I didn't want to wake her, but I had to talk to you right now. There's a video," she says; she can barely catch her breath.

"Slow down. What—what do you mean? What are you talking about?"

"There's a video of Caleb," she says, and I feel like I'm supposed to know what that means. "Someone was there— they took a video after he got hit. It's— He was dying. God," she says, and tears spring to her eyes. "He had been hit, and there's a video."

"Wha—what are you saying? I don't understand. Who was there? Who took a video—of what?"

"It was Mia. But that's not the point right now. I don't know why she didn't tell anyone, but that's not... She pulled up right after he was hit. Someone in the car with her turned the camera on the whole thing, but the point is there is a car. Just...look," she says, and my palms go clammy, and I swallow hard, waiting to see what she's going to show me. She opens her phone, goes to her email, and pulls up a video. I cup my mouth with my hand when I see him lying there. I suck in my breath, wanting to turn away. I see Mia come into the frame, and Cora pauses the video. I look at her, still not understanding.

"Look." She points to something in the frame. "There's a car racing from the scene right when Mia pulls up, before she even knew it was *a scene* at all, obviously. Look. It's your car—it's the BMW. Those are your plates!" she says, with a mixture of horror and excitement. She waits for a reaction, and I feel like my lungs have filled with water. Bile rises in my throat, and an electric shock pulses through me. Then the tears fall, and I have no way to stop them. This is it. This is how it all ends. The evidence is right in front of me. There is no way out of this anymore. I'm caught. It's on video. Lying can't help me now.

"Please. Please, Cora, you have to understand that it wasn't intentional. I never meant to kill him. That's not what happened," I say, and she stands frozen with her mouth open. Her eyes narrow in confusion, and it feels like she stays that way for a very long time. The silence in the room rings in my ears as I wait for her to speak.

"I said your car, but I— No, I meant—I was saying a general *your* family car, but I meant Lucas. I didn't mean— Oh, my God. Nicola. What are you saying?"

I realize my mistake, but it's too late to swallow the words back. It's the most careless move I've made, but on the other hand, the relief of telling someone is profound. And it's too late anyway.

"It's not how it sounds," I say, but Cora is watching the video again on her phone with fresh eyes, trying to understand.

"That's you?" she asks, and I look down at my hands and try to think about how I could possibly explain what happened.

"Please, just please at least listen. Let me tell you what happened before you hate me," I beg. She runs a nervous hand over her mouth and swallows. Her eyes are wide and fearful, but she sits at the very edge of the bed, giving me permission to try to explain.

"I told you once that I gave all my money to a guy in the neighborhood for an ID card, but he screwed me over and used it on drugs. That was Caleb. We knew each other."

"H-how? How is that possible? Like, what? I feel like I've been fooled, like you aren't who you're saying, or— I thought you were being held. I thought—"

"Nothing that I told you has changed! I told you that when I first came here, there were a few months where I thought everything was normal. There was a time I had no idea what was about to happen. He was establishing me in the community in a certain way, grooming me. But in that time, I lived normally. He made me feel like I could make friends, take classes…all normal stuff. I met Caleb one night when I walked over to the park behind our house. I just wanted some fresh air after Lucas fell asleep. I sat on the swings, and he came over and offered me a pull of his joint."

"All this time, all the… Paige getting involved…and she never even knew you knew him? I…" she says.

"I know. How could I tell her?"

"Because you just do, because she's desperate for answers, and how can you—" But I cut her off to explain.

"Caleb and I became friends. I know that seems weird to you, but we are only five years apart in age. Lucas was becoming strange and controlling, and I already knew I wanted out, back when I still thought that was a choice. I was unhappy, and I told Caleb about it, that I wanted to go home. We became… close," I say, and then I feel my face contort into an ugly cry, but I can't let myself break down. She needs to understand. I dig my nails into my palm to keep control.

"How close?" she asks with a judgment in her voice I haven't heard before.

"Very close," I say, quietly.

"Jesus," she mumbles.

"He was a mess, though. You have to believe me. He was an addict. He was selling. It started out small, but he was a full-blown addict, and he did desperate things. I know you don't believe me. Paige thinks he was some honors student, that he was perfect, but he had dropped out of school months before. Paige and Grant were clueless. He was selling their shit for drugs. He was all in. You have to believe me. I swear to God, I'm telling you the truth," I say, and I see in her eyes some sense of familiarity, like she isn't shocked, like it isn't the first time she's heard this.

"I knew about the drugs," she says, and I almost cry with relief. That's something, at least.

"That's why he screwed me on the ID. He needed drug money. He kept trying to get me to give him money, but I couldn't. And then—" I start, but then stop. I want to tell her the worst part—the part she'll never forgive me for—but I don't know how. I go to the small refrigerator and pull out the open bottle of wine and lift it up, looking to her.

"Sure," she says, softening around the edges just a little. I pour two large glasses and take a sip, then sit again.

"This isn't easy to say, but I trust you. I really pray to God you trust me," I say, and I don't look at her because I don't want to see doubt in her eyes, and I need to say this.

"He was strung out all the time. He stayed away from Paige and Grant when he was like that. He was a master at hiding it from them, but he didn't hide it from me. We met all the time when Lucas worked late, but finally, I needed out. It was toxic. He needed rehab. But he wouldn't let it go."

"Let what go? What?" she asks.

"He wanted money from me. I stole as much as I could from Lucas to give it to him, because Caleb threatened me. I gave him the last of the small amount I had myself, then I started selling things, pawning things from around the house that Lucas wouldn't miss, but I was tapped out."

"What do you mean *threatened* you? How? Like threatening your life? What do you mean?"

"Sort of. He didn't know he was threatening my life. I didn't know it at the time either," I say, knowing how evasive that sounds.

"That doesn't make sense."

"He threatened to tell Lucas that the baby I was pregnant with wasn't his," I say, so quietly I'm not sure I actually said it. I hear her sharp intake of breath and see her hand flutter to her lips.

"Oh, my God in heaven. Is that true?" She stands and paces a few steps, then stops and sits, then gets back up. She stares at

me, waiting for something, and then points at Avery. "Is she…
Caleb's?" she asks, in a strange, high-pitched voice.

I want to scream and run out the door. I want to throw up.
It's all imploding, and I can't escape the truth any longer. I nod.

"That's how he was threatening my life. If Lucas found
out that Avery wasn't his baby, he'd kill me, but Caleb didn't
know that," I say, and Cora sits down again. Her face crum-
ples. I see her eyes well, and she shakes her head quickly and
then nods and stands again. I don't know what's happening.
She sits again. I feel dizzy with her anxious movements. She
looks me in the eye.

"That's Paige's granddaughter," she says in the same high-
pitched, emotional squeak.

"She can't know that," I say, much louder than I mean
to, and we both look at Avery, who, thankfully, doesn't stir.
Cora doesn't rebut this right away. She regroups and tries to
stay calm.

"I don't understand. Why— What happened to Caleb?
What did you do?"

"He thought I had money just because Lucas does. He
wouldn't believe me when I told him I couldn't access it. He
wanted more. I was just driving home that night. Lucas was
out with Finn, having drinks or whatever, so I went out, too.
Nothing interesting—I saw a movie—and then when I drove
in, he was there. He flagged me down," I say, and the memory of it steals my breath. I remember seeing him and feeling
a longing: I wanted him to be clean. I hoped we'd sit on the
swings and talk the way we used to. I just wanted him to be
okay, to be stable, to be the person I could run away with. He
was so amazing when he wasn't high, but he was that night.

"I saw him there," I say, "standing in the rain. He was crying, he was totally fucked up—higher than I'd ever seen him.
I rolled down the window and asked if he was okay. He was

angry. He was apologizing, saying he just wanted to talk, but when I realized the state he was in, I said I needed to get home. He demanded money. I said again that I didn't have any. And that's when he pulled a gun," I say, and I start to shake.

Cora puts her hands on top of mine to steady them.

"The gun at the scene they never figured out. That was his?" she asks.

"I don't know where he got it. It was untraceable, I read in the paper. No prints, probably because he was wearing gloves. It was winter, it was cold, and with the people he ran with, keeping his prints off an illegal gun was probably something he knew to do. They never figured out what the gun and the hit-and-run had to do with each other. It never made sense," I say.

"But it never was a hit-and-run," Cora says in stunned disbelief.

"He pointed it at me," I say. "He even cocked it. He was high as a kite and ready to shoot. He wasn't the real Caleb, he was the high-on-coke Caleb. He was screaming at me, demanding I give him money or he'd kill me. He'd been on a bender for a few days. He was out of his mind. Then—I couldn't believe it—but he fired. He was so shaky and messed up, he missed by a mile, but then he cocked the gun again and used both hands to position it, aimed at me, so I just..." I can't stop the wail creeping up my throat. "I just pushed on the gas!" I cry. "I thought about the baby. I knew he wasn't himself, and he was ready to kill me. Cora, you have to believe that I did the only thing I could. There was no reasoning with him. There was nowhere to run. He had the gun cocked and pointed at my head. I never thought the impact would kill him. I was just trying to protect us. That's all I've done since I've been in this fucking country—I was just trying to stay alive," I say and then double over, sobbing.

I don't know what to expect from her. If she hadn't already

had the shock of her life, now she has. She clasps her hands together in fists and rests her forehead on them. She stays that way for some time.

"I need to think," she finally says, and without another word, without making eye contact or giving any indication of what she's thinking and what she plans to do, she's gone.

29

PAIGE

Paige stands in the dark kitchen with her mouth open, frozen, unable to speak. She's holding a glass of water she never brought to her lips because when she came down to get it, she heard Cora's voice coming through the baby monitor Nicola left on the kitchen island when Avery was napping upstairs earlier.

At first, she couldn't put together why she was hearing Cora's voice in the baby monitor, and she'd thought she was dreaming, but then she stood still and listened.

The words she was hearing didn't fit together. The characters in the story Nicola was telling were all wrong. Finn hit Caleb, not Nicola. Caleb was the victim, not the villain. What was happening? Her first instinct was to run into Nicola's room and lunge at her, pin her down and rip the flesh from her face with her fingernails and scream for Caleb until her chest burned and her eyes blurred and she was hoarse from his name in her mouth.

She can't do that. Avery. Somewhere in between her rage and confusion, she tries to let the weight of that one detail settle in. Avery is Caleb's. Her head swims. Caleb needed help, and she didn't know. He was in trouble. He was a criminal? He wasn't who she thought he was. The pain of this is unbearable, suffocating.

Nicola could have stopped all these months of agony and searching and not knowing, but…how could she? Can Paige blame Nicola, now that she knows what was happening to her? Yes, she decides, she can. She's overwhelmed with anger. She needs someone to blame. She *has* someone to blame. She's not sure, though. Could Caleb have been that unhinged addict Nicola described? How could Paige have never known any of that? What kind of mother would be so blind to all of it?

She needs to sit, to breathe. She needs to think, but she is still frozen in shock with a glass of water vise-gripped in her hand and her eyes wide and unblinking. She thinks about Finn in jail and wonders how she could have gotten it so wrong. She thinks again about Caleb and how he wasn't faultless. She's drowning in thoughts that are coming too fast to process.

Her shock shifts into something else, a slow realization of the truth. The items in the room around her don't look real. Her head feels light, and she feels like her knees will buckle from the sudden dizziness. Her hands quiver violently, and before she can put down her glass of water, she loses control of it, and it falls to the ground and shatters.

Nicola appears from the bedroom immediately to see what the crash was. Paige stares at her—the woman who killed her son.

"What happened? Are you okay?" Nicola asks.

"It was you."

30

CORA

I resort to taking a muscle relaxant. After the last few days, sleep refuses to come, and I feel like if I'm forced to know one more horrific thing against my will, it could literally kill me if I can't get at least a small amount of sleep first. The ceiling fan is off, and Finn is gone, and I feel more desperately alone than I ever thought possible. They say feeling alone with someone else is worse than really being alone, but right now, I don't know.

After just a few hours of sleep, my anxiety wakes me up. My mind is racing, but the medicine makes me feel sluggish and groggy. Still, I force myself to the coffee maker and start a pot, then I text Mia to come home right away. When she responds asking why, I just text back, Now, and to my surprise, by the time I finish my first cup of coffee, she's pulling into the driveway.

She sprints into the house, dropping her stuff, and stops cold when she sees me at the kitchen island, looking her up and down.

"What's the freakin' emergency?" she asks, and I look at her in her stupid pajamas and beautiful, unkempt hair she got from me, and her innocent face, and I wish I could take away what she saw that night, but I can't, and she's almost an adult, and she needs to answer for what happened. I ask her to sit down, and she does. Then I turn my phone around and play her the video. Her face goes pale and ghostly.

"Oh, my God! Why are you going through my stuff?" she says, and I see her eyes dart, her mind racing for an explanation.

"No. You don't get to say that now—not about this." I smack my phone down on the counter and look at her. "Why, after all we've been through with Paige searching, with Caleb, with— Why would you hide this?"

She stares at the floor.

"Mia," I say. She keeps her head down.

"I wanted to help him. We were just coming home and saw him. I was gonna call the police, but we heard them coming, so…"

"Who's *we*?" I ask, sharply.

"Ryan," she says. The boyfriend I thought she was moping over all this time after they broke up. I guess she was carrying something much bigger than that.

"You didn't call the police or tell me or anyone else because you heard sirens coming? That doesn't add up." I think about Caleb in the video. Unmoving, eyes open. The fear he must have felt. Even though I know he was high, and I know Nicola had to protect herself, it wasn't the real him. Maybe Finn could have helped him instead of buying drugs off him.

My heart breaks for Caleb, and I'm furious at how so many secrets built this fortress around the truth.

"Ryan got some pills. Some…"

"Some what? What does that have to do with anything?"

"Some Molly," she says, not making eye contact.

"What the hell does that mean?"

"Mom."

"It's a drug. You're telling me you were on drugs?"

"I promise, I never did it again. I hated it. I was so sick the next day. He had a party in his basement. He said it would be fun just one time. Mom, if we called the police, my life would be over!" Now she starts to cry. "The police were coming, and there was nothing I could do, so I listened to him when he said we had to get out of there."

"So you not only took the drug, but let a completely high kid drive you home?"

"Mom, I'm sorry. It never happened again. That was almost a year ago, and I've never touched anything since then. I promise. I thought I'd never go to college, I'd have a record—I didn't know what would happen, but I couldn't tell. And I didn't know Ryan recorded it. He sent the video to me. He thought it was cool he had it, and I broke up with him—that's why, 'cause he was such a creep about it," she says, and then walks over to the sink and pulls a paper towel from the roll to wipe the streaks of mascara from her cheeks.

"Why did you keep the video?" I ask. She throws the towel away and takes another, blotting it under her eyes, then sits back on the stool and sighs.

"I didn't know if Ryan would try to get revenge. He was angry about the breakup. I didn't even know what he would do—give details about the scene, somehow point the finger at me. I just kept it, I guess, because it proves I tried to help and that he was the one trying to leave the scene and the one driving in case anyone thought *we* hit Caleb…" She's rambling. I pick up my phone and find the video.

"Look at this again," I say, and she does.

"Okay? What?"

"That car. Do you remember seeing it drive off?" I ask, and she watches it again.

"Yeah, I guess."

"You guess?"

"Yes. I remember, because my first instinct was to flag it down for help, but it must have not seen him because it was driving past, I guess," she says, and I take in a deep breath and blow it out hard through my lips.

"Are they gonna arrest me?" she whimpers and starts crying again. I stand and put my arms around her, pressing her head into my chest. "I'm sorry. I should have told you. The news said someone heard a gunshot and called the police, but Caleb was dead before the police got there, so I knew there was nothing I could have done. Mom, if there was—if the ambulance weren't coming, I would have said something—I would have stayed!" She's sobbing now. I hold her close to me.

"Shhh. They're not going to arrest you, okay? I promise. But there will be a lot of questions. We have to turn this in," I say, and she pulls away, horror on her face.

"Why?"

"I can't explain it all to you right now, but I can promise that you're not in trouble," I say, even though I want to rage and tell her how sitting on this all this time left Paige drowning in pain—the not knowing, the suspicion of everyone—but on the other hand, if she had turned it in before, there'd probably be another life lost—Nicola's. So at this point, it's a damn good thing she didn't.

"Hang out at home today, okay?" I say, and she nods obediently and hops off the stool and walks toward her room without another word, happy to be done with the conversation.

I sit in the stillness of the kitchen. I look across at the windows and watch the wind whip the fallen leaves into spirals on the sidewalk. I cross to the gas fireplace and turn it on, then sit in front of it, staring into the artificial embers. Finn sits in jail for something he didn't do, and we can't turn in the person who did do it. What have we done?

31

PAIGE

Later that morning, Cora and Nicola sit in Paige's living room, each holding a coffee cup on their lap as the sun peeks through the sheers on the windows and bathes the room in yellow light. Paige takes a sip from her mug and stares out into the yard. After Cora explains Mia's video, nobody speaks for a very long time.

Nicola cried and pleaded apologies in hiccuped sobs all night, and in the back of Paige's mind, she felt so much pity for the poor thing. Nicola's done what she needed to defend herself, to protect Avery. Paige's logical, reasonable side knew this, but she still harbored an irrational bitterness she tried to suppress. She should have offered forgiveness to put Nicola out of her misery after everything she'd already been through, but Paige just sat numb through most of Nicola's explanation, which only reiterated what she'd already overheard.

Nicola's face is red, and her eyes swollen and bloodshot. She dots at her eyes with a tissue now and then, and Cora just looks down at her lap. Nobody knows what to say next. The air is heavy and charged with one question: Will Paige turn her in? What other choice is there? Finn is a son of a bitch who Cora thinks deserves a few nights in jail but obviously can't be charged with murder. Well, sometimes she thinks that might not be so bad, if she's honest, but no. They need to figure a way out of this mess.

Paige stands and goes to the kitchen. She pulls a bottle of vodka out of the freezer and brings it back to the living room, pouring a generous portion into her coffee. Then she holds it up asking if anyone else wants any.

"It's—" Cora starts to say, but her words get caught and she clears her throat. "It's eight in the morning," she says. Nicola holds up her mug, and Paige splashes some in and then pours some in Cora's anyway before she can protest. She then sits on the edge of her armchair, takes a chug, and looks at them.

"We have no choice but to go to the police and let them know that Lucas killed Caleb and we have the video to prove it," she says, confidently. Nicola shrieks, and Cora sits speechless, so Paige goes on.

"He is responsible. It's his fault his wife was pushed to find safety in someone else. It's his fault she couldn't tell anyone who her baby really belonged to. It's his fault we suffered all this time because he kept her captive and she couldn't tell the truth about what happened to Caleb. As she said a thousand times last night, she would have explained it all to the police right when it happened if doing so wouldn't have gotten her killed. Lucas is to blame. But all of that is second to why he really needs to go away forever. What he did to Nicola is un-thinkable. That alone justifies this, but if we don't put him away and it's discovered Nicola was involved instead…"

"Then, he'd get Avery," Nicola says flatly, following where Paige is going.

"And that can't happen. Over my fucking dead body will that happen," Paige says. Cora pours another splash of vodka into her coffee and leans back in her chair, sipping it, her eyes darting between Paige and Nicola.

"The video shows him fleeing the scene, but they think if it's an accidental hit-and-run, he could be out—"

Paige doesn't let her finish. "We have motive. He found out Caleb was the father. And we have the audio recording that proves he was holding you against your will. We have your testimony that backs up the audio—that you were being held—and they'll investigate and find the room in the basement, the excessive surveillance, all of it."

"But it could go wrong," Nicola says, still dotting at her eyes, panic in her voice. "Men like him get out all the time with a slap on the wrist for abuse. And what if they don't believe the motive? What if it looks like an accidental hit-and-run and this blows up and he gets out and finds me? You think he wanted me dead for getting away? Imagine what will happen after I put him in jail and—" She stops talking suddenly.

"What?" Cora asks, taken aback by Nicola's sudden blank stare and colorless face.

"That means I have to tell them about Avery. He still doesn't know. Oh, God, he'll know about Avery—that she's not his. Oh, my God," she says, placing her head in her hands.

"Yes. That's motive!" Paige says. "So listen. Just listen. What is the alternative? You tell the truth without pointing the finger at him and get arrested yourself? At least he'll be the one arrested and you'll be protected."

"We'll get a protection order," Cora agrees quickly.

"I've seen the movies. They don't work," Nicola says.

"Then, we all absolutely have to be on the same page and

make sure we do everything we can to get him put away. This is what happened. You told him about Avery—and Caleb. He *does* know. Got it?" Paige says, going to Nicola's side and lifting her head up to meet her eyes.

"Right," Nicola agrees.

"He found out a few days earlier, before the hit-and-run, and then that night, they saw Caleb on the way into the community entrance, and he dropped Finn off and went back. Okay? Lucas was going to confront Caleb. Caleb tried to protect himself with the gun, but Lucas—"

"Got him first," Nicola says, and they look at each other.

"Yes," Paige says.

"Yes." Nicola nods in agreement. "Okay," she says, starting to see that this story is pretty tight. Something in her eyes changes: a darkness lifts. She finally has real, concrete leverage. She's so close to freedom. She pulls on her bottom lip, stands, and paces, looking around the room.

"He'll be arrested first. We have to make sure they have audio—the proof that nails him. They have to have him in custody with all that other evidence, too, before I tell anyone about Avery."

"We will," Paige confirms, and Cora vigorously nods her head.

"Okay, then…then, we should do it now. Before there is any more risk that he'll find me."

"We will, but I think we need one more thing for this to work," Paige says. "We need Finn to be in on pointing to Lucas. He'll seal it all if he says Lucas dropped him off at ten."

"No! How?" Nicola asks.

"They record everything in jail. You can't tell him to lie. It could ruin everything," Cora echoes, confused. "Finn drove that night. What if he already said so?"

"He probably did," Paige says, "but he can say he lied because he was trying to protect his friend. There is so much evidence against Lucas with this video that Finn's lie will be one of the last things for them to worry about. Cora will go and visit him, have a talk."

"Okaaay..." Cora says, with wide eyes and uncertainty in her voice.

"She won't tell him to lie. Just trust me. I have a plan," Paige says. And what other choice is there really? So they all agree, each of them terrified of the fallout.

32

CORA

After they take all my personal belongings and wave a metal-detector wand around my body, there is paperwork. I didn't know what to expect visiting a jail. I thought it would be like the movies I've seen, and I'd have to sit across from Finn through plexiglass and talk on an old-looking phone receiver. That's not how it is. I'm escorted to a room that looks like a small cafeteria. I sit on a green plastic chair at a small table and watch them bring him into the room. He's in a jumpsuit. I had forgotten about that, and seeing him looking so submissive and afraid makes me feel pity for him despite how little he deserves it.

He sits across from me. His eyes are pleading.

"Cora, I—I didn't do this. I know you hate me. I know, but you gotta believe me," he says, with a hopelessness and despair I've never seen before—not in all the years of ups and downs. He's never looked like this. There is still a small part of me that wants to walk away and let him suffer, but just because he's a terrible husband and shit human being doesn't mean he deserves this.

"I know. I believe you," I say, and his eyes shift, he straightens up. It's the last thing he ever expected me to say, I can tell.

"You what?" he says. And I know we're being watched and recorded, so I try to keep eye contact so he knows what I'm doing, how I need him to respond.

"Is there anything else? The warrant? Anything I need to know besides what I told you myself?" I ask, because I do need to know if there is anything more we are dealing with so I can maneuver around it, but the script Paige gave me feels stiff and unnatural, and Finn can tell. He's confused, but he's following my lead regardless.

"The only thing the warrant found that they didn't already have was his DNA. A hair in my car. Cora, I swear to God on my life that kid was never in my car. All of this is—"

"Don't worry about that. Mia hung out with him sometimes. That explains the car. Is that it?"

"What? She what?" he asks.

"Is. That. It?" I repeat.

"Uh, you mean besides the massive box of bullshit evidence Paige gave them?" he asks.

I make sure to speak clearly when I explain to him what happened.

"Look, there is a video. It shows Lucas's car leaving the scene that night at 10:33."

"I'm sorry. What? I wasn't there, so there is no way—"

"Stop. What I'm saying to you is that I know that you were covering for him when you said you drove that night, but you don't have to cover for him. You need to tell the truth," I say, trying not to leave any breathing room for him to interject something stupid.

"He dropped you off at ten and went back out to confront Caleb. It's on video, so you should be released as soon as we turn this video over," I say, and he's blinking as he stares at me like I am someone he's never met before. This side of me he's never seen was suppressed by years of self-doubt and insecurity, but now he's seeing the real Cora. I gain more confidence as I see he's catching on and this could work.

"So you can tell me the truth. You were covering for Lucas, right?" I say, giving him a look so piercing I think I will him into nodding his head, but he doesn't.

"What?" He tilts his head. He's smart enough to know he needs to pick up on something but doesn't really have a clue what.

"It's okay," I say. "We know it was Lucas. The video shows it, so just stop. It's serious now. You could be in real trouble if you don't just tell the truth," I say, and his eyes dart, his brow is furrowed. Then he nods and swallows hard. I know that it might work to say Finn drove him home and then Lucas must have left again, but it's not a clean story. Between the DNA in our car and the front-bumper repair, I want to keep that out of it and create something that makes more sense, feels more seamless.

"You said you passed Caleb hanging out by those park benches at the neighborhood entrance on your way in, and Lucas said he wanted to go back and talk to him," I say. "I remember you telling me that. We didn't think anything of it then."

"Right," he agrees, still unsure.

"But now it's time to tell the truth. You can't protect him," I say. "We'll get you out of here." Then I stand up and walk out. I relish the thought of being the one to save his ass. After everything he's done to me, I had the last word. I had the knife at his throat, and I could have pressed it in, but instead I let him go.

He gets to watch me saunter out of his life with my head held high, not crying and begging the way I have done so many times—from the first time in an Applebee's parking lot years ago when I found a text saying Come over, baby and he said it was just his coworker making a joke to all of the times in between until the last when I flipped a table on the redhead at a wine bar and was scolded like a child all the way home. That woman doesn't exist anymore. I feel him watch my back until I am out of the room, clicking the door shut behind me.

Realistically, they could both go down, and I hold the power to make that happen. What I just did was a kindness, yet somehow, the high road feels like the best revenge.

On my way to my car, I call Paige to tell her it worked, and I share the whole conversation: that he did exactly what we needed him to do, and we all agree it's time for her to go to the police.

I don't want to go home right away. I don't want to face the empty house. I don't want to fill it with mindless television and too much wine. And right now, I don't want to be with Nicola. The talking about Lucas and planning and crying has all been exhausting. It's almost over, and right now there is nothing more I can do.

I pull into the Moretti's parking lot as dusk is settling in. The only time I have felt like myself in weeks, or maybe years if I'm honest, has been in the company of Grant. I long for a moment where I'm not worrying or mourning or angry— where I am just in the moment, feeling listened to and understood. Sometimes even feeling wanted.

I see him in the warm glow of the restaurant window. He's in a white apron. He's leaning on the bar, talking to a patron, a tall, bony man with a napkin tucked into his shirt collar. I can tell from here that he is describing, in too much detail, the bottle of wine he's holding in his hand. I could turn off the ignition and go inside. He'd be surprised to see me. I could ask to talk to him privately, in his small office in the back, maybe.

I could start something we've both been resisting for a long time—something we both deserve. We wouldn't talk. I wouldn't answer him when he asks why I'm here and if anything is wrong. I'd simply kiss him, hard, against the wall until his surprise gave way to reciprocation and...

I stop myself then. I watch him pour the man at the bar a sample with a smile that doesn't reach his eyes. I am simultaneously angry at Paige for throwing him away and at myself for my willingness to betray her friendship after knowing what the deepest of betrayals feels like. I pull away from the restaurant and drive back to my lonely house.

33

PAIGE

After nightfall, Paige is putting a kettle on the stove to make tea and try to decompress her nerves, even if it's just for a few minutes. When she walks into the living room to ask if Nicola wants some, she sees her standing at the front bay window, looking down across the street at two police cars, their red lights like a strobe in the darkness. Nicola's hands are cupped over her mouth as she watches Lucas being forced into handcuffs on the front lawn. Paige looks out to see what's going on, then she lunges at Nicola, tackling her to the floor. Nicola howls.

"Are you insane?" Paige hisses. "He could see you!"

"I—I... He didn't. I just looked out when I heard the... It happened fast. I didn't—"

"Stay down. The lights are all on. He could glance up here and see you," she snaps, and Nicola's eyes fill. She knows how careful Nicola has always been but is surprised she wouldn't think about the risk, even if it's unlikely he'd have the where-withal to look at which neighbors are witnessing his humili-ation.

"He's getting arrested. I can't believe it," Nicola says from her crouched position next to a wingback chair.

"Well, after everything I brought them, they had to, but I'm surprised that they did it this fast," she says.

"Make sure you see him actually go. Make sure they don't let him do something—say something—to get out of it. That could happen," Nicola says frantically. Paige watches out the window, a sense of satisfaction washing over her as she sees him struggling, arguing with the police.

"My wife is missing, and this is how you're spending your time! You're following ridiculous accusations. Stop! I demand to talk to the chief before— Stop!" he yells.

Then, his eyes dart around as he starts on another train of thought about calling his lawyer before they take him any-where, and while he's shouting and wriggling, he looks up. He looks right up at Paige, standing in the window, backlit by a table lamp.

She wants to smile and give him a small, condescending wave, but she resists the urge because it would give her away—could give Nicola away. Jail or not, she can't have him know where she is. He's too powerful. It wouldn't be safe.

All his resisting and threats don't do him any good. She watches them push his head down to duck under the roof of the car and into the back seat. She's surprised when he looks out the window and up at her again, but it doesn't really mat-ter. He's gone.

"Look, they're gone. They took him. It's okay," she says, feeling a surge of emotion she swallows down. Nicola stands next to her at the window.

"You saw it. You saw him in the actual car," she says, seeking confirmation.

"Yes. Thank God. They actually did their job this time," Paige says, and Nicola exhales.

"Are there things in that house you need? Do you want me to get anything you left behind there?" Paige asks.

"There is nothing in that house I want. I never want to step foot in there again," Nicola says. Paige looks at her and nods, then they both watch the red lights illuminate the distant main road until they are out of sight.

After Nicola goes to bed upon Paige's insistence, Paige rocks Avery softly in her bassinet in the living room. None of them have really slept in days, but Paige needs to finally tell Grant what's happening, and just in case Lucas is on the news before morning, it should happen tonight. On the phone she has only really told him that Georgia, the neighbor he's seen once or twice, was trafficked, and that Lucas has been holding her hostage, but now he's been caught and arrested, that Georgia/Nicola and the baby are staying with her for the time being. Grant was stunned into silence on the other end. Then he just repeated, "Lucas Kinney?" a few confused times and said he'd have the bartender close the restaurant tonight and come over.

An hour later, Grant is sitting next to Paige on the sofa with the drink she's poured him.

"It's good you're sitting," she says. She doesn't know how to lie to Grant. She can't remember ever lying to him. He probably deserves the truth, but what good will it do? What does it matter to him whether it is Nicola or Lucas who is guilty? He's healed as much as a father is able. She was the one obsessed with the truth, with justice…which is exactly what she feels like this is. Still, it feels strange to not tell him everything. She might be difficult and fanatical, but she is always blunt and straightforward.

But she and Cora and Nicola have made a vow that the truth would stay between them. With every other person who knows the truth comes a higher risk of it all falling apart, and she will not lose Avery. Not for anything.

"There's a video that surfaced showing Lucas fleeing from the accident—from Caleb—that night," she says and then studies Grant's face. Red blotches appear on his cheeks, and the crease in his forehead tightens. He doesn't ask how the video has shown up. He puts down his drink and perches at the edge of his seat. He runs his hand over his mouth.

"Was he drunk? Is that why he didn't... Finn is the one with the DUIs. It made sense that—"

"No. It wasn't an accident," she says, resting her hand on his knee, and just then, Avery starts to make a low, whimpering sound. Paige sees she's waking up and goes to pick her up. She stands and props her on one hip, swaying her back and forth rhythmically.

"Okay, Paige, but you always say that, so what are you saying, exactly?"

"Lucas found out that his wife was having an affair. With Caleb. He found out she was pregnant."

"Wait. I'm sorry. What? You're not just saying this because you have a hunch? This is for real?" he asks, fidgety and wide-eyed.

"Yeah. The proof is all there. The video, proof of abuse and him keeping her captive, the motive, everything...and Nicola told me," she says, and he stares for a minute, unblinking, trying to come up with a response.

"Wait. Wait. Stop. What? You're telling me..." His eyes light up. They look at each other a moment, and then he looks to Avery, who is nodding back off to sleep in Paige's arms. She places her on Grant's lap, and before she can say anything else, she sees his tears fall in fat droplets onto Avery's pale forehead as he holds her into his chest. Then, he sits her on his knees and holds her under her armpits and stares at her. He studies her. His head just shakes slowly in utter disbelief, and she can tell he's not sure if this is real.

"How can this be?" he whispers into the top of her warm little head, and he holds her without ruining it by saying anything else until she's fast asleep.

After Avery is asleep again in her bassinet and Grant has regained his ability to speak, he and Paige move into the kitchen so they don't wake her. There are too many questions to ask and so much information that Grant hasn't been able to digest in small bits the way Paige has, so he doesn't know where to begin.

"Where will they live?" is the first thing he asks, which is one of the first things she thought herself—the selfish and overarching instinct to wonder, *Will I get to see my granddaughter?*

"She wants to go home," she says.

"There?" he asks, indicating across the street.

"Jesus. No. England. I mean, I can't say that I blame her. But I'll go with her if I have to."

"But he's, like… After everything you told me, my God, how could he ever get out? Isn't she safe here?" he says, and the desperation in his voice is something she understands well because it's how she's felt for the last year.

"Hopefully. Right now, they only have the domestic abuse and trafficking evidence—" she starts to say, but he interrupts.

"Only?" he scoffs. "The man sounds like a complete psychopath—like something you see on a *Law and Order* episode. That's not enough?"

"What I mean is they don't even know about the motive

part. They have the video that shows Lucas's car screeching away from the scene. Which is, I don't know, damning, but when they find out about the reason—about Avery—I hope it's enough."

"You hope?" he asks. "How could a fraction of what you have told me not be enough?"

"I don't know. I've heard of pot dealers getting life and the guy who puts a hit out on his wife getting five years. Plus he's a—whatdyacallit?—*pillar of the community*," she says, using air quotes. "Gag me. And, of course, he's white and male, so there's that. I mean, I just think she has reason to be freaked out that he wouldn't die in prison and then he'd find her. But at least he'll be held, and if he doesn't plead out, there'll be a trial, right?" she asks, having thought through every scenario a thousand times, even googling some of her questions to try and get a sense of how this could play out.

"Even if he pleads out on murder, he'll still be gone a very long time. She has time."

"Yeah," Paige agrees.

"They should stay here," he adds. "They're staying with you, right?" he asks. And Paige tries to make her mouth smile. She doesn't know how to feel. Of course she wants Avery there. But Grant doesn't know what Nicola has done, how hard it is for Paige to look at her sometimes. She doesn't want to feel that way. She wants to separate the truth from her pain, but that will take time.

"If there's a trial, she'll have to be here."

"Yes, I've— Yeah, she knows she can stay here," she says, but Grant gives her a sideways look.

"Is she afraid of you?" he asks. She scoffs, an almost laugh.

"What kind of question is that?"

"Have you been nice to her? Will she want to stay? You know exactly what I'm asking," he says, and he's right. She's not unaware of the way she comes off, but he, of course, doesn't know the half of what's happened.

"She's here, isn't she?" Paige says, and he doesn't reply. She walks away from him and goes to sit on the couch. Grant follows her and sits next to Avery's bassinet, watching her sleep. He stays that way for an impossibly long time.

"Can I stay on the couch?" he finally asks. And she resists saying what she always says when he asks about something in his own house. *It's your house, too!*

Instead she sits next to him and lays her head on his shoulder, a gesture that surprises him: she can tell by the way he tenses and then softens.

"I'll stay with you," she says. He lifts his head and looks at her. She knows it's something he's been longing to hear her say for almost a year. She gets up and goes to the linen closet and grabs a pile of sheets and blankets. They top up their drinks and curl up close together with Avery next to them.

Paige looks through the dim room out the front window and sees a fingernail moon against a black sky. She finally knows what happened. There is some modicum of hope that she could come to peace with it. In due time, Grant will find out more about what Caleb had become in his last months of life, but right now, she will relish this moment. She remembers hearing the moon described as a dead star that is caught in the earth's gravitational pull and suspended there forever. This is exactly how she feels—like a dead star being held up by forces beyond her control. She wishes she could stay like this forever.

They sit with their bare feet intertwined and her weight on his chest. She knows she doesn't deserve his grace, his forgiveness, but she wants it.

"We'll probably need some help around here," she says. She thinks she feels his heart quicken, but it's like him to not respond quickly, especially when it comes to her and the sometimes unpredictable things she says.

"A baby's a lot of work," he says, and his voice is calm, but the speed of his heart gives him away.

"Would you wanna help?" she asks. "Maybe move your things back in?" He doesn't say it in words because she can tell he's trying to keep his emotions in check. He nods his head a few deliberate times in response, and she can't see it, but only feels it against her shoulder.

"Good," she says, and they sip their drinks in the silence.

34

CORA

Finn has been released from jail, and as I get ready to go and pick him up, I think about all the ways I could kill him now that there is no chance some inmate named Face, with a soft spot for middle-aged corporate guys, will shank him in prison. I could drive out to the middle of nowhere, and with each passing mile he would panic, asking over and over where I was taking him until he is finally forced to fling himself from the car onto Highway 6 and get run over by a Freightliner truck.

"Mom!" Mia interrupts my fantasy.

"What? Why are you yelling?"

"I've been calling you. Angie Hilliard said that her mom heard from Bevvy Nielson that Dad's in jail. What the fuck? He's supposed to take me to soccer at three," she says.

"Uh…he will. I'm going to pick him up. And don't use that language. You know better."

"Was he drunk?" she asks.

"What?"

"Did he get arrested 'cause he was drunk?"

"No. No. Of course not. Why do you think that?"

"He's drunk a lot. I don't know, what else could it be?"

"No... It was just a bit of a misunderstanding. I'll explain later. I gotta go, but don't worry. He'll be back before you have to leave," I say.

When I go out to the driveway, I click the auto-open on my trunk and stand waiting for the hatch to lift when I see Grant across the street. He pulls a small rollie suitcase from his back seat and slams the door of his car shut. I toss a few bags into the back of my car, then shield my eyes from the sun with the palm of my hand and call over to him.

"Morning." He seems startled.

"Cora, morning," he says, walking over to me. I know Paige was going to tell him the gist of what's happened, so he's probably still in a bit of shock. I'm not surprised to see him, exactly, but I guess I'm reading into the suitcase if I'm honest. Although it's absolutely none of my business. He looks to Lucas's house.

"Crazy what's happening. Paige told me you saved the woman's life." He nods his head to the house again, meaning Nicola.

"I don't know about that," I say. "You must be— I can't imagine the shock of hearing everything and about Avery, and— Are you doing okay?" I ask, and he smiles, the sun reflecting his dark eyes and making them sparkle, the first I've seen them do in at least a year.

"Despite everything, I'm thrilled. Yeah."

"Good," I say, not sure if I mean it. Of course I mean it, but there is something leaving my body in this very moment as I see him, not as the man I kissed and became so close to—that I could have run away with if things were different—but as a neighbor, my friend's husband, someone so unavailable to me it aches. Is this what hopelessness feels like? I nod to his suitcase.

"Going somewhere?" I joke. He looks at his house and back to me. There is a kindness in his eyes. It's not pity. It's maybe something mixed with a recognition of what could have been and an apology for the something that was between us. I don't know, but I do know what he'll say next.

"No, staying this time, actually. Moving back in," he says, and I nod and close my trunk. I want a satisfying slam, but it closes automatically with a soft click. A disappointment.

"That's great," I muster. "I'm happy for you." We offer one another an awkward flash of our palms as a goodbye. He goes inside, and I get into the car to pick up my serial-cheater husband.

As I drive across town, I think the sadness will hit me—that the loss of something that was never really mine will take its crushing toll on what's left of me, but somehow it doesn't. After a few miles, I find my mood lifting. It's not just the fantasy of taking a bat to Finn's man cave, smashing his Xbox, eighty-inch TV, and gold memorabilia—but no, not a bat. I could use his clubs. The putter could take out his forty-year-aged Glenfiddich. The wedge, whatever the fuck that is, could do some nice damage to the felt on his hideous pool table. Ohh, I was feeling…

No, that's not what is making me keep it together. I guess, if I'm honest with myself, it's that I feel more hopeful knowing that Grant is going back to Paige than I would if he and I pursued something. No matter the hell she put him through, he waited. He knew it was the insurmountable pain talking, and he still loved her. And what kind of love must that be?

That is what gives me hope right now. It gives me pleasure to imagine Finn jumping out the door of my speeding car, but Grant's character is what is keeping me from falling apart today.

When I pull up to the jail, I still can't believe this is my life—that I'm someone who's getting used to this otherworldly setting every day. Last week I hosted a Girl Scout craft fair, and now I'm...what, exactly? Very different, that's what.

There is waiting and more paperwork before they release Finn. They act like they're doing me a favor, reuniting us or something, when they open the door and he steps into the lobby. I want to cup my mouth with one hand and yell, *You can keep him!* I almost chuckle because it's funny to me. Maybe funny because it's so new. My desperate need to cling to him my entire adult life has not only dissolved but become hard and bitter. Exactly where I should have been long ago. It feels...invigorating.

He looks hollow and emasculated somehow. His eyes are watery, and his chin has grown shaggy in a couple days. He smells strange, and I don't feel sorry for him. His shoulders twitch toward me like he wants to embrace me, but only momentarily. I'm sure he can see that I have no intention of doing anything but picking him up, and I'm only doing that to fill him in because he'll need that story I fed him later on, when this case blows up and goes to trial.

We walk to the car in the cold, bright morning without speaking. We drive a few miles before he says anything.

"So are you going to tell me what the fuck's going on?" he asks.

"I already told you when I visited, and you're out, aren't you?"

"You said Lucas did this. Are you serious? I feel like you're so off in left fucking field I don't even know what I'm supposed to think. All of a sudden they drop the charges against me?"

"He did do it. But we needed to make all that circumstantial stuff around you go away. So you weren't lying, exactly. You were backing up the truth. Don't worry. There is plenty of proof he did it."

"So why are you doing this for me?" he says.

"Oh," I say, and a laugh escapes my mouth before I can stop it. "It's not for you. Not even a little. It's just the truth," I say, and I can see him frown and sigh and look out the passenger window.

"Wait. Where are we going?" he asks. And for a second I think again about him jumping out of a moving car or, better yet, me pushing him, and I smile. "What?" he asks again.

"I'm dropping you at Jerry Tucker's. I already called. Well, I called his ex-wife, who said you two like to hang out at nightclubs together. Funny, I always thought Jerry was just a golf buddy. And I didn't know people over thirty went to nightclubs still, but anyway. I packed a few bags for you, and you can stay there," I say, calmly, matter-of-factly. "Oh, and I'll drop your car off so you can take Mia to practice at three."

"Or I can stay at my own goddamn house. Enough with the bullshit, Cora," he says, and I wonder if he actually thinks that we live in some parallel universe where I will overlook all of this just because it turns out he's not a murderer and just go back to business as usual.

I don't have to say the word *prenup*. I just reach into the back seat with one hand and hand him a manila folder with preliminary paperwork I had my lawyer draw up for the divorce. He doesn't even open it. He sees our lawyer's name on the envelope and tosses it into the back seat again.

"You always get it wrong, don't you?" he says, as I pull onto Jerry's block.

"Yep!" I agree, not buying into whatever bullshit argument he's trying to pursue.

"You think I'm a...what? A murderer! And you put me in

fucking jail because you're pissed. That's way more psycho than me having an affair."

"Zzz," I add.

"What?"

"Just making *affair* plural. Affair*zzz*."

"Jesus, Cora. You don't think this is a little much? Now you have Lucas arrested? Who's pissed at *him*? Well, it didn't work 'cause he got out already. Tell me, who will you and your crazy little witches' circle get arrested next? Whose lives will you totally fuck over for your perverse pleasure next?" He's screaming now. I screech the car to a halt before we reach Jerry's house.

"What?" I match his volume.

"What, what?"

"You said they let Lucas out. What are you talking about? He was arrested last night. On major charges."

"Yeah. And he was arraigned and posted bail this morning. Like, two-million-dollar bail from what I hear, so good job there, witch-hunt sisters. Another man down." He tries to go on, but I lean over him and open his passenger door and push him out. Once he lands on the pavement, he slams the door and raises his arms.

"My stuff!" he hollers as I screech away. But there's no time.

I call Paige. No answer. I call Nicola. No answer. Oh, my God. He's out. What if he knows where she is? I call the police and just hope I beat them there.

35

NICOLA

It seems like weeks since I've felt the sun on my face. Even though the morning is cold and drizzly, I sit in Paige's back garden under a covered awning and watch Avery as she sits on a blanket and bounces, smiling at me and looking around, mesmerized by the bird and squirrel sounds. Grant left for the restaurant early, but this morning I was able to meet him finally, properly, and he and Paige seemed...cozy. Paige is showering before we take a trip to town to buy some clothes and get lunch. Lunch out. It seems like such a simple thing, but I literally have no recollection of the last time I experienced that. I feel elated. I know it's not over, but I am a little more than cautiously optimistic.

And then, just as Avery looks up at me, flexing her little hands inside the knitted mittens I've dressed her in, I feel a sharp explosion of pain on the side of my head, and the world goes black. Only for a moment, though, because then I see him. Through the blur and colors behind my eyes, I see him standing over me. I scream for Avery, but he leaves her outside as he drags me in by one arm, my body limp against the ground as he pulls me over the threshold and into the adjacent kitchen. The metal runner cuts my side as he pulls me through. God, he wants to bring me somewhere where nobody will hear what he's about to do.

I open my mouth to scream again, but he quickly covers it. He has duct tape. I see the kitchen drawer ajar. Is he prepared for this? Did he grab it out of desperation or is this rage-induced and he has no real plan? I don't know which is worse.

My pulse hammers against my skull, and I try to hold my arms behind my back, keeping them from him so he can't bind them. I lie on the cold tile just inside the sliding glass doors. I can hear Avery screaming, crying, and my heart breaks.

"You really thought you'd get away with all this?" he says, hovering over me, a smirk on his face. All I can hear is my baby, and I heave my hips up and kick my right leg as high as I can, landing on his jaw. It knocks him back; he falls to his knees, and I'm able to scramble up. I run to the opposite side of the kitchen island and rip the tape off my mouth. It's not far, but I can't leave her alone. I hear her cry again, and I scream, "What do you want from me?"

"I gave you everything! Look at that house. Look at all I gave you. You were never grateful. You only complained," he says. Tears roll down my face, and I shakily pick up a carving knife from the counter. I can barely hold it steady, and he laughs. He walks slowly to me, thinking I won't use it.

"I saw you. Looking down at me, thinking you won," he says, laughing. He saw me in the window. This is my fault. I wasn't careful enough.

I hold the knife out with my shaky right hand as he creeps

closer, smiling at me. I back up, but then he lunges so quickly I don't see it coming, and he takes hold of the handle. He holds it to my neck. I look out the glass doors at my baby. Her face is red and swollen, and she's crying so hard she's shaking. The dull blade presses into my flesh, and I can feel it break the skin.

"What do you want? Tell me, and I'll do it," I say in a hoarse whisper.

"Tell them you lied," he says. I realize he doesn't know about Avery yet. I haven't given up that big piece of the puzzle to prove his motive quite yet, so in his mind, it's just the abuse, and a hit-and-run he knows he didn't do. Does he think this will go away if I agree? If I say it's not true?

"Okay," I agree in a whimper.

"It was all part of your fantasy, fetish shit. We scream. We play kidnapper and victim. Whatever the fuck you gotta say. I told you, goddamn it, so many times, that no matter what you did, it would always end up like this. You got me good, Georgia, you sure did, but this will still end the way it's supposed to."

"Okay," I say again, choking back my screams for Avery. "Just tell me what to do."

"We're going home." He lets the knife fall loose in his hand and faces me. "You'll call the police and tell them you lied. That you—" and then I grab the knife while his guard is down, and even though it's not very big, I push it as hard as I can in the first place I can. I don't aim, I just close my eyes and hope he doesn't get hold of the knife before I can somehow hurt him first. It plunges into his left shoulder. He grabs at the knife with his right hand, trying to pull it out, howling in pain.

"You fucking bitch!" he screams. I don't know whether it's safer to go and grab Avery or leave her as far away from this as possible even though she's terrified. I decide I need to get her. What if he does know the truth about her? What if he would hurt her to spite me either way? I can't risk it. I can better protect her if she's close.

While he's doubled over on the ground, trying to pull the knife out of his flesh, I run and pull Avery into my arms. I think the best thing to do is to try to run toward Cora's house—at least be out in the street where someone can see us. But before I make it out of the yard, there is a hard yank in the back of my head. He has me by the hair. It's twisted into his fist, and he controls my every movement with his tight grip on the back of my scalp.

"You will never outsmart me. You were a fucking wait-ress when you met me, so don't think for one minute you are capable of winning this," he hisses in my ear as he pushes me back inside, out of sight. I hear a noise upstairs. Paige! But he hears it, too. He looks up. He looks surprised. He's so care-ful. He knows Grant doesn't live here. Maybe he waited until he saw a car pull out of the drive this morning, assumed it was hers, was sure I was alone, and now he doesn't know. He looks to me and then up again.

"What is that?" he spits, holding my hair so tight I can feel parts ripping out.

"The dog," I say, hoping the tone in my voice sounds con-vincing and not hopeful that there is help coming.

"We're going. Now," he says. His shoulder is dripping blood on the ivory-tiled floor, and he holds the knife, sticky with blood, shakily in his hand. If he gets me in that house, I know it's over. No one can save me. I'll never get out. I know that with everything I have in me.

"We're gonna walk home. Now. Got it? Pull any shit, and I have no problem pushing this into a kidney," he says, look-ing at the knife. "I may go down, but at least you won't have Avery," he says, and I lose my breath.

The pain and the smell of his breath in my face as he spits threats are familiar as rain, but no matter how many times I find myself here, I still will never understand the sick mind of someone like him. Why he needs absolute command over someone to fulfill a fantasy. I always thought it could have been anyone he targeted at that resort that day. If it were anyone else, maybe I'd be free. But he'd rather go to prison forever just to hurt me—just to make sure I was separated from the only person I love. He's an absolute monster.

"Okay," I say, "we'll go. We want to go," and he nods to the open sliding doors. I hold sobbing Avery against my chest and take a step outside. He follows behind, the knife against the skin between my shoulder blades.

All of a sudden, we hear sirens, and he stops in his tracks. They're distant. Maybe headed this way, maybe not, but that moment of hesitation gives me an opening. He's dropped his arm and is looking up. His guard is down. I turn and dart past him as he looks over the fence to see if they're close. I run inside the glass doors, slamming them shut and locking them behind me. I try to catch my breath. I can't tell if it's me or Avery howling, but I put her down on a chair so I can breathe. I hunch over with my palms on my knees and try to calm myself enough to think. He could kick that glass in any second, but I need to breathe first. I just need to—

And then I see Paige walking down the stairs in a bathrobe with her wet hair plastered to the sides of her face, carrying a shotgun. I see Lucas see her. She walks right past me, and Avery screams as the sirens shriek, getting closer and closer and hurting her ears. Lucas stops kicking the glass door when Paige aims the shotgun at it, but he laughs when he takes her in.

"You that little bitch who broke into my house?" He snorts. The look on his face goes from mockery to fear when Paige flings open the glass doors and aims the barrel of the gun at him. She walks out into her yard slowly, keeping her aim. He backs up and stumbles over a rosebush but then regains his composure and starts to run. When I see Paige move closer to him as he runs away, I don't know what she'll do.

"The police are coming!" I say. She can't shoot a man in the back. But then he trips on a low row of barbed wire around the lettuce meant to keep rabbits away. He falls and bloodies his shins. When he gets up, he's facing Paige. She stands near her beloved Adirondack chairs with the gun pointing at Lucas, his hands held up in surrender.

"Okay! Fuck!" is all he says. The police will be here in seconds, and she can hold him there until they arrive. She looks back at me and Avery, who's still screaming and red in the face. She turns to Lucas, and without one word, she pulls the trigger. A spot of red blooms on his chest and expands, and then he falls to the ground, soundlessly.

Paige holds the gun still in her outstretched hands, and I see her whole body shake uncontrollably. I look at Lucas's body, still and lifeless. I hear Avery's cries and the sirens so close now. Are they coming to us? How? It's so loud. Paige doesn't move. I think she's in shock.

She's saved me. He can never come back now. I hear car doors slam and the sirens stop. Cora's voice is calling my name. She's banging on the front door. It's happening so fast and in slow motion at the same time. I see a drop of blood fall onto the back of my hand, and I reach up to touch the gash on my head from that first blow Lucas gave me. No one can know he had tried to flee and had his hands up when he was shot. This was self-defense. They'll see me and know it was. He came for me, and I need to finish this.

I take the gun from Paige. She doesn't move to stop me, she just stares at the dead body. I hold it in my trembling hands and point it down at his body just as police officers, followed by a distraught Cora, push their way through the brush at the side of the house and into the back garden. Once they see me with the gun, they draw theirs out of caution, but I drop it immediately and fall to my knees.

Paige rushes to my side and puts her arms around me. I know they will separate us to ask questions, so I grip her hand tightly and look in her eyes. "I shot him. I had to." She gives a slight nod of her head and squeezes my hand back.

"You had to," she agrees.

"It's over," I say again and again, on my hands and knees in the muddy earth. "It's over."

EPILOGUE

ONE YEAR LATER

NICOLA

I'm on my way out the door when it comes. The postman asks me to sign, and then casually nods and walks off like he hasn't handed me my future in an envelope. I push it into my handbag with shaky hands and place Avery into her pram.

The familiar, salty breeze from the Celtic Sea is bitter as I pull a blanket up around Avery and make my way toward the pier. Since returning to Cornwall, I never take one solitary thing for granted, not the cold drizzle or the perpetually gloomy sky. I even smile at the vendors, the pushy fortune-teller who hollers for us to come inside, the elderly man at the pasty shop, bent over a small chalkboard, writing out the daily specials in block letters, and the smiling, portly woman at the bakery kiosk where I stop for tea and two blueberry scones. I hand one to Avery, and we sit on a weathered bench facing the sea. I breathe it in and savor it.

I pull out the contents of the envelope, and my hand flutters to my chest when I see it. I think of Cora and Paige. None of us stayed in Brighton Hills. Last month Cora sent me a photo of herself in front of a Sold sign on a beach bungalow in Fort Lauderdale after dropping Mia off at the FSU dorms, and Paige said she and Grant should have left that house a long time ago. I understand the need to get as far away as possible. Paige and Grant will visit us here over the Christmas holiday and then maybe Maine, Paige told her. They could move there or Cape Cod; they haven't decided yet.

I never expected this. There was no trial because the DA didn't prosecute: the evidence of self-defense, along with eye-witnesses supporting that claim, didn't merit one. The history of abuse was documented and undeniable. So that was it. I was just so happy it was over. That was enough.

But the money. I didn't ask for it, but here it is in my hands. The statute that prohibits a spouse from collecting on life in-surance covers unlawful and intentional killing, but when it's self-defense and the state doesn't prosecute, it does not apply, as it turns out. Plus, there was the estate. There is a part of me that doesn't want it because of what having it means, but there's the other part of me that thinks it's a sort of poetic justice. I look at the number on the check, and it just doesn't seem real. I examine the back, the watermark, then the amount again. I close my eyes and clutch it to my chest.

I'm free.

★ ★ ★ ★ ★

ACKNOWLEDGMENTS

A huge thank-you to my agent, Sharon Bowers, and my incredible editor, Brittany Lavery, for continuing to believe in me and navigating me through this new world of publishing. Not only are they remarkably talented, but they are also patient and available, and I am very lucky to be working with them both.

To my wonderful superhero of a husband, Mark Glass. I could not have done any of this without him. He's always been my biggest cheerleader and unconditionally supportive.

Thank you to my family, Dianna Nova, Julie Loehrer, Tamarind Knutson, and Mark Knutson, for always being supportive and encouraging throughout this journey.

And a special thank-you to my Dallas girls, Alexa Marrach Cariffe, Cheryl Price Ginn, and Laura Neathery, for making this transplant city finally feel like home.

And of course, from the bottom of my heart, thank you to my readers.

If you loved what you just read,
keep going for an excerpt of Such a Good Wife,
another explosive thriller from Seraphina Nova Glass!

PROLOGUE

The door was open when I arrived. I didn't think it was strange. I thought maybe he'd left it that way to let in the breezy night air. Perhaps he was enjoying a glass of wine on the porch and had run in for a refill. I didn't know what it would mean that the door was ajar, and I shouldn't have shut it. I shouldn't have touched anything.

I called his name, setting my purse on the counter and cocking my head to listen for maybe a shower running or footsteps upstairs. No answer. No sounds. That's when I noticed his phone on the floor of the kitchen. The glass screen was smashed, but it worked. That gave me pause. Why would he leave it there like that if he'd dropped it? When I looked through into the living room, I saw the couch cushions tossed on the ground. It was so quiet. What the hell was going on?

I called his name again; my heart sped up as I yelled for

him and threw open doors to find him. Had there been a robbery? I raced up the stairs and started to panic a bit. He should be home. The television in the upstairs family room was on, but no one was watching it. When I turned it off, the silence rang in my ears. I saw that the French doors to the balcony off the bedroom, which overlooked the pool, were open. When I walked out onto the balcony, I felt a tremor of unease even before I saw it.

The backyard was canopied with Spanish moss dripping from the trees and it hummed with the sound of cicadas, invisible in the branches. The humidity was palpable in the thick night air. I thought of calling him, but remembered I'd just seen his phone downstairs. All of a sudden, I wished, desperately, that I could take back every decision I had made over the last couple months that landed me here, witnessing what I could never unsee.

He was there. I saw him in the shadowy blue light that the swimming pool cast across the patio. He was lying on the concrete slab next to the pool with ribbons of blood making a river from the back of his head down to the pool-deck drain. I could tell from the eerie, lifeless stare and gloss over his eyes that he was dead.

1

BEFORE

The August heat hangs heavy in the wet air. I try to keep Bennett occupied in a way that doesn't involve a screen, so we sit barefoot on the back steps behind the deck, peeling muddy red potatoes and snipping green bean ends, discarding them into the rusty buckets we hold between our knees. He loves this. The ritual of plucking off each knotted end soothes him. Inside, I see Rachel and her friend from school eating strawberries over the sink, throwing the green tops into a soggy pile in the drain; she rolls her eyes when I call in to tell her to run the disposal and pull the chicken out to defrost. It's only a few weeks until school starts back up, and I'm using the advent calendar left over from Christmas to count down the days. Bennett helped me tape cutout images of book bags and rulers over the old Santas and stuffed stockings.

He starts a new school in September, one he's been on a

waiting list to attend because his doctor says it's the best for kids on the spectrum. He should have started in kindergarten, and now, as he goes into the second grade, I try to curb my resentment at the bougie place for keeping us waiting that long, even after a hefty donation we made two years ago. But I'm hopeful the new school might be a better fit for him because it specifically caters to neurodivergent kids. He can be rigid and set in his ways. He can also be easily agitated and this school is the best in the area. I've read every book, I've gone to every specialist, and still feel like I'm failing him when I struggle to understand what he's feeling.

Ben gets the little chocolate Santa out of the pocket taped over with a cutout of colored pencils, and we cheer in anticipation of the exciting first big day (only eighteen days left), and I get a secret reward of my own. I'm a day closer to a few minutes of peace and quiet. I swell with love for him as he opens the foil around the chocolate with the care and precision of a surgeon. He is my joy, but I'm so very tired these last weeks.

The heat is getting to him—making him irritable. I can tell because he loses interest in counting each green bean end, and stares off.

"There's a firefly!" He begins chasing it along the bushes near the fence. "Did you know they're bioluminescent?"

"Pretty cool," I say.

"And they eat each other. Does that make them cannonballs?"

"Cannibals," I correct him.

"What's the difference?" He has come back over to the deck after losing the insect, now genuinely interested in the answer.

"Well, a cannonball is when you jump in the pool and splash everyone, and cannibal is the thing you said." I decide on this explanation rather than going into descriptions of weaponry.

"They eat each other!"

"Yes."

"Cool, can I see if they like ice cream? I can leave some out for them."

"Mom!" Rachel yells from inside the sliding glass door she's cracked open, "I don't see any chicken!" All I have to do is give her a warning look and she shuts the door and goes back inside, muttering "whatever" under her breath. She knows yelling will almost always set Ben into a panic. As recent as last year, she'd be immediately remorseful if she did anything to upset him, but now that she's headed into junior high, the arm crossing and annoyed sighing is a constant. The unkindness of puberty has changed her. Now, when we drive past the Davises' house down the street, and their boys are out front playing in the drive (or "hanging" in the drive because, as she points out, kids don't "play" anymore), one of them will shoot a basket or tackle another boy at that very moment—like birds of paradise, putting on a show—a primitive mating ritual. Rachel always giggles and avoids eye contact with me. It's maddening. She's just thirteen.

"Bennett," I say, smiling, "I think there's some mint chip I hid in the back of the freezer." I pat his back gently and his eyes light up. He bolts inside before I can change my mind.

I pile the buckets of beans and potatoes on the patio table and step my feet into the pool. I sit on the edge and close my eyes, letting the cool water caress my feet and whisper around my ankles. It's momentarily quiet, so I allow myself to think of him for just a few minutes—just a small indulgence before bringing Claire her medication and starting to make dinner.

He's practically a stranger. It's so shameful. I think about the way we tumbled in his door and didn't even make it to the couch. He pushed me, gently, against the entryway wall and pulled my shirt over my head. The flutter in my stomach is quickly extinguished by the crushing guilt I feel, and I try to push away the thoughts.

"Mom!" Rachel calls from the kitchen.

"Dad's on the phone!" She walks out holding her phone, and hands it to me with an annoyed sigh. My hands tremble a little. It feels as if he overheard my thoughts and interrupted them on purpose. Rachel notices my hands.

"What's up with you?" she asks, standing with a hand on a hip, waiting for her phone back.

"You just startled me. I'm fine. And stop yelling."

"He's in the living room," she says defensively, glancing in the screen door to make sure Ben is truly out of earshot. She sits in the patio chair and twirls while I talk to Collin.

"Hi, honey. Honey? Hello? Collin?" There is no response. My eyes prick with tears. It's totally irrational, but suddenly, I imagine he knows what I've done and he's too angry to speak. Someone's seen us and told him. I sit, weak-kneed, and strain to hear. "Collin?"

"Sorry, hon. I was in an elevator for a sec," he says, upbeat. The ding of an elevator and muffled voices can be heard in the background.

"Oh. Why are you calling on Rachel's phone?" I ask.

"I tried you a few times. I wanted to see if you needed me to pick up dinner. I'm on my way home."

"Oh, I must have left mine inside. I was in the yard with Ben. Um…no that's okay, I've already got things prepped, but thanks." I wonder if my voice sounds guilty or different somehow. I never leave my phone, not with Bennett's condition and Collin's ill mother living with us. So, that seems out of character. He's too kind to say anything, but I'm sure it struck him as odd. It's a pact between us as we juggle all the health issues and crisis calls from school. Both of us will stay available. As a high-profile real estate agent, it doesn't bode well for Collin to have his phone ping during a showing or a big meeting, but he won't let me carry all the weight of this myself. It's his gesture of solidarity, I suppose. The same way he stopped drinking beer when I was pregnant, both times. If I couldn't have my wine, he would suffer with me. That's just the way he is.

My face is flushed with shame. I can feel it. I turn away from Rachel slightly.

"Roast chicken and potatoes. Ben helped," I say with a forced smile in my voice.

"Sounds great. See you in a bit, then."

When we hang up, Rachel snatches her phone back. She crosses her long legs and hooks a foot inside the opposite ankle. It looks like they could wrap around each other endlessly. She's always been thin. Her kneecaps practically bulge compared to the rest of her threadlike legs, which seem to dangle loosely inside her too-short shorts. I don't say anything about them, choosing my battles today.

On my way inside, I stop to smooth her hair and kiss the top of her head. As if each good, motherly thing I do is a tiny bit of atonement for my sins. She smells like sickly sweet Taylor Swift body spray, and doesn't look up at me, just scrolls on her phone.

Dinner is quiet, but when Collin tells Rachel "no phones at the table," she fires back.

"You haven't looked up from yours since we sat down."

"That's different. It's work and it's urgent." He gives her a twirly gesture with his hand to put her phone away. It's true, Collin almost never uses his phone during dinner, but I know he's working on a huge commercial sale and lately all he can talk about is how a train track is too close to a hospital they invested in and it's causing the building to vibrate. I pour a little more wine into my glass than I usually would, but take advantage of his distraction. He wouldn't say anything if I drank the whole bottle, but sometimes that's worse—wondering if someone harbors quiet disappointment in you, but is too kind to ever point it out.

"How's Mom?" he asks.

Jesus Christ. I can't believe I forgot Claire.

"I poked my head in before dinner, but she was asleep. Should I bring her a plate?" he asks.

I never brought her her 4 p.m. medicine. Shit. I'm so distracted. I leave my phone, I forget important medication. I try to cover quickly.

"I told her I'd bring her something later. She wanted to sleep awhile," I lie.

"You're a saint." He smiles and kisses me.

"Barf. Can I go now?" Rachel doesn't wait for an answer; she gets up, scrapes her plate in the sink, and leaves, too much homework being her staple excuse for getting out of dish duty, which is fine. I usually revel in the quiet kitchen after Collin is parked in front of the TV, and the kids are in homework mode.

"Why don't you let me get this?" Collin playfully hip-checks me and takes the plates from my hands.

Recently, he feels like he's burdened me beyond reason by asking to have his ailing mother come to live in the guest room last month. Of course I said yes to her staying. Not just because of how much I love and would do anything for Collin, but because I cannot imagine myself in her position. She's suffered years with atrial fibrillation, and now lung cancer and dementia. Isn't that what we should do, take her in? Isn't that what makes us shudder—the thought of being old, sitting alone at a care facility that smells of stale urine and casserole. Spending your days staring out at an Arby's parking lot outside the small window of an institutional room, or sitting in a floral housecoat in the common area, watching reruns of *The Price Is Right* while putting together a jigsaw puzzle of the Eiffel Tower.

Maybe it's human nature to care because it's a reflection of ourselves—what we can't let happen to someone else for fear of it happening to us someday—or maybe it's compassion, but I could never let Claire be cast off and feel alone in a place like that. Even though having her dying in the back bedroom is breath-stealing and unsettling, and very hard to explain to your children.

I let Collin take the dishes so I can bring Claire a plate and her pills. I pad down the long hall to her room, carrying a drab-looking tray with chicken cut up so fine it looks like baby food. I tap lightly on her door even though I know she won't answer. When I enter, I resist the urge to cover my nose so I don't hurt her feelings, but the air is stagnant and the odor is hard to describe. It's vinegary and acrid, like soured milk and decay.

"Evening, darlin', I have some dinner for you."

The light is dim, but I don't switch on the overhead because she complains of the headaches it gives her. My heart speeds up when I don't see her shape under the blankets.

"Claire?" The room is hot and a box fan hums at the end of her bed, propped on a chair. The smell and humidity make me lose my breath a moment, and I notice she's opened a window. No wonder it's so unbearably hot. August in Louisiana and she opens a window. Shit. I should have checked on her at four. I close the window and cover my nose with my arm. When I turn back around, I can see Rachel down the hall, and her expression is enough to betray Claire's whereabouts. Rachel stares, frozen with tears in her eyes, looking at Grandma Claire standing, exposed, in an unbuttoned robe without her wig. She's been sick on the bathroom floor, and stands in the hallway, hairless and breasts bared, disoriented, looking for her room.

"Honey," I try to say to Rachel before I help Claire back to her bed, but she's run off, crying, traumatized by what she saw. I should have fucking checked on Claire at four. What I've done—my distraction—now it's hurting my kids and poor Claire. I need to pull it together.

I help Claire to bed and switch on a rerun of *Frasier*, her favorite. I leave her a tray and give her her pills, then I clean up the vomit on the bathroom floor without telling Collin about what's happened. He'd worry and he'd want to help, but this is my negligence, so I'm glad he has a work disaster of some sort and is drinking a beer out on the patio, making calls.

Rachel has her door closed when I finish, and I hear an angsty, acoustic, festival-sounding song turned up loudly in the background, so decide to leave it until tomorrow.

In the living room, Bennett is sitting at the coffee table, coloring. My sweet baby. I wish so desperately that I could wrap him up in my arms and kiss and hug him, tickle him, and joke with him, but he's the most sensitive soul I've ever known, so I pour myself a little more wine and sit by his side, hoping he lets me have a moment with him. He doesn't say anything for a minute and then...

"You wanna color the Big Bird? You can't have the Transformers page 'cause it's mine, but you can have this one." He pushes a ripped-out page across the table. It's Big Bird with one yellow leg colored in. "It's for babies, so you might not want to," he continues.

"I still like Big Bird. I guess that makes me kinda baby-ish, huh?"

"He's not real; he's just a guy in a suit."

"Right." I smile, taking the page and finding a crayon to use.

"Adults can still like that stuff, though. Mr. Mancini at school calls it nostalgia," he says. I stifle a laugh.

"That's very true."

"Is Mr. Mancini in the Mafia?" he asks, without taking focus off his Transformer. I don't let my expression show my confused amusement.

"Pretty sure he's not. Why?" I say, matter-of-factly.

"'Cause his name is Mancini, like Vincent Mancini."

"Vincent Mancini?"

"You know. *The Godfather.*"

"You watched *The Godfather*?" I ask, wondering when he would have seen it.

"It's only the best movie ever written."

"Says who?" I laugh.

"Uh. The internet." He looks at me, hoping that I agree.

"Oh, well, that's a good point. But I don't think he's any relation."

"That's good," he says, the topic apparently resolved.

"Yeah," I agree, coloring the rest of Big Bird. I'm so incredibly in love with my son in this moment. The times I see the true Ben come out, and he's totally himself, are breathtaking.

When the kids are asleep, I take my time before getting into bed. I gaze past myself in the mirror, removing eyeliner with a makeup wipe and closing my eyes against the intrusive heat I feel between my legs at the thought of him. I push the thought away and undress, pulling on a T-shirt and clean underwear. In bed, Collin is on his laptop, but he closes it when I sit down.

"Hey, beautiful."

"Hey. Everything okay with work?" I ask, knowing the answer.

"Eh. It will be. Sorry I got busy there." He puts his readers away and shakes his head.

"The hospital project?" I feel obliged to ask.

"Can you imagine having a spinal fusion and a goddamn

train full of Amazon Prime packages paralyzes you? It's un-fathomable." He says this like I'm hearing this for the first time. I smile at him.

"Sorry," he says, holding his hands up in surrender. "No work talk in the bedroom. I promised."

"It's okay." I pull the down comforter over my legs and rub lotion into my hands and up my arms.

"No. It's a sanctuary. Who said that? Someone wise, I think." He always pokes fun at me and my insistence that no TV, work, or arguing belong in the bedroom. He pulls me over to him and kisses me. So comfortable, so innocent. I breathe into that familiar, faded scent of Dolce & Gabbana left on his neck, the feel of his sharp whiskers, grown out from this morning's shave, sandy against my skin, and I want to cry.

All I see are threads of memory strung together from the other night. The ride home I should have refused, a benign acquaintance turned more, his mouth on mine, the keys un-locking his door, every time I said yes, never trying to stop it. I can't bear it. As tears run down the sides of my face, I push them away quickly before they fall on Collin's bare skin. Sweet Collin, kissing down my neck, his discarded reading glasses about to tip off the side of the nightstand in front of a photo of Ben and Rachel.

What have I done to us?

Need to know what happens next?
Grab your copy of Such a Good Wife
wherever you buy your books!